GREETINGS

—|— FROM —|—

WITNESS

PROTECTION!

GREETINGS

— ⊢ FROM ⊣ —

WITNESS

PROTECTION!

JAKE BURT

FEIWEL AND FRIENDS

NEW YORK

A FEIWEL AND FRIENDS BOOK
An imprint of Macmillan Publishing Group, LLC
175 Fifth Avenue, New York, NY 10010

Our books may be purchased in bulk for promotional, educational,
or business use. Please contact your local bookseller or the Macmillan
Corporate and Premium Sales Department at (800) 221-7945 ext. 5442
or by e-mail at MacmillanSpecialMarkets@macmillan.com.

Library of Congress Cataloging-in-Publication Data is available.

ISBN 978-1-250-10711-4 (hardcover) / ISBN 978-1-250-10710-7 (ebook)

Book design by Vikki Sheatsley

Feiwel and Friends logo designed by Filomena Tuosto

First edition, 2017

7 9 10 8 6

mackids.com

For Lauriann

GREETINGS
FROM
WITNESS
PROTECTION!

Dear Dad,

Being an orphan sucks. One hundred thirty-two letters, five foster families, and three suitcases later, and I'm back at the good old Center. They're thinking about naming my bed after me. That was Wainwright's joke.

Ha.

Ha.

I'm still waiting, of course. Any day now, a bald billionaire with a heart of gold will adopt me, and a half-giant will come to take me to a school for wizards. Two simple farmers, longing for a child, will pick me up and discover I'm faster than a speeding bullet. I'll find out you were eaten by a rampaging rhino, which would explain a lot, and I'll hop on a peach to sail to the Emerald City. Along the way, I'll learn that with great power comes great responsibility, and if you're clever enough you can get everyone else to whitewash the fence for you.

Yep, I've done my reading.

Speaking of which, the library at the Center got a new donation—about a hundred more. I've already read forty-nine of them—as many as I could find that still had covers, and some that didn't. Doesn't matter to me. It's like Grammy used to say—it's what's on the inside that counts. Yeah, I know, she was talking about wallets at the time, but still. . . .

Anyway, Chrissy wants to play, and I think Wainwright just realized I stole her pencil. Write back if you want—you know, so that I know you're not shivved, or dead, or just gone. It doesn't have to be a letter like mine. You can write anything. I'd love anything.

Oh, and if you read this stuff, Warden, hi! I was kidding about stealing the pencil! Really!

Missing you, for the one hundred thirty-third time,
Nicki

P.S. Still saving my adventures for you!

CHAPTER ONE

Kind of Home

I'm working on making a world. I've got the mountains and valleys, an ocean, and continents. It's a slow process, though, since I use only my hands. Well, my hands and a couple of tennis balls.

As I work, pieces of plaster rain on me, but I don't care. I'm digging my trenches just a little deeper, carving my roads a little farther, and when I manage to break off a bigger chunk, I get new lakes and hills. Each time, I name them—Lake Nickisia. Mount Andew. The Trenchbull. There's something calming about the *thwackathwackathwacka* of the balls off the ceiling, the dance my hands do as I throw faster and faster, until I can't hardly see my fingers anymore. Fast hands. I've always had fast hands.

"God, Nicki . . . slow down! How am I supposed to do

that? I can't even keep the ball going. You're doing two at once!"

I catch both and glance apologetically at Emmy.

"Takes time and practice," I offer. "You'll get there."

"I'll get fostered again before I get there, Nicki. And I just got my own top bunk, too!"

"Stay here as long as I have, and it'll be no sweat."

"I . . . I'm sorry, Nicki. I didn't mean it like that. . . ."

Swinging my legs over the edge of the bed, I drop down to the concrete. My toes instantly seek my slippers, and I cram my feet in as quickly as possible. Mid-October and it's already thirty degrees outside, every bit of that cold happily taking up residence in our floor. Tossing an afghan around my shoulders for good measure, I sidle up to Emmy's bed.

"No worries. I was joking, Emmy."

"I wasn't. I stink at this."

"Not as bad as I stink at sticking."

Sticking—that's what we call it. The lucky kids stick to their foster families. I seem to be covered in nail polish remover or something. I've been with five—count 'em, five—families in five years since Grammy died, and I've spent as much time in the Center as I have in homes. It's not like I have any major horror stories to tell—nobody hit me, or starved me, or touched me. Sometimes things don't work out, and things just didn't work out for me. A couple of those *did* involve legal issues on my end, but the others? Finances, leases running out—heck, one of my families got deported two weeks after I moved in.

They were all nice enough. I just didn't stick.

Emmy finally tosses the tennis ball away and curls around her Minnie Mouse pillow.

"You going to the art course with me this morning?" she mumbles into Minnie's ear.

"If I can finish unpacking, yep. Wainwright's been bugging me about it. Two weeks back and I haven't emptied my suitcase yet. Wishful thinking, I guess."

"I know! You haven't even taken out Fancypaws!"

That'd be Ms. Fancypaws McKittenfluff, my sole remaining stuffed animal from a childhood menagerie. My grammy bought me many more—Doggy the Dog, Findango, Corduroy-If-You-Please, and Sullen Moomelstein, to name a few. I can still remember Wainwright explaining to nine-year-old me that they'd gone to foster care, too. I liked imagining them finding new families and kids to play with. Of course, that was before I knew about Goodwill.

"I guess she just got comfortable in there," I muse. "Can't say I blame her."

"A suitcase is no kind of home for a lady!" Emmy exclaims, fanning herself like a southern belle. With her blond curls and tiny mouth, she actually looks the part.

"It might be if the lady is missing her left ear and has cotton leaking out of her armpits," I reply. It's true. Two and a half feet of well-loved and clumpy-haired stuffitude, Fancypaws is a few years removed from her debutante days. I shuffle over to the suitcase and gently extract her from the jumble of jeans, socks, books, and bracelets. My fingertips automatically find the velveteen patch of her belly and worry at it, carefully avoiding the holes and little rips. I remind myself to check out a book on sewing and fabric repair—Fancypaws is long overdue for a makeover, especially now that she's retired from the thieving business.

Emmy asks me if I want to get breakfast, but I'm not even dressed yet, so I let her go ahead. I clear a bit of space in the middle of my blankets for Fancypaws and nestle her in there, then slipper-slide my way across the concrete to my little closet. The chill in the air says sweaters and jackets, though for some reason the tights, long black skirt with the sequined hem, and a white T-shirt are whispering to me. I throw on a hoodie with big pockets and my grammy's Swarovski crystal earrings for good measure, then scoot out to breakfast.

All the rooms in the Center are off one long hallway. Wainwright has it set up so that the entire space reads like a timeline of kids' lives. At our end, where the boys' and girls' rooms are, the walls are plastered with pictures of families. Most of them are from the 1980s, when the Center opened. Beneath each picture is a little brass plate that says the family's name, the kid's name, and when she or he was adopted. Down the hall, the pictures get newer and newer. The best part is looking at how stuff like clothes and haircuts has changed. You know those fringed lizards that pop out their neck skin like a gigantic umbrella to frighten predators? That's like the girls' hair in the '80s. I'm not sure who they were trying to scare, but I'm betting it worked.

As the hallway goes on, the hair gets better. Toward the end, near the kitchen and the art room, are the newest pictures. Mine's not up there, since I haven't stuck. Wainwright never lets us see the moment she takes our pictures down when we come back, but I've heard her sniffling in the bathroom after she does it. I think it hurts her almost as much as it does us.

I pass by thirty years of bobs, bowl cuts, and bangs on my way to grab a bagel, and it's just as I'm turning around, bagel in my mouth and a milk carton in either hand, that I spot the guy. Or rather, The Guy. I murmur a "Whoa" right past the pumpernickel between my teeth. The Guy is one of those who goes about six-foot-six, but seems ten feet. You could fit four kids, comfortably seated, across his shoulders and balance a cafeteria tray perfectly atop his crew cut. He spots me and reaches up to slide his sunglasses a centimeter down his big, oxygen-vacuum of a nose so he can size me up. It takes him all of a second.

He makes me nervous. He's wearing a black short-sleeved polo shirt despite the cold, and it's got a star, like a sheriff's badge, sewn into it. Black belt, black pants, black shoes. Looks all uniformy. What's more, hooked to his belt is a holster. Conspicuously jutting from the leather is a blocky plastic handle, as yellow-and-black as the business end of a hornet. It's smaller than a gun, but still big enough that I can read the word "Taser" along the side. All people in uniforms make me twitchy, but especially armed ones, and my fingers get to tapping on my milk cartons, my toes curling in my slippers. Yeah, I know I haven't done anything wrong recently, but I'm still feeling the urge well up in me. It's a kind of tightness, crouched behind my heart, above my intestines, and in my sinuses, all at the same time. Once my left thumb starts to waggle, I know I've got to get out of there. So, speeding up, I round the corner and duck into the art room.

The art room is tiny, with just a table and four chairs. Still, there's a lot of color there—it's wallpapered in waxy, curling drawings made by kids over the years. Mr. Jordanson doesn't throw away anything. Even if it's a three-year-old's scribble-scrabble, he's taping it to the wall. We like Mr. Jordanson because he makes us feel like Rembrandts. Seeing him and Emmy calms me a little, but I still can't stop thinking about The Guy out there. He wasn't a prospective parent, for sure. I set my bagel and milk down and hide my hands behind me.

"Oh no . . ." Emmy whispers. She's the only one who ever notices when I'm twitching.

"I'll be all right," I mutter.

" 'Kay," she says, offering me a sympathetic smile—and something else. She's midway through a tree, and she's probably going to need her lime-green crayon again in a second, but she's positioned it at the edge of the table, just behind her elbow. She turns away from me for a minute, pretending to listen to what Mr. Jordanson is explaining to Halla, the Center's newest arrival and resident baseball expert.

Emmy's a good friend. . . . The crayon is gone before

anyone notices, and I'm holding it in my big old pocket, left thumb rubbing at the tip, which is still warm from her vigorous shading. I'm not shaking anymore, and I can breathe again.

"Here, Emmy . . . you dropped your crayon," I whisper, and she takes it back, thanking me. Have I mentioned how awesome Emmy is yet? Now that the urge has passed, it's no sweat to grab the chair across from Halla and settle in.

"Need a sheet of paper, Nicki? We're doing fantasy gardens," Mr. Jordanson announces, and he points to Halla's work. Halla has drawn trees coming from the ceiling, a baseball bat growing out of a pot, and some sort of viney monstrosity. "Art class" is a joke. We basically think of something to draw as a group, then tackle it. It's silly, but it passes the time, and we get to chat for a while. Right now, that's exactly what we need to do.

"So," I offer casually, "anyone catch that big guy out in the hallway? He looks like a Green Beret or something."

"I saw him!" Emmy blurts. "I bet he's on steroids!"

"Alex Rodriguez did steroids!" Halla adds.

Yep, this is usually how our conversations go.

"Let's change the subject, guys," Mr. Jordanson suggests, and he tries to talk to Halla about stippling.

I scoot closer to Emmy and whisper, "So you *did* see him? What do you think?"

"Can't be here to foster. Did you do something?"

"No, did you?"

"No . . ."

9

"What was he doing outside the transition room, then?"

"Not sure. Maybe he's a health inspector?"

"Does he break your knees if you aren't up to code?"

"Ahem!" Mr. Jordanson huffs, glaring at us. He goes right on glaring at us, even after the second look up. That's how you know a teacher means business. When one tells you to be quiet, you wait thirty-five seconds, then look up. If the teacher isn't watching anymore, you can start whispering again. If he's still staring at you, you best zip it.

Humbled, I bite my lower lip and give Emmy one more glance, just in time to see her stick her tongue out at me. I try to suppress a giggle, but it comes out all snorty, and Emmy starts snickering. Halla joins in, and we're a mess. Even Mr. Jordanson can't stop us at that moment.

But Wainwright can.

She opens the door, then knocks on it in the way grown-ups do—the old "Hey, I'm barging in, you can't get me to go away, but it's okay, because see? I *knocked*!"

Emmy and I both stiffen. Wainwright doesn't usually interrupt classes, and her face seems drawn tight, even her wrinkly forehead.

"Wonderful news," she says softly. "Nicki, dear, there are people here to see you."

She always begins this announcement with "wonderful news," but the second part is different. Emmy nudges her crayon toward me, and I grab for it instinctively. She noticed, too. Normally, Wainwright says, "There's a family that can't wait to meet you!"

Normally, Wainwright smiles.

My chair screeches as I get up, and I wince. As I start to trudge out, Mr. Jordanson says, "Congratulations, Nicki." He's trying to be cheerful, but it comes out more like a question than an exclamation. Fingering my right earring nervously, I follow Wainwright out of the room. It doesn't even occur to me to turn around and hug Emmy, to find Chrissy for one last game of Uno, to ask Halla about baseball, or to shake Mr. Jordanson's hand. It should have, though.

After all, I might never see them again.

CHAPTER TWO

Careful What You Wish For

I follow Wainwright out into the hall, pretending not to notice that she stops every few feet to peer at me. She's trying to figure out if I'm okay. I've got my hands in my pockets, so she can't see my left thumb twitching, and I'm keeping my eyes locked on The Guy, still standing at the doorway of the transition room.

He's smiling.

I'm not.

"Wainwright, am I in trouble or something?" I dare to ask, pausing halfway between my friends behind me and The Guy up ahead.

"No, dear, nothing like that," she says, taking off her bifocals and squinting down at them while she pinches at the lenses with her cardigan.

"Then why did you just call me *dear*? Like before, in the art room. You don't do that. Not ever."

No response. She just takes my shoulder and eases me forward. A step at a time, I'm getting closer to The Guy, and proximity isn't helping. He's even more menacing up close. When I see that there's a woman in the room behind him, also wearing a uniform, my nerves go into overdrive. It feels like no matter how deeply I breathe, I'm not getting any air. If something doesn't give, I'm going to bolt, and that only ever makes more trouble. So I decide to do my thing.

"Hello, sir! It's nice to meet you!" I chirp as I extend my hand. I flash him my most dazzling smile. My other hand sweeps my hair over my left shoulder.

He seems surprised, which is what I expected. Good.

"Yeah, Nicki. You too. Nice to meet you," he says, reaching out a big paw to shake. I pull back my own hand before he can grab it, though, and leave him looking at his palm like he's checking for a rash.

Hmmm . . . he knows my name already. They've probably read my file. Still, I'm betting he won't see this coming.

The Guy is so big it's nearly impossible to slip past him. But I use that to my advantage. I let my shoulder glide gently against his chest. I twist my head just enough to allow my earrings to sparkle, and my hands go to work. Once I'm inside, I stow what I've scored in my pockets and manage a grin. The woman is sitting at the table and leafing through a big stack of papers. I say, "Hello, ma'am," in a syrupy singsong, but she doesn't even glance up. It's all kinds of awkward, but that's to be expected.

This is the transition room, after all.

Ironically, the place is decorated to be as soothing as possible—shelves full of brightly colored books, stuffed animals perched on every available surface, a huge alphabet carpet dominating the floor. There are three comfy chairs, a globe, and a massive toy chest. The idea is that you come in here, and the family that's adopting you "gets to know you." This usually consists of sitting at the table and watching while you play with toys you're too old for. Occasionally, they ask you a question—"What's your favorite ice cream?" or "Do you like to read?" or "Isn't that a pretty dolly? Do you like dolls, Nicolette?"

No. Seriously. I was twelve, and they actually used the word *dolly*.

As I turn to watch Wainwright close the door, my throat tightens. Just this once, I wish she'd stay instead of watching through the closed-circuit camera.

I make my way over to the corner with the toys. This is Chrissy's favorite spot in the whole Center; we actually have to stop her from sneaking in. Granted, she's six and hasn't been in here enough to associate it with disappointment, but I'd think there would be some lingering ghost of doubt and sweaty anticipation that might spook her. I sure feel it. Grabbing the biggest teddy I can find, one about the size of Fancypaws, I turn back to watch the two uniforms.

The Guy sits next to Ms. Filemonger, who slides him a

folder. When he opens it, I see that it's got *Nicolette Demeer* written across the tab in red Sharpie. My nose crinkles. They've switched the final two letters of my last name. I whisper this to the bear and use the uniforms' distracted paper rooting as an opportunity to check out the items in my hoodie. Courteously, the bear shields my hands, so when The Guy and Filemonger do finally look up, all they see is a smiling thirteen-year-old with a scruffy grizzly.

"She's pretty enough, don't you think?" The Guy says, and the creepy factor shoots up to about fifteen.

"Yes, very much like the mother."

Filemonger is holding a photograph. I can't see the image, but they're both squinting at it, then me, then it, nodding the entire time. I'm trying to stay still, but my foot is doing its best to grind a hole through the letter *Q*. Filemonger is pointing at a chair with her pen. I sit down and put the bear next to me on the table. He's staring, unblinking, at The Guy, and I'm across from Filemonger. Teddy seems a lot cooler than me right now; my leg is bouncing so badly it's rattling my teeth.

"Nicolette Demere," Filemonger begins. "Age?"

It takes me a few seconds to realize she's asking me a question. I say, "Isn't it in my file?"

Wrong answer.

"Age?" she repeats, louder and slower, like she's trying to translate it into whatever language she thinks children speak.

"Thirteen. My birthday was three weeks ago."

"Happy birthday!" The Guy says, and I offer him a little smile.

"Height?"

"Huh?"

"Your height. How tall are you, Ms. Demere?"

I stare at her for a second, trying to figure out if she's serious.

"I dunno. About five and a half feet? I'm kinda tall for my age, I guess."

"You're five-foot-five," she corrects, reading it from a paper hidden behind the folder.

"If you knew it, then why did you ask?"

"Weight?"

I look at The Guy for this one. He arches an eyebrow. I have no idea what that means.

"A hundred pounds?" I venture.

"Closer to ninety."

"My shoe size is seven and a half, if that helps."

"Race?"

I peer up into the camera in the corner, less-than-cleverly disguised in a hanging flower basket.

"Is this a TV show or something? Do I get a prize if I figure out that I'm being pranked?"

The Guy leans forward. "It's not a prank, Nicki. We're making sure you are who the file says you are."

"Yeah, but what for? You're not taking me home to practice parenting a rebellious teenager."

The Guy snorts. "Smart mouth on you. Why so defensive?"

"Let's see, two scary people who didn't identify them-

16

selves have me closed in a room. They're asking questions about me even though they already know the answers. They're carrying weapons. Yeah, I think I'm good with defensive."

"You never asked who we were, Nicki."

"You're U.S. marshals. Your name is Edward Harkness, but I'm betting you go by Eddie. You're thirty-nine years old, you were born on the fifth of July—tough luck there, patriot—and you've got blue eyes underneath those sunglasses. You have a kid already, but not with her. She's probably your partner. You drive a Buick, drank coffee this morning, and you used to smoke. How's that?"

"Wh-what? How did you . . . ?"

Filemonger has frozen mid-file-flip, and The Guy . . . I suppose I should call him Eddie now . . . is still fumbling his words.

I look over at the bear and shake my head knowingly. My leg actually slows its bounce. From my pocket I produce Eddie's wallet, which I slide back to him.

"I'm not Sherlock Holmes or anything. Your driver's license gave me your name, eye color, and birthday. There's a picture of your wife and kid in there, too. He's cute in that little football helmet! Oh, and the insignia on your shirt says you're a U.S. marshal."

"Where did you get this?" he demands, though by the way he's holding up the wallet and blinking at it, he's more wonderstruck than angry.

"Your back pocket. Pretty close to where I got these."

I toss his car keys across the table next.

"And this, which I'm guessing is the change from a cup of the cheap coffee at the bodega across the street, since it's ninety-three cents with tax."

I roll a nickel and two pennies his way.

"I've got your badge, too, but I'm keeping that until I know what the heck is going on. The nicotine gum you can have back. I'm betting you'll want a piece after this."

"You realize we just caught you stealing from a U.S. marshal, young lady?" Filemonger says through gritted teeth. I glance at her, but I can't bring myself to look for too long; she makes me twitchy. Her lips are pursed. Her eyes are narrowed. Her watch squeezes her wrist so tightly you'd think she was using it as a tourniquet. And whereas Eddie's shirt is comfortably unbuttoned at the collar, Filemonger has hers worked up her neck like the sheath around a knife. Makes sense, I guess, what with the way she's staring daggers at me.

"It's not stealing," I explain. "It's creative ownership reassignment. Besides, you didn't catch me. Nobody has, and nobody will. Been found with the goods a few times, but never caught in the act. Now, if you want your badge back, you'll give me some answers."

I let that sink in for a couple of seconds and then smile innocently. "Pretty please?"

Eddie starts laughing—little chuckly snorts at first, then a proper Brooklyn belly-bray.

"Got a deal for you, Nicki. You tell me how you did all

that, we'll tell you what you want to know. Then you can decide whether to give my badge back."

"Harkness, that's not why we're—" Filemonger begins, but my main man Eddie waves her off.

"Aren't you curious, Janice? Let her talk."

Janice crosses her arms, but she gives me a go-ahead nod.

"Fine. Deal. I got your badge first," I begin, handing it over to Eddie. "It was clipped to your belt, and I worked my left while you were trying to shake my right—you didn't see because you were watching my hair. I got your wallet when my shoulder touched your chest on the way in, since your body can really only process one point of contact at a time. Then, when I twisted out of your way, I brushed my hand against my earring. It caught the light, you glanced over, and I nabbed the gum and keys from your right pocket. Took your change from the other pocket as you walked past—you didn't hear the jingle because I said hello to Filemo . . . um, to Janice here. Oh, and I could've taken the Taser, too, but I didn't want to risk panicking and shooting you in the leg with it. Anyways, cool Taser."

"Oh, Janice, I really like this one," Eddie says, nudging her with his elbow.

"Your turn," I declare, staring at Janice.

She eyeballs me with no small amount of suspicion. I think she believes I'm going to rob her blind as soon as she looks away. That's silly, of course. I wouldn't do that.

But I could.

"We are United States marshals, members of the oldest and most versatile federal law enforcement agency. We protect the courts, track down fugitives, and shield witnesses from retribution. And you are Nicki Demere," she says, reading from the file, "daughter of Christian Demere, convicted felon, sentenced to nine years' imprisonment at FCI Otisville for class B robbery one and possession of a weapon two. Paroled in March of 2012."

My heart is suddenly thumping so hard I can hear it.

"Wait . . . wait, wait, wait," I exclaim, my hands fluttering in the air before my face, like the info she just dumped on me is a host of sparrows all trying to dive-bomb my brain at once. "My dad is out? As in, he's free?"

"Yes, Nicki. For two years. Now let me continue. You wanted answers, you listen."

I grab the teddy bear again, squeezing him so tight something rips. The world is crumbling, and Janice just keeps on talking.

"Mother unknown, abandoned family shortly after daughter's birth. Father imprisoned when child was six. Child raised by paternal grandmother, Florence Demere, until her death in 2009. Is all this correct?"

Those sparrows have decided to stick around for a while, building their little nests in my throat—my mouth feels dry and powdery, and the lump in my windpipe won't let me talk. I'm blinking away tears as I barely manage to squeak, "Go . . . go back to the part about my dad being out of prison?"

Janice nods. "He is."

"And he's been out for a long time?"

"Yes," she states flatly.

Eddie jumps in. "I know it's a lot to take in, Nicki, but you've got to bear with us. We're not here about your dad, or your grandma—"

"Grammy."

"Or your grammy, or any of that. That's the past. We're here about you, now, because . . . well, because we need you. The U.S. marshals need you. A family needs you."

I'm spinning, or the room is, or something. Now I know why my dad never wrote back. Pretty hard to get the mail your daughter sends to prison if you're not *in* prison.

He's had two years. To get me. To take me home.

Two years, and he never came.

About five hundred dreams I've had of him showing up at the Center, of him telling me about prison over pie, of me sharing my adventures with him . . . they all come crashing down.

And my adventures! Every crappy little thing that's happened to me! Every family that's ever dumped me, every friend I've had to say good-bye to, every last bit of trouble I've made for myself . . . they were adventures only because I was going to tell my dad about them, match him story for unbelievable story. Now they're just . . . just what? Stuff, I guess. Bad things. They're all skittering out of my brain, roaches from a bright light, black and shiny and every bit as ugly.

I hadn't even realized that Eddie had gotten up and put his hand on my shoulder. Janice keeps on reading: "Grandmother had a rap sheet: petty larceny, pickpocketing . . ." She pauses, staring at me for a moment. "Taught her granddaughter the ropes, apparently. Grandmother dies, granddaughter is picked up by the foster care system. Diagnosed with an impulse-control disorder, specifically kleptomania, likely as a result of separation and abandonment issues. Weekly court-mandated therapy sessions."

Not adventures. Just bad things.

"Nicki," Eddie whispers. He's squatting next to me now, looking up past the teddy bear's ears. "We're going over this because it's vital that we know where you've been, who you are. I'm so, so sorry you have to hear this from us, but it's for a good reason. All this, I'm thinking, has made you strong, and we're looking for a strong girl, one with your kind of grit, smarts, and skills. We're looking for a girl who has dealt with all that stuff and come through still spitting fire and throwing jabs. Nicki, kid—we're looking for you."

I sniffle, wipe my fingers across my eyes and nose, and level a red-eyed stare at him. Through clenched teeth, I growl, "For . . . *what?*"

He smiles.

"The adventure of a lifetime."

CHAPTER THREE

An Offer
I Can't Refuse

"Look at this, Nicki."

Eddie holds out his hand to Janice, who scowls for a second. He snaps his fingers. Shaking her head, Janice forks over the photograph they were staring at a minute ago. He flips it around and holds it up for me.

It's a family—they look nice enough. Father a little bit bald and a little bit beardy. A boy about my age stands next to him, a soccer ball under his foot and a baseball cap shielding his eyes. A mom . . .

Good God, the mom! I instinctively reach up and grab a lock of my hair, pulling the strands in front of my eyes. It's as black as the woman's in the photo. And her eyes? They're mine, too, down to the flecks of green in the gray. Face thin as a razor, long fingers, pixie ears. She could be my future body double. She could be my much, much older sister.

Heck, she could be my mom.

"Nicki?"

Eddie's talking to me, but I can't take my eyes off the picture. She's not my real mom, of course—Grammy had a few photos of *her*. The lady in the photo looks ten times more like me than the one who gave birth to me and skedaddled.

"Nicki?"

"What? What do you want? Who are they?"

"Nicki, have you ever heard of WITSEC? The Witness Protection Program?"

"Who is she?" I ask, tracing my fingers along the silhouette of the woman.

"It's not a she. It's a what."

I sniffle again and roll my eyes. "No, Eddie. I know what the Witness Protection Program is. I watch TV. Who is she, in the picture?"

"Nicki, meet Elena Sicurezza. There next to her is her husband, Pietro, and their son, Lucas. They're a nice family, and they need you badly."

They do look like a nice family. Happy. Close. She's got one of those powder-blue sweaters draped over her shoulders. He's got a Mets shirt on. The kid is wearing cleats and white kneesocks.

"Here's the thing, Nicki. Elena is brave. Very brave. Because of her bravery, many evil men and women are in prison. However, there are other evil people out there who are looking for her, who want to punish her."

"You mean she ratted on someone," I murmur.

Eddie scratches the back of his neck but then nods. "There are those who would see it that way, yes. Mostly, those are the people we're trying to protect Elena from."

"How do I factor into this again?"

"Times have changed, Nicki," Janice says somberly. "Twitter. Instagram. Facebook. Digital everything. It's much harder to hide a family now. We've had to take drastic steps recently. One of these steps is Project Family."

"Project Family? Is that, like, one of your cool acronyms? What does it stand for?"

"It's not an acronym. It's just the name of our initiative."

I twist my mouth to the side, unimpressed. "I thought everything was an acronym for you guys."

Janice ignores me, which I suppose is fair.

"It used to be we'd change people's identities, give them new cities, new names, new jobs, new schools, even new appearances. But that's not enough anymore. Bad people have caught on to how to look, where to look, and what to look for. We have to evolve, and Project Family is one of our strategies."

Eddie jumps in. "That's right, Nicki. We're evolving, and we're hoping you can help us with that process. Help the Sicurezzas, too. We don't just want to change their names. We want to change their family. That's where you come in. With you, their dynamic is different. A credible daughter of your age completely changes their past, beefs up their backstory, and gives their lives an entirely new trajectory. Not only do you look the part—which, I'll grant you, is a huge reason we're here—but you're street-smart and book-smart, you know what to look for if danger does show up on their front porch, and you can handle yourself. Combine all that with your own unique background, and you're our girl."

"You want me to join this family?"

"To help hide them, yes."

And here it is, the final stage of wigging out. I've pretty much covered them all. Started with nervous, jumped to thiefy, moved to sarcastic, moseyed on into weeping, and now that beautiful numbness. I'm actually able to think again.

And now that I can, this all sounds totally ridiculous.

"You want me to become a U.S. marshal?"

Janice shakes her head emphatically. "You will report to us, but there are age and field test requirements for marshals. You're far too young. You could consider yourself a consulting asset, but there really isn't a name for someone in your position."

"I'm not in a 'position' yet. You're trying to get me adopted by a family that isn't looking for a new kid, that is about to move to who-knows-where, and that's being chased by, as you describe them, evil people?"

"We're arranging your placement with this family. It's not a foster situation. Not an adoption. Those leave paper trails. No, you will become one of them, after a brief but intense training session. And they've already agreed to it."

"You mean, like, they can't get rid of me if they don't want me?"

"No. If your performance is unsatisfactory, if you endanger the family, WITSEC would reevaluate your placement, but absent that, you'll be the permanent contact person for the Sicurezzas."

"But if I screw up, I just come back to the Center again?"

"No, Nicki . . ." Janice pauses, glancing at Eddie. Clearly this next message is one that needs a bit more sugar to deliver.

Eddie clears his throat. "Nicki, to do this, to have this opportunity, some things are going to need to change. The biggest of these is who you've been. We can't allow any evidence that you aren't a member of the Sicurezza family. In essence, Nicki Demere has to disappear."

I whistle softly; it's a good thing I'm not still in the weeping phase. Sure, there have been dozens of times I've wished I could just disappear: the day Grammy got picked up by the cops and I had to sit in the police station for four hours, the time in fourth grade when Ms. Dresker found out I'd been swiping clothes from the school store, and after that one thing in sixth-grade gym class. Now, though?

"How would I . . . disappear?"

Eddie tries to take my hand, and I pull back sharply.

"Don't touch my hands," I warn.

He backs off, his own hands in the air. "Easy, Nicki. Sorry about that. I should've known. Bet you rely a lot on your hands."

"They're my treasure."

I watch the cliffside of Harkness's forehead avalanche a little bit in confusion.

Grammy always told me that no matter what I stole, my hands were the real treasure. I guess I must have taken that to heart. My therapist tells me it's part of my "issues." Yep. A little anxiety to go along with my uncontrollable urge to swipe things. Another gift I should probably thank my dad for.

"I can't even wear gloves," I explain. "Just the feel of them, all itchy and squeezy around my fingers, freaks me out. So yeah, nobody touches my hands."

Eddie nods solemnly. "That's my bad. It's clear you've been through a lot. But this is tough, see, and we wouldn't be asking if we didn't think you could do good here, that you could help."

He stands up, leaning his backside on the edge of the table. Man, can he loom. He looms like nobody's business.

"Part of this, Nicki, is that you need to sign your records over to us. Ms. Wainwright told us she wouldn't do it without your approval—and good on her for saying so. Kid, you should've seen the hoops she made us jump through just to get this far. We had to have our director Skype with her from his office, forms signed in triplicate, multiple IDs. . . . The lady does right by you, let me tell you."

I cast a glance up at the camera, giving it a little nod. Eddie continues.

"This is a big decision, because once your records are

the property of the U.S. marshals, we're going to destroy them. Nicki Demere will no longer exist. If your father . . ."

I wince. Eddie sighs sympathetically, but goes on.

"If your father or mother come around looking to reconnect, they won't find a trace of you. If some long-lost uncle researches his family tree, he'll find no evidence that you were ever here. All your records destroyed. You'll be issued a new birth certificate, new social security number, new identity, and Nicki Demere will be erased from the government's memory. It's a big commitment, but . . ."

I think I already know the "but." Yeah, I have fostering papers and school reports, but there's another kind of record that I wouldn't mind obliterating.

"Does this also mean my juvie record will be . . ." I start, sitting up and meeting Eddie's gaze.

"Yes. You'll be forgiven. No evidence will be kept of any trouble you've been in, and as a result of your cooperation any sentence you may have received will be considered served in full."

"Let me get this straight. No community service. No prior record. No court-mandated therapy sessions. No nothing?"

"No nothing, Nicki. A fresh start."

"And . . . and these people will take care of me? Like an actual daughter?"

"Their safety depends on it. Anything out of the ordinary might draw attention and put them at risk. In fact, that's your number one priority—making sure everything stays normal. Nothing to draw notoriety, or shine any sort of spotlight on the family. Remember you said you've never been caught stealing? It's your ability to lay low, to assimilate into new families and schools quickly, that makes you ideal for this most important task. Other foster kids—"

"Kids in foster care," I correct.

"Sure, Nicki . . . anyway, they don't all adapt like you. They haven't done as well in schools, have acted out, have had problems that make them unfit for what we're doing. You're strong, though. You've made it through."

I almost laugh. Oh yeah, I've adapted just swimmingly. Have they seen my rap sheet? And I've "made it through"? All those nights I spent latched on to Fancypaws, unable to sleep, crying quietly so I wouldn't be a weepy burden on whoever I was with and get sent away again? Yep. I've been making it through just fine.

I give Eddie an archy eyebrow.

"But let me guess—I do this, I don't get to see anyone here ever again. I don't get to say good-bye, or tell them where I'm going. I just . . . disappear."

He nods. "We'd leave immediately. You and Janice would collect a few of your things and pack them right away. Our training center is in Georgia, and we'd fly there this afternoon. You'll be taught the protocols—how to act, what to look for, how to lay low. You'll also learn more about the Sicurezza family and your new home."

I run a hand through my hair, pulling it over my face

like a blanket on a birdcage. Hiding behind that veil, I'm able to think more clearly.

"What's she doing?" Eddie asks Janice after a few minutes.

"She's thinking," Janice replies.

Janice might be the stuffiest lady I've met in a while, but she gets this, at least.

Okay, Nicki—pros and cons. Pros: No criminal record. New family. New responsibilities. An amazing secret to keep. Maybe my own Taser. Cons: No more friends at the Center. No more dreams of meeting my dad in a diner and having a slice of Dutch apple pie. No more Nicki, except in my own mind.

Oh, and there's a criminal organization hunting down my new family.

Twenty minutes ago, when my world seemed sane, this would have been a much harder decision. What if I left with these two, and the next day my dad showed up, fresh out of prison and ready for a new start? But he's had two years' worth of days to do that, and he just hasn't. I run through every possible excuse. The law won't let him near schools or orphanages? The parole board told him he couldn't see me? He developed a weird pathological fear of telephones and taxis? No matter what I come up with, though, it's not good enough. None of that would have stopped *me* from finding *him*, so the only excuse I can think of that makes sense is the most painful one.

He just doesn't want me.

Something tells me it's probably not a good idea to do this to spite him, to say "Two can play at this never-coming-back game. . . ." Something's telling me I'm not in the right mental state to make this decision, and especially not so quickly.

Then again, the vindictive, petty, angry, hurt part of me is saying it's a fabulous idea, and sometimes you've just gotta give that girl her due.

I slowly sweep the hair from my eyes. Eddie offers me what must pass for him as a soft, reassuring smile. Looks more like someone chiseled a horizontal line in a block of well-tanned concrete.

"Nicki, I know this seems out of the blue, and strange; that it's not normal—"

I raise my hand, cutting him short. I learned three foster families ago that a kid needs to have a flexible definition of *normal*.

"Where do I sign?"

Janice and Eddie exchange glances. His is triumphant. Hers is more "What did we just do?" Warily, she slides several papers from the file toward me. "Going to need you to sign at all the Xs, Nicki. And make sure your signature is clear."

Grabbing a pen from the center of the table, I brush my hair behind my ears and get to reading. I think I understand most of it, or would if my head wasn't swimming. I carefully sign each form, thankful that I'm right-handed.

When I'm finished, I swallow once, think a tiny prayer, and toss the pen to Eddie, who fumbles with it for a minute before setting it down.

"All set, Nicki?"

I nod. Janice grabs the papers and hurriedly jams them into a folder. I try to smile but find that my teeth are starting to chatter, to go along with my quivering left hand and bouncing leg.

I'm totally about to freak out again.

I just joined the U.S. marshals.

CHAPTER FOUR

Smelling as Sweet

I'm expecting about an hour to pack up my stuff, to run my hands over the blankets on my bed, to touch the grooves and dips in the ceiling. I get five minutes. No walking the hallways to look at the girls with their big hair. No stop in the art room to tear down a memento. I'm not even allowed out on the playground to say good-bye to Emmy. Basically, as Janice watches, I shove a few things into my suitcase, starting with Fancypaws.

"Do you really need that ratty old thing?"

I don't answer. Fancypaws is nonnegotiable. Janice fights me on a bunch of other stuff—trinkets and tokens, mostly—and wins. She doesn't even let me go get my toothbrush: "We have them in Glynco," she explains.

In the end, I leave with two shirts, a skirt, a couple of pairs of underwear and socks, one bra, Fancypaws, and the clothes on my back. Everything else, Janice says, Wainwright will be instructed to incinerate. Now that I've signed the papers, Janice is even twitchier than me, as if she has a time bomb ticking in her back pocket. By the end, she's scooping up handfuls of things from my drawer and dumping them into a brown paper bag.

"Wait," I say when I see a particular flash of color.

"What now?" She sighs.

I peer down into the bulging bag and spot it immediately. It's my only picture of my dad and me—I'm six, it's about a month before Dad got sent upriver, and we're at the Bronx Zoo. It's your classic family-on-a-carousel photo—well, sort of. I do look happy, and my dad seems about as amused as you can expect a thirty-year-old guy to be while spinning in a lazy circle for seven minutes straight. He's got his old U.S. Army sweatshirt on, hood pulled up to hide the pale of his closely shaven head, and he's glancing down at his flip phone. What sets this picture apart is that the whole carousel is made of bugs. Not horses, or unicorns, or camels. Bugs. I'm riding on an enormous praying mantis, screaming with warrior-woman glee as I chase my father around and around. He's being unceremoniously rolled along by a hardworking beetle, sitting on a fiberglass bench crafted to resemble a massive ball of dung. Now that I think about it, I suppose it's a pretty darn good metaphor for my life up to this point. If I couldn't catch him while astride a wicked-cool mantis steed, how was I ever going to do it with hundreds of stupid letters and wishful thinking?

Besides, now I can see exactly what I've been chasing, and it doesn't amount to much more than that pile of dung.

"No, Nicki. The director has already given us what pictures we need. You're not permitted to keep—"

I cut Janice off with the sharp sound of ripping photo paper. In fact, I shred the thing, letting the bits of bug and baby girl flutter back down into the bag.

"Just making sure no one can connect me to that particular piece of history," I declare. Janice nods, and she covers the remnants of the photo with the last of the knickknacks I didn't have room to pack.

When we're done, Eddie and Janice lead me past Wainwright's office. I strain to see through the glass, but the two hands on my shoulders, especially Eddie's big paw, hustle me down the hall before I can get a proper look. Still, I think I can see Wainwright in there, looking down at the playground, biting her nails. There's a moment when it seems like she sees me, too, maybe in the reflection in the window, and she pulls her pinkie from her teeth just long enough to crook it in a little wave good-bye.

A wicked New York wind whips around the buildings, shearing past us as we step outside. I bury my hands in the giant pockets of my sweatshirt, glad Janice didn't rip it off my back. In just a minute or so, we're in front of a black SUV, which Eddie unlocks with a click of his beeping button before tossing my suitcase in.

When we're seated, Janice starts the engine and Eddie cranks the heat.

"I'll be glad to be back in Georgia," he offers from the passenger seat. Janice grunts in agreement. I'm too busy twisting around to see the Center.

"Seat belt, Nicki," Eddie says jovially. I can tell he's trying to be as friendly and upbeat as possible, mostly because that's what every other adult has done, in every other car, every other time I've been taken from the Center. Only this time, I doubt they'll be driving me back in a few months.

As we pull away, my fingers never leave the handle of my suitcase. I can't help but think of Emmy, Halla, Chrissy, and the rest. I hope they get a chance, and soon. Maybe not like this one, but a chance.

We drive for some time in silence, and there are enough red lights that I get to mentally say good-bye to the City. I can't say it's properly been home for me—nowhere has—but it kept me alive for this long, and I owe it that. Some of my friends at the schools I've been to have sworn up and down that they're City girls. It's in their blood, they claimed, and it filled their hearts, guided them to love ShackBurgers and hate the Red Sox. I never quite felt that way, and I don't know why, but I'm having pangs all the same, especially when we exit the tunnel into New Jersey and start seeing signs for Newark International Airport. For someone who signed those papers so quickly, I sure am looking back a lot.

I snap out of my reverie when Eddie suddenly claps his hands. "Say, Nicki—have you given any thought to your new name?"

"My new name?" I ask. It hadn't occurred to me that I'd

37

need to change it, though I suppose it should have. I spot the *ND* on my suitcase, and my hand slips over it.

"Sure! The Sicurezzas obviously won't be the Sicurezzas anymore. They're going to be the Trevors. Trevor—that's your new last name."

"But I get to pick my first name?"

"And middle, if you like."

Oh, so much potential here. I mean, I love my name. It connects me to my grammy, and it's all I've ever known. Then again, it also connects me to my dad. . . . And getting to pick a new one? After all the drama of the last hour? It's like eating those nasty little Valentine's Day hearts with the words on them for a week, suddenly to be offered a box of Swiss chocolate. I momentarily forget my nerves, my emptiness. I get to pick my name!

"Elegancia Florence Trevor."

Janice coughs loudly, and the SUV swerves a little before she recovers. Eddie laughs out loud.

"Sorry, kid. It can't be anything strange. You've got to blend in. Remember—normal is the key. Everything from here out has to be normal."

"So Titanium Ravenlocks is out, too?"

"That's a safe bet."

"No Baroness Quicksilver?"

"Nope."

"Smoothness von Fruffelburg?"

More choking sounds from Janice. I grab a piece of hair and chew. This is going to be harder than I thought.

"What about Anne?" Janice murmurs.

"You're kidding, right?" I say.

"What's wrong with Anne? It's a perfectly fine name."

"Yeah, if you're going to be tromping around Avonlea."

"What? Where's Avonlea?" Eddie asks.

I smile. "Oh, shelved somewhere after Frank and Raggedy, I imagine."

That one just gets silence.

"Anne Frank? Raggedy Ann? Man, I should've slipped a library card into your wallet before I gave it back, Eddie."

"I still don't get it."

"Lots of time to read at the Center. I like books," I explain. "And besides, I'd like to avoid names that don't bode well for kids my age. Anne's one. So is Joan. Or Juliet. Did you know she was only thirteen when she borrowed Romeo's happy dagger? I need a name that gives me a fighting chance to make it to high school someday."

"Hey!" Eddie bubbles enthusiastically. It's the first time I've ever seen a two-hundred-pound man do jazz hands. "I get it now!"

I smile, then get back to thinking. "How's about Trevor? Like, Trevor Trevor?"

I swear, the way she's gripping the steering wheel and muttering, Janice is just going to pull the car over right here, like some angry minivan-mom with a load of fourth graders in the backseat.

"I'm kidding, of course."

Doesn't matter. She's still white-knuckling it. My own

digits get to drumming on the plastic seam of my suitcase as I think, long fingers skittering across like the legs of some quickly crawling . . .

"Charlotte?" I blurt.

"Charlotte," Eddie pronounces slowly. "Charlotte Trevor. Hey, kid, yeah! I like it!"

Actually, I kind of do, too. It's no Titanium, but it shares a bunch of letters with my actual first name—Nicolette—without sounding like it. I can still end my signature with the flourish through the double *t*'s, and I've never known a Charlotte before, so I don't have any other kid's face in my head when I think about it. My brain isn't conjuring up any unfortunate famous Charlottes, either—just the spider, a Brontë sister, and a Doyle. This could work.

"How's that, Janice?" I say, leaning forward and watching her eyes in the rearview.

"It will do for now," she replies, not even glancing back.

"No famous tragic Charlottes, huh?" Eddie inquires, chuckling.

"Nope. At least, none that didn't live full lives and have hundreds of babies first."

Eddie's face scrunches up as he thinks about that one.

We spend the rest of the drive in silence—well, okay, they do. I'm back here quietly having conversations with myself. "Hello, Charlotte Trevor! I'm Charlotte Trevor. Can I introduce you to Charlotte Trevor? Really? Your name is Charlotte Trevor, too? What a coincidence!" Every time I say it, it rolls off my tongue a little easier. Soon I'm trying different accents—"Charl'a Trevvah, guv'nah, iffn' yah please," and "*Oui*, I em ze one called Charleaux Trev'veh." It's only when I get to my spot-on Brooklyn accent that Eddie turns around and shakes his head, and I shut up . . . for about five minutes. Then, without even realizing it, I'm singing the Beatles's "Yesterday," only I'm replacing all the words with "Charlotte Trevor." After that it's Billy Joel, Taylor Swift, and half of the first act of *Wicked*. By the time we get to the airport, I'm feeling pretty comfortable with my new name. I still have to pick a middle—something with an *A*, I'm thinking, for "CAT," but I'm saving that thought-thread for the flight.

When we get to the airport, Eddie grabs my suitcase. I notice we're going past everyone else—they all seem to be standing in lines at counters. Sure, I've seen airports in movies and on TV, but this is my first time actually being in one, and Janice has to snip at me to keep up since I stop to stare so frequently. After the marshals flash their badges and check their Tasers at a security station, we're through. On the other side, there's a massive board of arriving and departing flights, and I'm mesmerized.

"Nicki, please keep moving."

"It's Charlotte, if you please," I murmur, still looking at the board.

Janice sighs. "Charlotte, then."

"There are no flights soon that go to Georgia."

"We don't fly coach, Charlotte."

I don't really know what that means, but I nod anyway and throw in a "Figures," just to be safe.

After the big board, the airport blooms into this weird mix of mall, festival, golf course, campground, and middle school hallway the moment the bell rings. Two ladies walk past—one is decked out in a gorgeous black business suit, silk blouse, pumps, leather purse, the works. The other, chatting with her, is wearing pajamas and moon boots. We dodge a dude driving a little train of elderly people down the middle of the way, and I nearly bump into a guy shoveling a massive cinnamon roll into his face at the same time he's texting on his phone. And everywhere, everywhere, there are people rushing, zipping, bouncing from stall to stall, store to store, desk to desk, barely paying attention to anybody else around them. They have to avoid folks who are sleeping, actually sleeping, in torturous positions near just about every gate. My first time in an airport is noisy. It's chaotic. It's frenetic.

It's beautiful.

This is a pickpocket's paradise. My eyes are wide, my hands slicing through the air, swerving and sweeping in that sweet dance. I'm not actually taking anything—*willpower, Nicki, willpower*—but I'm pretending, practicing. A man stops in the middle of the flow, looking down at a map of the terminals. My hand brushes lightly against his pocket, and he doesn't even glance up. Could have had a smartphone there. A college-age girl has her purse next to her on a bench, and she's chatting with her friend on the opposite side. She's not even looking! I casually time my movements with the beeping of one of those golf carts that's passing, and I manage to flick open the clasp of her purse, pick up her wallet, and drop it back down again without her, or Eddie and Janice, noticing. And this is all while we're still hurrying along.

A girl could get rich in an airport.

"Sorry we're rushing you, Charlotte," Eddie says as we navigate our way around a kiosk of prewrapped muffins, water bottles, and gum. "Gotta get to our gate, though."

"Oh, it's fine," I reply, only half listening—there's a boy ahead of us with a backpack on, and it's half unzipped already. I'd just match him stride for stride, slip my left hand in there, take what's for taking, and then spin him around with a cute little smile. He'd be blushing while I skipped away with a new PlayStation Vita.

Eddie smiles. "You're taking all of this remarkably well, Charlotte. We had in your records that you've never flown before. What with how nervous you were at the Center—totally understandable, by the way—I'd think you'd be worried here."

"No, big crowds are kind of my thing. They keep me distracted, keep me from being afraid. I feel safe here," I explain, leaving out the part about everyone else not being safe from me. "Because, like, if you were to suddenly turn out not to be U.S. marshals, but just clever kidnappers, well, I could scream all sorts of things here. Or I could run, and I'd have about eight phones in my pocket before you caught me, all of them dialing nine-one-one at the same time. Being trapped in the transition room with you two gave me the heebees much more than this."

Eddie slows down, casting me a look. He's just remembered he's escorting a first-rate pickpocket through a bustling airport. I smile innocently and turn out my pockets, and he takes a deep breath. Then he adds, "Yeah, sorry about the Center. Had to be done, though."

"No worries," I offer. "I'm excited about all this, really. Haven't quite wrapped my mind around it yet, but I'm excited."

Our conversation carries us all the way to our gate, which is really nothing more than a glass door and a couple of rows of chairs. Two other marshals are there, each one a cookie-cutter copy of Eddie, right down to the brick-wall build and the pockets where they keep their wallets. When they step aside to let us through, I gasp. There are two other kids here!

I quickly sweep my hair behind my ears, using the cover of my hand to check them out. The girl is a few years older than me, and the boy is my age, maybe a little younger. They're both obviously from the system like me: small suitcases; wide, darting, and distrusting eyes; and crossed arms.

"Hey," I say to the girl. She's a little taller than me, with frizzy hair and a great pair of chunky glasses.

"Hey," she replies. No turn of the shoulder, no blink and glance away.

"My fake name I chose ten minutes ago is Charlotte. What's yours?"

She laughs, just a titter at first, and then giggles properly. "Erin," she replies. "I forget my last name, though."

I snicker at that, and so does the boy. He stands up and joins us. He's got the blondest hair I've ever seen, and it's cowlicked all over the place.

"I'm A.J., but I haven't decided what it stands for yet. Are you guys with the marshals, too?"

"Nah," Erin deadpans, "I just like guys with crew cuts."

I giggle again, but A.J. looks confused.

"She's kidding," I offer. "I'm here with the marshals. Headed to Georgia for training or something."

"Me too," both reply in unison.

"Project Family?" I ask, glancing Janice's way. She's watching, but not too closely; one eye on us, the other on her phone. I wonder if she's playing solitaire or something. Probably not.

A.J. and Erin nod. "Yeah," A.J. says, "Project Family. Do you know what it stands for?"

I shake my head. "Nothing, apparently. Though I think it should. Been working on it, too. Federal Agents Masquerading In Life . . . Yogurt?"

"Foster Assets Making Invisible . . ." A.J. loses steam, scratching in that blond bird's nest of his. ". . . Licorice . . . Yogurt. Yeah, I got nothin'."

We spend the next five minutes or so coming up with new ones, all of them ending in "Yogurt." It continues as we board the plane, and between talking to Erin and A.J., thinking of a middle name, and playing "most useless thing on the page" with our copies of *Skymall*, I survive my first flight without getting too jittery. I only hope I'm just as distracted in Georgia.

Oh, and it's Ashlynn. Charlotte Ashlynn Trevor. Pretty nice ring to it, I think.

Dad,

I'm gone. Done. Not even going to sign this letter. I don't know where you are, but I know you're alive, and that you're out.

I know you don't care.

So have fun sweeping floors, or fixing cars, or moving furniture, or doing whatever other crummy post-jail job you scored. Maybe rob somebody again, if that's what you do for fun. Does it beat going to the park with your daughter?

My therapist, if I still had one, would call this letter "venting." And I've got to admit, it feels pretty good. So don't look for me. I'm disappeared. For real. Of course, you and ol' birth mom know just what it's like to disappear, don't you?

Tell you what—I'm going to do you a favor that neither of you ever did for me.

Check it out.

Here it comes.

Are you ready?

                                                    Bye!

CHAPTER FIVE

Backstories

Glynco, Georgia, is a whirlwind. The complex is huge, like they took Central Park, doubled it, and replaced the playgrounds and monuments with shooting ranges and dorms. There are troops of men and women jogging around, all wearing T-shirts and track pants. At first, I think we're going to be doing the same intense boot-camp stuff; I'm half expecting to army crawl through mud with Fancypaws held above my head like an AK-47. Fortunately, our physical training never gets quite that intense. Most of the time we're in courses on math, writing, and science meant to get us ready for our placement schools and grades.

Erin, A.J., and I, it turns out, are a fourth of the kids in Project Family, and for the first two weeks of training, we're together. We train together, we eat together, we relax together, and we speculate together. That's the big pastime—trying to figure out what the heck we're doing and where they'll ship us off to. I have to say, these are two of the best weeks of my life. The weather is so much better than in New York, I'm busy, I'm learning, and I'm in it with other kids just like me.

I haven't even felt the urge to nick something this entire time.

Not that I completely abstain, of course . . . I just don't feel the urge. A.J. loves putting on his jacket, loading his pockets with stuff, and walking by me. Then he tries to guess what will be missing. He gets it wrong every time, though I think he might be doing it just to flirt with me. He's always all, "That's incredible! Do it again, Charlotte!"

The kid seriously needs an Xbox.

Erin and I, meanwhile, grow closer and closer. Her background is similar to mine—dad in jail, grandma taking care of her. She's also been in and out of foster homes, and we get to swap descriptions of the cruddiest bedrooms we've had, compare our shortest stints with a family, and see which one of us has had the weirdest foster experience overall (she wins; I can't beat staying with a couple who collected taxidermied housecats). Through conversations like these, and laughing at A.J., we become as good of friends as you can in two weeks.

It can't last, though.

. . .

On the morning of our third Wednesday, they herd all of us into a room. It's got tiers of padded seats that swivel. At the front of the room is a big table, and on that table are envelopes. As I file in and sit down, I manage to catch a glimpse of the topmost envelope. It says *Charlotte Trevor* on the label.

A short, matronly lady comes in after a while, and twelve swiveling kids all come to an abrupt stop. Well, eleven of us. There's one kid, made-up name of Charles "Chuckie" Islip, who doesn't notice the lady and just keeps working that chair back and forth, eyes closed and lower lip sucked in as he hum-grunts "We Will Rock You." It's only when the rest of us back him up with a little chorus of "Go, Chuckie! Go, Chuckie!" that he opens his eyes, blushes, and apologizes. The lady takes off her glasses and pretends to clean them as she waits for us to stop laughing. Her gaze never leaves us, though, and our snickering dies off. There's almost pity in her look, like she's saying, "Enjoy that laugh. It's the last you'll have for a while."

Erin is clearly spooked. She reaches down to hold my hand, but I manage to yank mine away in time, pretending to pick at something between my teeth.

"For those of you who have formed bonds over the last few weeks, I am sorry," the lady begins. "Your lives have been defined by relationships cut short, and I want you to know that we sympathize and understand. I am Special Deputy Marshal Dr. Helena Coustoff, and I'm Glynco's on-site psychiatrist. I am here to talk to you about the next phase of your training."

I cast a glance over at Erin. She's got both hands pressed between her thighs and is leaning forward intently, shoulders frozen. My leg has started bouncing a bit as well.

"Starting today, you'll be separated, because each of you will be learning about your new family and relocation site. We cannot under any circumstances allow you to share this information with one another, as it would jeopardize the safety of both you and the people you're helping to protect. I'll call your names one at a time, and you'll come down to get your information packet." She pauses, holding up the first envelope on the table—mine. "Then you'll be escorted to a soundproof room, where you'll be joined by the marshal who will be your point of contact with us from here on out. I'm sure you'll have lots of questions, and we'll try our best to answer them."

A few kids raise their hands, but she subtly shakes her head, and the hands go down. I guess by "try our best" she meant "just not right now." As she starts riffling through the folders, we get the sense that it's time to say good-bye.

A.J. taps my shoulder, and I turn. "Good luck, Charlotte. You'll be great at this! And who knows—maybe we'll meet each other totally randomly one day, like, in college or something."

I grin. "Yeah, and if we do, we'll go out for coffee. I'll buy."

"Awesome."

"With your wallet," I add under my breath.

Erin overhears me. She half laughs, half sobs, and it comes out like a hiccup. Covering her mouth in alarm, she waves at the air with her other arm and leans in for a hug. Hand-holding I can't do, but hugs I can, and I squeeze her tightly. It's brief, but it's enough, and when we pull away, we both nod at each other. Short, intense, and awkward—the foster farewell.

"Charlotte Trevor," Helena announces, staring right at me. "Room one."

I get up slowly, aware that everyone else is watching how I handle this. I ease my chair back into position and tug the hem of my marshal-issue T-shirt down. With my head held high, I stride along the row, screaming at myself not to trip over anyone's foot. A couple of kids want high fives, but I pass them by. I grab my folder quickly so nobody sees my trembling left thumb, and I head toward the door. Just before I leave, though, I turn back. Making sure I've caught Erin's and A.J.'s eyes, I whisper, "Good luck!"

Then I'm gone.

There's a marshal waiting outside the door to move me along, and he points to a hallway off the central room. It is carpeted, unlike the rest of the facility, and it has a single track of fluorescent lights. I follow the lights until I get to the numbered rooms, march all the way down to the end, and slip through the glass-and-steel door labeled *1*.

It's small, sort of like a converted closet, and it smells like fresh paint and drywall. There's a round table in the center of the room, a U.S. marshal logo mug situated in the center, bristling with pencils. Three chairs flank the table, and I pull one out. As I sit, I grab a pencil, slipping it into the seam of my envelope and ripping it open in one smooth motion. A picture of the Trevors—the same one Eddie and Janice had back at the Center—falls out, and there's a thick stack of papers as well, loosely clipped together. Upending the envelope, I allow them to shuffle onto the table.

At the top is written *Sicurezza Case File*, along with a bunch of numbers and random letters, probably to help with filing it in some sort of system. I scan it quickly—it's mostly data about the family, like their birthdays, hair color, income (whoa, nice work, Elena!), and driver's license numbers. I'm guessing all of that will change. Will I get a new birthday, too? Maybe I can wrangle an extra one so I can turn fourteen ahead of time.

I'm still skimming along, picking up tidbits of info here and there, when I flip the page. At that point, I freeze. There, smack-dab in the middle, is a picture of a dead man.

No, not just dead.

Murdered.

Very murdered.

The picture is grainy, but a few things are clear enough: He's been shot repeatedly. What's more, someone has done something horrible to his eyes, and even worse to his mouth. I'm no expert, but I've been around enough to know how to read this. The guy had snitched. The eyes mean he had seen something, and the mouth? He had talked.

I take a moment to rub at my temples. It suddenly feels colder in the room, and my arms are covered in goose bumps. I inhale deeply and flip the picture over.

The next page is a dialogue, like a transcript or something. I dive in.

"Please state your name for the court."
"Elena Sicurezza."
"Is that your family name?"
"No."
"Married name?"
"Yes."
"Please state your maiden name."
"Elena Cercatore."
**"In addition to your family affiliation, what are your
ties to the Cercatores?"**
"I am, or was, a lawyer in their employ."
"And what were your responsibilities as their lawyer?"
"I was one of many lawyers, responsible for the
day-to-day document processing and oversight for
their legitimate businesses, such as Facciata Cleaning
Services and the West Nook Bistro."
"But you had other responsibilities, too, correct?"

CLERK'S NOTE: Mrs. Sicurezza hesitates.

"Mrs. Sicurezza? Your other responsibilities?"
"I drew up contracts."
"What kind of contracts?"
"Agreements between the Cercatores and small
business owners for protection, primarily against the
actions of the Cercatores themselves."

"In other words, you personally witnessed key members of the Cercatore family engaged in protection racketeering, extorting money and favors in exchange for protection against the Cercatores' other criminal activities."

"Yes. Some of the contracts stipulated that the syndicate would agree not to sell or make drugs, launder money, or house their enforcers in a two-block radius of those who paid the monthly bribes."

"And how much money did the Cercatore crime family . . ."

CLERK'S NOTE: Defense objection: inflammatory. Sustained.

"How much money did the Cercatore family make from these activities?"

"Upwards of seventeen million dollars a year from the racketeering alone."

"Thank you, Mrs. Sicurezza. No further questions."

I blink several times, then swallow slowly. The Cercatores . . . no wonder the Sicurezzas need WITSEC! Everyone has heard of the Cercatores, at least enough to know you don't mess with them. It was big news when eight of their most powerful members were sent to prison last year. It never occurred to me that for that to happen, some- one would have had to talk. For that someone to be a Cercatore herself, for that someone to be my new mom . . .

Grinding through the rest of the papers reveals more

information about the Cercatores and the Sicurezzas. I read as hard and fast as I can, until my eyes water. It's heavy stuff—some of the legal jargon I don't understand, but this much is clear: When Eddie said that Elena was a brave woman, he wasn't kidding. She ratted out her own family. Even I know you don't rat out blood, and I don't have any blood to speak of.

I'm about to sneak another scare-myself-silly peek at the picture of the dead guy when I notice one more form. It's not about the Sicurezzas or the Cercatores, or about Nicki Demere. It's about the Trevors. As I scan, I realize it's *all* about the Trevors. I'm looking at their entire history, conjured up and laid out neat.

Apparently, I'm from Indian Hill, Ohio, just outside Cincinnati. The Trevors—Jonathan, Harriet, Charlotte, and Jackson—lived there until Jonathan's company moved its headquarters to Research Triangle Park in Durham, North Carolina. Jonathan's a consultant—for what, it doesn't really say—and Harriet is joining the legal team at IBM, the computer place. Both Charlotte and her younger brother, Jackson, will be attending Loblolly Middle School in Durham.

Loblolly? I'm going to a school called Loblolly?

That's what has me crinkling my nose as the door opens behind me, and I'm still wearing that expression when I turn around. There, standing in the doorway and shooting me a nearly identical look of disdain, is Janice. I shake the half cringe, half sneer off my face and find my smile as quickly as possible.

"Hello, Janice! I haven't seen you in two weeks! How have you been? Because I've been good. Well. Good."

"Have you read the file yet?" she asks curtly.

"Yeah, Janice. It's unbelievable! The Cercatores! Why didn't you guys tell me the first time we talked? Oh, and by the way, isn't it weird that when I first saw you, you were reading files about me, and now you come in and I'm reading the files? Coincidence? I think not!"

She acts like I'm puking words all over the floor, rather than just making conversation. Sighing, she sits down across from me, adjusting the collar of her shirt while she arranges her papers just *so* on the table.

"Memorize that, Charlotte. All of it. You have exactly one week to learn who you are, and you can't take that envelope with you once you leave for North Carolina. While there, you must maintain your persona at all times. A single slip may jeopardize the safety of the Sicurezzas."

"You sure do put the *nice* in *Janice*, you know?"

"Charlotte, it is precisely that flippant attitude that will endanger this entire operation. Focus!" she says, slapping the table for emphasis. "Now, for the remainder of this week, we will be training you in how to avoid detection. This will include intense exercises in surveillance, local customs, and communication. Do you understand?"

I nod quickly. Janice really does seem to be in a mood; her hair is pulled back so tightly she can hardly blink, and she's keeping her teeth bared as she talks, even though they're not moving much.

"None of that, however, will be as important as you learning the rules for staying hidden."

"The rules?" I ask as meekly as I can.

"Yes. The rules. Everything from this point forward is about maintaining an air of normalcy. That is how to avoid detection by the Cercatores, who, we are confident, will be looking for Elena and her family."

"So, basically, stay normal?"

"Basically, yes. We have done considerable research on families in the Durham area in general, and on girls your age in particular. Via the data we procured, we have distilled a profile that you will adhere to as closely as possible."

"So I'm going to act like the girl in this profile?"

"What you're going to do, Charlotte, is act normal."

"Implying I'm not normal right now?"

She scowls at me. I think she's trying to say "Well, obviously," but she doesn't want to stoop that low. I get the message anyway and shrug.

"Rule one," she snaps, plowing right through the drifts of awkward that piled up just then, "you will not commit any criminal acts, including theft, breaking and entering, trespassing, or vandalism. Again, Charlotte: no theft."

I hold up my hands. "Got it, got it!"

"Rule two: You will maintain a B-minus average in school. No higher, no lower."

"Holy hell, are you serious? An exact B-minus?"

I've always been more of an A girl. When it's not family

you're going home to, it's a whole lot easier to jump into your homework after school. Other kids I know haven't been as lucky as me; my grammy taught me to read like nobody's business, and I didn't get put into any absolute pits like Emmy did. She'd been with only one foster family, but it was a nightmare, and she lost an entire year of school because of it. I feel like I owe every A I get to all the other kids at the Center who struggled. Now I have to get B-minuses?

"First, watch your language. And second, yes, that is the average for a seventh-grade Caucasian female in your school district in North Carolina. Now, the Sicurezzas—that is, the Trevors—have requested that their son be placed in a high-achieving school. Loblolly Middle School has been recognized as a school of distinction, and its students consistently do well on state achievement tests. A B-minus there should allow you to maintain a low profile."

"So a B-minus at another school would be . . . what, good?"

"We're taking no chances, Charlotte."

"Can you pay for college? Not exactly scholarshipping it up with a B-minus my entire academic career."

"This is serious, Charlotte. B-minuses will ensure that you do not garner attention for your academics, whether your grades are too high or too low."

I'm imagining a big, white refrigerator, the entire front plastered with papers covered in red B-minuses, held on by *Great Job!* magnets. Yeah, that's normal.

"Rule three: No online presence. You will not create a Facebook page, a Twitter account, or any other social media avatar, unless expressly required by your school. You will be given an e-mail account by the marshals' tech department for communications with us only, and we will monitor all incoming and outgoing messages."

"Can you clean my spam folder?"

"Rule four: You will maintain a clean, moderate appearance at all times. Attire will be preapproved by this department, as will haircuts and other body modifications."

"Body modifications? Does that mean my SpongeBob facial tattoo is out? Because I was going to get Plankton on my left cheek, Patrick on my right, and SpongeBob on my forehead. Well, okay, not SpongeBob. Just his pants. What do you—"

"Enough!" Janice barks. I jump in my seat, thankful that kids don't get heart attacks as a general rule.

"Sorry," I mutter. "I didn't mean . . . I mess around sometimes, when things get to be a lot . . . I . . . well, I'm sorry."

She snorts like a bull deciding a puny matador isn't worth charging. I grab my shaky left hand with my right. The urge is suddenly overpowering, but . . . rule one. Instead, I just whisper, "Go on. I'm listening."

"You will engage in two extracurricular activities—one sport and one nonathletic. Our studies show this is the median number for a child your age. You will not excel at either of these activities, but you must maintain your position in the groups."

I nod, even though this makes no kind of sense. I'm starting to question whether Janice was ever a kid herself.

"You will also maintain regular friendships: do not withdraw, or become a loner, deadhead, goth, vamp, emo, punk, or skater. These types are regularly targets of school administration probes focusing on antisocial behavior."

I want to ask her how many of those names she had to Google before coming in here, but I keep my mouth shut. And anyway, deadhead? Is that even a thing?

"Nor are you to achieve too prominent a social position. Popularity, though alluring, is not your ally here."

I sigh. "So fit in, but don't stand out?"

Janice's eyes widen briefly. "Yes," she says slowly. "Yes, Charlotte. That's it exactly. Thank you."

I wonder how much pressure you could lift off new kids at a school if they could say, "Sorry, I'd try harder, but the U.S. government ordered me not to be that cool."

She continues, "Rule five: Maintain a respectful, caring front in your familial relations when you are in public. Do not, under any circumstances, let on that there is something unusual about your family dynamic, and do not do anything destructive in private to erode their trust in you. Your father is normal. Your mother is normal. Your younger brother is normal."

At that point, I have to clear my throat.

"Yes? Something the matter, Charlotte?"

"Well, it's . . . it's just that nobody, and I mean nobody, not in the history of ever, has had a normal younger brother."

"You do, starting now."

I think she thought I was kidding. . . .

"It's just that no kid I've ever known or read about, no girl my age, has ever said, 'Oh, that's my normal little brother. Look at him trying to drink Coke from a saucer like a dog. Totally normal.'"

Doing her best to stampede over what I think is a valid point, she demands, "Repeat those rules as I've given them to you, Charlotte. They are your new code of conduct. You don't leave this room until I'm satisfied that—"

"Rule one: No crimes.

"Rule two: B-minus.

"Rule three: No Facebook.

"Rule four: No personality.

"Rule five: Happy family."

She raises a thick eyebrow, but then she nods, satisfied. She gathers her papers and stands up to go. But she pauses, seeming to suddenly remember I'm still there. Grumbling, she says, "Oh, yes. Do you have any questions?"

Only about five billion.

"A couple, yes."

She purses her lips, throwing a snarl in there for good measure, and sits back down.

"Proceed."

I take a breath to steady myself because I don't want to forget any of these. They've been beating against my brain for two weeks, and I need to let them dance a bit.

"How will I get in contact with the marshals if I

need to? I know I've got the e-mail, but what about dire emergencies?"

"You'll have a contact person here. We will provide you with a phone number to call. If you notice something of concern, call your contact, and you'll receive the assistance you need."

"Who is my contact?"

Janice taps her left index finger on the table a few times. Oh, lord . . .

"You? You're my contact?"

"And supervising officer. I trust that won't be a problem?"

"No," I say, smiling broadly, trying really hard to make it seem genuine. "No, that's great, Janice. Fine. Yes. I'm sure it'll be fine. You . . . you and Eddie . . ."

"Not Eddie. Eddie is assigned to another case. He doesn't even know where you're going, for the safety of all involved." She pauses and then waggles her and-another-thing finger at me for good measure. "You really should refer to him as Deputy Marshal Harkness. And me as Deputy Marshal Stricker, for that matter."

"Yes, I will. Deputy Marshal Stricker. Got it."

"Now, if we're finished . . ."

I raise my hand. Silly habit, but I'm a kid, after all.

"What now?"

"Well, you wanted me to look presentable at school. I . . . I don't exactly have the clothes for it. In fact, I really don't have anything for it. I'm betting you don't want me wearing my U.S. marshals sweats, and rule one implies you don't want me taking care of the problem myself."

"Shopping. When you get to Durham . . . we've given your family a thousand dollars on a preloaded debit card to take care of those things you'll need for school. We can't buy them here, because there are regional fashion considerations to take into account."

I lean forward. "I get a thousand dollars?"

"Your family does, though it's earmarked for you. Each family member has a similar budget."

Score.

I decide to press my luck.

"And if I need to protect my family? Myself? Do I get a Taser?"

Janice mutters a curse under her breath. "What is your obsession with Tasers?"

"They're cool! Haven't you ever seen any of the videos on YouTube?"

Her dour look leads me to believe she hasn't.

"Oh, you totally should! There's loads of videos out there, just of guys getting tased, and they're all hilarious. There's this one of a dude who's drunk, riding around on a lawn mower, and he starts just cruising through everyone's lawns, like all their flowers and stuff, right? And the police tase him while he's on the mower. His hands come up by his chin and his teeth pull back—guy starts chittering like a psychotic squirrel wearing sunglasses. It's all like *gikkagikkagikkagikka . . .*"

I'm doing a darn good impression of tased lawn mower guy at this point, but Janice is having none of it; she's giving me the old arms-crossed head shake. I wipe a little bit of spit from my chin, lower my hands, and cough. A good ten seconds of silence pass, and then I say, "So, um, yeah. Can I have a Taser?"

She's still shaking her head—though to be fair, I think that's just her natural state.

"C'mon! You've seen what the Cercatores do to people!" My hands wade through the papers until I find the photo. "How am I supposed to protect them from this? I've learned a few cool moves in my classes this week, but seriously . . . check out this poor guy's mouth. . . . I think they actually shoved a bird in there. I'm pretty sure that's a real canary! And it's not like I'm asking for a gun or anything. You want me serious? I'm being serious. This is me taking this seriously."

I tilt my head forward, looking up at her through my lashes. I've got my jaw set, lips sealed, and nostrils flared. As far as faces go, mine can't get any more serious than this. Granted, it might have helped to avoid the Famously Fuchsia glitter lip gloss this morning, but other than that, I'm gravitas personified.

Janice leans in, bringing her own face about a foot from mine.

"No."

Heck. She does serious face better than me. She even has a poppy vein up there. I can't compete.

"Okay," I mutter grudgingly. "But pepper spray?"

"You're not here to protect the Trevors. You're here to help hide them. The best way to do that isn't with a Taser, or pepper spray, or with your ridiculous attitude. It's to be who we're telling you to be. So pick up your files, Charlotte. Take them to your room and study for the rest of the day. Also, review the included list of extracurricular activities at Loblolly Middle School. You'll need to choose two—one sport, one academic. Make sure none of your choices compete for awards. No geography bee, no choral competitions, no debate club."

"But what if we win whatever sport . . ."

"You won't. Loblolly Middle School isn't known for its athletics. The Sicurezzas requested academic excellence."

"Two extracurriculars. Got it."

"Oh, and Charlotte?"

I pause my search for the form.

"Yes, Deputy Marshal?"

"Set your alarm for six a.m. Make sure to take a shower. You're meeting the Trevors tomorrow at seven."

"Wait, Janice . . . I mean, Deputy Marshal . . . but . . . hold on. . . . They're . . . they're here?"

Without responding, she stands up and marches out. I lean back, both hands in my hair as I look out over the tableful of strewn papers.

The Trevors.

Tomorrow.

Whoa.

CHAPTER SIX

Tea with the Trevors

I'd like to say I'm as cool as a cucumber this morning, but I'd be lying. It's 6:45 a.m., and I'm not even dressed yet. I'm still staring in the bathroom mirror, practicing faces. Do I go in all serious? Miss On-a-Mission? Or should I go with calm, confident, ready-to-be-the-daughter-you've-always-wanted? One thing's for sure, I can't be panicky, nervous-giggle girl. Unfortunately, that's who keeps showing up in the mirror, despite my best efforts: I even use my fingers to try to squishify my face into a more professional look. That doesn't work, either; I end up looking like a Muppet. Finally, I pull my hair back so it doesn't seem like I'm hiding anything, put in my Swarovskis, and use just a little bit of the rose lip gloss Erin lent me; it's not the Famously Fuchsia, but I'm thinking that's not a bad thing.

I've haloed out all my clothes on the bed, and it's pathetic.

Basically, my choices are the outfit I flew in with, a pair of jeans and a *Sweeney Todd* T-shirt, or some of my U.S. marshal couture. That thousand bucks can't come fast enough.

I decide on my black skirt and a gray marshals tee, though I quickly wish I had some color to throw in there. Just as I'm slipping into my shoes, there's a knock at my door. It's Janice, and she's wielding a clipboard in one hand and the biggest mug of coffee I've ever seen in the other.

"The Trevors are waiting for you in Special Deputy Marshal Coustoff's office. Come. I'll lead you there."

If Janice's lips part more than a centimeter at any point, I don't see it. Apparently, my already-grumpy contact isn't a morning person. Great.

I follow Janice down the hallway, up a short staircase, through a doorway, and into a well-lit, inviting foyer. There are several office doors that open onto this central space, and they're all closed, the occupants hidden behind panes of frosted glass. Janice sits down on one of the blue couches lining the walls of the room, and I start to sit next to her.

"See the door with the doctor's name on it?" Janice growls. "Go knock. They're waiting."

I swallow, take a deep breath, and stride toward the door. Instead of knocking, I listen at the glass for a moment. There's a man's voice, then a woman's, then another woman's. Yep, they're in there.

"Knock," Janice commands from behind me.

"Just . . . um . . . gonna get a drink first," I ad-lib, spinning off toward the water fountain nearby. It's one of those obnoxious ones where you push the bar as hard as you can, but only a trickle comes out. You're basically French-kissing by proxy whoever used it before you. Still, I'm supposed to be stalling here, so I take a sip and churn it across my teeth about fifty times.

When I turn around, Janice is standing behind me. Good thing I swallowed, or I'd be doing a scared-stiff spit take into her face.

"Get in there, Charlotte," she whispers.

"Can you come with me?"

Janice shakes her head slowly.

"Fine! I'm going, I'm going! Just give me a second."

I feel like a year wouldn't be enough time to get ready for this. However, Janice is already taking the liberty of knocking. Dr. Coustoff answers, sees me, and smiles, ushering me in with a broad wave of her clipboard.

"Come in, dear, come in! We're all very excited to meet you!"

I smile too, nod, and hide my shaking left hand behind my back. Then I walk into her office.

The man and the woman from the photograph are there, in living color. She's standing, holding a bouquet of flowers in her left hand, and he's seated on the edge of the doctor's desk, fretting over the arrangement of the baby's breath, carnations, and yellow roses. He murmurs, "It's fine, hon. I'm sure Charlotte will be happy just to—"

He looks up and notices that I'm standing there, and his hand drops from the flowers to his lap. "Goodness," he says, and again, "Goodness . . ."

Elena, or Harriet, I suppose, gasps. She presses a hand above her heart and stares at me. I can actually see tears welling in her eyes. They're just like mine, only darker, more strained than they were in the photo, like she's seen a hurricane or two in her time. It makes my skin prickle and my heart race.

I've met with many families in the last few years, and it's been so businesslike. We meet in the transition room. They ask me questions. I behave politely, and they go to sign the paperwork with Wainwright. This? This is just paralysis. I want to say something. I want to seem eloquent, and strong, and brave. I have to say something. Someone should say something. Someone should . . .

"Well, at least she's kinda hot."

That'd be Jackson Trevor, the shaggy kid sitting in the doctor's chair, his feet up on the desk. At first, it's hard to recognize him; he was clean-cut in the photograph. Now he's all greasy bangs and slumped shoulders. He sneers at me. Mr. Trevor—Jonathan—swats his son's shoes off the desk, mutters something harsh in what's probably Italian, and turns back, smiling.

"What he means is that your photo didn't do you justice, Charlotte. You're the spitting image of my wife."

"No, I meant she's kinda hot."

First, *ew*.

Second, I can tell when another kid is angry. Under normal circumstances, I'd be sympathetic. This can't be easy for him: moving away abruptly, all the danger his mom is in, suddenly having an older "sister" shoved into his family. I get it. However, this is supposed to be my moment. My debut. As a result, I'm going to have to go with you shutting your face up, Jackson Trevor.

I shoot him an absolutely withering stare, and he turtles his way down, eyes settling on the screen of his phone (better not be tweeting, kid. Rule three). Then I turn my attention back to Harriet. She inhales sharply, nods, and steps forward, holding the flowers out.

"Thank you," I say, accepting them with my right hand. "They're beautiful."

I don't expect to get crushed in a hug, but Harriet sweeps in before I can interpose any carnations between us. Her arms are around me, her cheek on my head, and she whispers, "I can't thank you enough for what you're doing for my family. There are no words."

She's right—at least, there aren't any words I can think of. Instead, I just stand there. I don't even return her hug, though I want to. Her scent is all lilacs and lotion, and I can still smell it as she pulls away.

"Charlotte is a brave girl for volunteering to help you," Dr. Coustoff says.

I'm already blushing, so a bit more can't hurt. Murmuring, I add, "Not half as brave as you, Mrs. Sicurezza. I read the files. What you did—"

"Better go with Mrs. Trevor," she interrupts softly, smiling. "We should start getting used to it now."

"Actually," Dr. Coustoff interjects, "Charlotte should be calling you *Mom*."

Jackson grunts at that. I think it was supposed to come off as a laugh, but instead it just sounds like a warthoggy protest. Dr. Coustoff narrows her eyes at him, but this time I'm inclined to agree with my new kid brother. *Mom* isn't exactly a term of endearment in my life, and I shuffle nervously at the silence that follows. It's Mr. Sicurezza, or Trevor, or Jonathan, or Dad, or whoever, who breaks it.

"I'm sure we'll all need a little time to acclimate to this new situation, Doctor. No need to rush things." He turns to me, his softening smile echoing Harriet's. "Charlotte, basically what we're all trying to say is, welcome to the family. We're lucky to have you."

I nod, grateful that I pulled my hair back this morning. Otherwise, I'd be chewing it like a cow.

Before another awkward silence can descend upon the room, Dr. Coustoff has us all sit in a circle, our chairs close to one another. She offers tea, which everyone refuses. I put my flowers on the table near the window and take a seat. Harriet is on my right and Dr. Coustoff is to my left. Jonathan drags Jackson over, using a few choice threats to motivate him. My favorite is "It's not too late, you know. We could still change your name to Dweezus." When he comes to the circle, I can smell him—Cheetos and Axe body spray. It's basically the calling card of every twelve-year-old boy I've

72

ever met. I have to stifle the compulsion to inch closer to Harriet's lilac hair.

Dr. Coustoff starts. "Welcome, Trevor family. From now on, you are precisely that. Charlotte is one of you, just as each of you is hers. As we speak, the U.S. marshals are hard at work creating photo albums, schoolwork, old family vacation itineraries—everything necessary to fill in your backstory. You will drive into the East Campus neighborhood of Durham, near Duke University, in a moving truck filled with exactly these sorts of items. Each one will attest to your identities."

Jonathan and Harriet seem impressed, though weary. He rubs his eyes slowly, then runs his fingers up his forehead and through his thinning hair. Harriet sighs softly. My gaze ping-pongs between the two of them, and soon I get it.

"I'm sorry," I blurt.

"Pardon, Charlotte?"

"Excuse me, Doctor—I didn't mean to interrupt. I just . . . well, I'm sorry, is all. I know what it's like to have to leave everything behind. New stuff seems cool until you realize you'd fallen in love with the old stuff."

I look right at Jackson—this is my olive branch. He rolls his eyes and slouches farther down into his chair, until his chin is resting on his chest. A stern *humph* from Jonathan has him sitting just a little higher, but as soon as his dad looks away he sinks back down again.

"That's a nice sentiment, Charlotte," the doctor says, "and a point well made. But this new *stuff*, as you say, may very well save this family. At the very least, it will help. The bulk of the work, though, of the camouflage, will come from you. That is why you'll be training together for the rest of this week. Every day, after Charlotte is finished with her classes, she will join you for lunch or dinner and an evening of role-play. We will simulate various public family events that you may encounter upon arriving in the city."

"What about the rest of today?" Jonathan asks.

"We'll be here, getting to know one another in a safe environment. We will go over each of your backstories, embellishing them with the details that will make the Trevors come to life. It is not enough to know one another's birthdays. You need to know what *happened* on one another's birthdays. Did Charlotte have a sleepover party? Did Jackson get a video game last year for Christmas? These are the details you have to share with one another."

"I don't get it," Jackson mumbles. Every head turns toward him.

Dr. Coustoff nods. "I'll explain it a different way, then. Lives become believable when there are shared details to give them authenticity."

"Still don't get it."

"What part don't you get?"

"Her," he says, pointing at me. I flush again and frown, slipping my left hand beneath my right arm and clamping down.

"Charlotte? What about her?"

"Why do we need to make up new stuff? Why can't she

just learn about us? I actually had a tenth birthday party. We went to laser tag, had pizza, and Matt Kroger threw up in the car on the way home. Make her learn that."

I manage to smile stiffly. "It's okay. I had a tenth birthday party, too. I wasn't just animated from dead girl body parts yesterday."

Nobody laughs. Nobody even acknowledges that I spoke. They're all still drilling holes into Jackson with their eyes.

"Jackson," Dr. Coustoff says softly, "those kinds of details—though precious memories, no doubt—are the very things that people might use to track you."

Some kid puking in your car after laser tag is a precious memory? Okay, Doc. . . .

Jackson apparently doesn't appreciate the doctor's analysis, either, because he screams, "It's not Jackson. It's Lucas!"

He shouts this so loudly that I jump, and my left hand pops free of my armpit. Though everyone's looking in horror at Jackson, I panic. Before I can stop myself, my hand shoots out, a viper's strike, and returns. Instantly I feel better, calmer, like I've just been sung a lullaby, heard a cat's purr, and spent an hour on my therapist's couch, all in the span of a second. I can breathe again. So it's perfectly cool, and I'm perfectly in agreement when Dr. Coustoff tries to reason with Angrypants von Outbursten over there.

"Jackson, you have a right to be upset. No one here will tell you otherwise. However, you're old enough now to accept the responsibilities that come with . . ."

clickaclicka

". . . with your family's position. For their sake and your own, the faster you come to grips with your situation . . ."

clicka . . . clickaclicka . . .

". . . the faster . . . faster that . . ."

clickaclickaclicka . . .

"Wait . . . one moment. Charlotte, would you please stop clicking my pen?"

"Oh, yeah, sorry," I mutter, and then freeze. There, in my left hand, is Dr. Coustoff's pen—the same one that about fifteen seconds ago resided quite happily at the top of her clipboard. Blushing furiously, I lean over and return it.

"Where did you get this, Charlotte?" she asks skeptically.

Sheepishly, I reply, "It must've fallen. There . . . there you go . . . oh, wait . . . yeah, there. Got it. All better. Carry on."

I can see her wheels spinning, her eyes flickering from my hand, to the clipboard, to the floor, back to my hand. Still staring at me, Dr. Coustoff finally declares, "Actually, I think perhaps a break is in order. Why don't we head to our rooms for a bit? It's been a big morning. We'll review our backstories in our folders, reconvene after lunch, say twelve thirty, and start with our role-plays."

"Yes," Harriet says, "I think that might be wise." From what I can tell, she didn't even register my theft of the pen. She's still fuming at Jackson for his performance. Standing up, she takes him by the wrist and starts for the door. I rise and offer her a little wave. Though her brow is knitted and her nostrils flared, she nonetheless manages to sneak me the faintest of smiles. I'm still waving when Jonathan steps in front of me. He extends his hand, which I politely decline, and he claps me on the shoulder instead.

"Well, it was lovely to meet you, Charlotte, and I can't wait to get together again after lunch, when hopefully your *brother* will be in a less sour mood."

"It's okay," I say. "He's going through a lot."

"Aren't we all!" he replies quickly. "Aren't we all."

"We'll do it, though, Mr. Trevor."

"Yes, Charlotte, I suspect we will."

He claps me on the shoulder again and turns to go.

I exhale softly. This might have been the weirdest fifteen minutes of the weirdest three weeks of my life, but I got through it. As I grab my flowers and bury my nose in the petals of the yellow roses, I push the thoughts of Jackson and the pen out of my mind. I concentrate on the way my heart skipped a beat when I saw Harriet. I focus on Jonathan's little message to me there at the end, and I smile. I have no idea if WITSEC's plan will work, if I'm cut out for this, or if we're doomed to fail like every other family I've ever been in.

What I do know, however, is that I'm not dreading twelve thirty, and that's a start.

CHAPTER SEVEN

Places, Everybody. Places.

I should have been dreading twelve thirty.

It turns out that after lunch, I'm having lunch again—only this time, it's fake. Dr. Coustoff and Janice lead me into a side room where they've set up a table like in a restaurant—checkered cloth, a little ceramic container of sugar and Equal packets, silverware and cups, and a single plastic tulip hanging limply from a vase. I'm the first there, so they tell me to wait, although they give me a menu to look at while I do.

"Before you make any snide remarks, Charlotte, that's not an actual menu," Janice explains. "This is a situational role-play to get you acclimated to spending time in public as a family. Inside that cover is your script, which we expect you to read line for line."

"Yes, Deputy Marshal Stricker."

"I wrote all the scripts for this week myself," Dr. Coustoff declares. "I think you'll be pleased, Charlotte. Adolescent socialization is one of my specialties."

I smile and flip open the leather-bound menu. Sure enough, the first page is a cast of characters. Oh, good. I'm playing Charlotte Trevor. It actually says *CHARLOTTE TREVOR played by CHARLOTTE TREVOR*. Four lines beneath that, it says *WAITRESS played by JANICE STRICKER*. My smile widens, and I look up at the deputy marshal. She glowers at me and shakes her head. I just keep grinning.

The rest of my new family is a few minutes late, and they make an awkward entrance, stage left. They all squeeze through the doorway at the same time, with Jackson leading the way and a parent's hand on either of his shoulders. I can tell by the scuffling walk and the way his nostrils are pulsing that Jackson received a talking-to. Harriet and Jonathan lead him directly up to me, so close that to avoid eye contact he'd have to look straight down at his shoes.

Which, of course, is precisely what he does.

"I'm sorry for before, Charlotte," he drones. "I should not have said those things, especially since it disrespects the incredible sacrifice you have made on behalf of our family. You have my assurances that it won't happen again."

I'm almost tempted to sweep my hand above him, just to check for strings. Instead, I reply, "Thank you, Jackson. I understand."

Both his parents nod, satisfied, and let go of his

shoulders. As he's wriggling free and dashing to the corner to wallow, he whispers, "No. You don't."

Before I can respond, Dr. Coustoff claps her hands twice and announces that it's time to begin. As Harriet and Jonathan wrangle Jackson into his seat, I flip to the first page of the script and read the little italic stage directions.

Family of 4 sits at reasonably priced restaurant. It has been a long day, but they are happy to see one another. After they receive their drinks, Mr. Trevor addresses his children.

Jonathan blinks, and then he clears his throat. "Oh yes. This would be me, I guess. Ahem. Right," he mutters, eyes scanning the text quickly while Dr. Coustoff spins her hands behind us to urge him on. "So, kids . . . how was your day at school?"

He smiles broadly and breathes a sigh of relief. The next line is mine.

"Thanks for asking, Daddy!" I read. "It was totes cray-cray!"

I only realize what I'm saying after I've said it, and I wince. Harriet forges on.

"Oh, Charlotte, you're so silly," she says woodenly, eyes riveted to the script.

I pause before reading my next line and look at Dr. Coustoff, who is beaming proudly and nodding to goad me on.

"No, Mom," I manage to mutter. "For realz. It was sooooo obvz!"

"What does that mean?" Jonathan whispers to Jackson. His son doesn't respond, but he's sitting up now, a weird smirk twitching at the side of his mouth. I think he's starting to enjoy the awkwardness, at least the part where I get embarrassed.

Back on script, Harriet turns to Jackson and says, "Was yours the same, dear?"

Now it's my turn to fight off a giggle. Jackson peers down at his menu, then gives Dr. Coustoff the pleading "Do I have to?" face. She nods vigorously.

"Yeah, Mom," he growls, "it was . . ."

"Go on," I say sweetly. "You can do it, Jackson."

I feel a breeze tickle my ankle, the hem of my skirt swiped ever so softly. Yep. He just tried to kick me. I smile all the wider.

Huffing, he finishes, "It was . . . awesomesauce."

I tilt my head toward him in mock appreciation, and he sinks back down in his chair, defeated. Score one for the older sister.

"Well," Jonathan reads, "I'm glad to hear it. Work for me was just fine. We're one step closer to consolidating the merger, and I got a promising text message from HR today. I think that promotion's just around the corner. That's why I brought you all out to celebrate!"

"That's so boss!" Harriet exclaims. She starts to blush

immediately and leans toward me. "I'm sorry, Charlotte. That was your line. Go ahead."

Despite my little victory over Jackson, I can't take any more of this. I put down my menu and wave Dr. Coustoff over.

"You're doing great so far, Charlotte. All of you. How does it feel? Developing any of the family dynamic?"

"Dr. Coustoff," I say gently, "it's, um, a nice first try, really. And I appreciate that you've watched the Disney Channel, read *Seventeen* magazine, and maybe Googled the word *tween*, but I'm . . ."

How do I put this?

". . . *slightly* worried about this dialogue."

Dr. Coustoff rests a hand on my shoulder. "Oh, don't worry, Charlotte. I had four of the other marshals read it, and they all thought it was great!"

"Yeah," I offer, "I'm sure they did. And that's nice, really. But trying to write the way kids talk is kind of impossible. Anything you put in here will be out-of-date before people even get a chance to read it; we evolve faster than you can write. So if you want us to blend in, let us figure out what that means. That, Dr. Coustoff, will seem normal. Not crash-landing in an unfamiliar city, busting out of our UFO, and boldly speaking . . . whatever this is . . . to the natives. No offense."

To my great relief, Jackson nods at my explanation. He may hate me and everything I represent, but he must detest having to say *awesomesauce* in front of an audience of adults more.

Harriet doesn't miss that little moment. "Dr. Coustoff," she says, "my daughter is one hundred percent correct. We have to be able to figure some of this out for ourselves. Otherwise, we won't seem authentic. And isn't that the point?"

She's staring at me now, smiling softly. A strange, terrible, incredible feeling sweeps over me. It's almost heart-stopping, and it brings tears to my eyes, which I blink away quickly. This woman I barely know, who looks like me, who agreed with me, just called me *her daughter* after knowing me for less than a day. I'm suddenly petrified by her, because it's finally dawning on me what I've truly gotten myself into.

Now, for the first time since my grammy died, I've got someone I don't want to disappoint.

SEARCH

Sign in

FacciataCSLLC

• • • • • • • •

SEARCH   Witness Protection Sicurezza

Your search produced 0 results

SEARCH   Elena Cercatore

Your search produced 0 results

CHAPTER EIGHT

Durham Bound

I'm quiet for the remainder of the rehearsal, which we ad-lib our way through. The rest of the week, I'm like a fanatic. I throw myself into every training exercise, every lesson with Janice. I actually know more about countersurveillance techniques than I do about algebra now. I'm seeing pages of Charlotte's backstory in my sleep. Thanks to the daily dialect classes Jackson and I take, I've weeded most traces of New York from my vocab—I'm even calling a can of Sprite *pop* now without having to think about it. And it's all because I've got this sudden weight behind me. It's like an Indiana Jones boulder rumbling along as I scamper ahead. That normally wouldn't be a problem—I'm generally pretty speedy in my own metaphors. However, in this one, I'm carrying the entire Trevor family on my back, and it feels like that stone is going to catch us any second.

So when Janice announces that we're meeting in our little room for the final debrief, I'm so hyper I can barely stand it.

"Deputy Marshal Stricker, should I go over the rules one more time?" I ask as I twirl my pen around my fingers like a miniature baton.

"No, Charlotte. You've recited them six times already this morning."

"What about more practice losing a tail? I'm basically a ninja in crowds, but what about if there aren't many people around, and somebody sketchy is chasing me down the street? What do I—"

"You could turn around and chat them to death," Janice grumbles as she checks off boxes on a to-do list.

"Hey!" I exclaim. "You made a joke! That's awesome, Jan . . . I mean, Deputy Marshal. Granted, you're trying to get me to shut up, but still, this is a breakthrough! I think that—"

"Here," Janice says, sliding a school health form across the table. "Sign this. You'll need it on your first day at Loblolly."

I flick the cap off my pen so hard that it shoots away, pinging against the wall. Sheepishly, I glance up at Janice, but she's peering at another piece of paper. "By the way, Deputy Marshal Stricker," I say as I scrawl out my new name, "I wanted to thank you for this opportunity. I won't let the Trevors down. Or you. I won't let you down, either. I've been working really hard, and I know our backstories as well as I do my own life. I've got Charlotte Ashlynn Trevor memorized but good."

"Next form."

She pushes another sheet toward me. It looks like there are fifty more where that came from. I continue to chatter as I sign page after page. She may think that she's wearing me out with all this paperwork, but I'm still bouncing around like a bug in a stiff breeze.

"I've been thinking, Deputy Marshal," I buzz, "and I'm pretty sure this is the best thing that could have happened to me. I mean, it's direction, right? Everyone needs direction. And you're right. This really is up my alley. Not that I hang out in alleys. That'd be all shifty."

I fling another form into the "signed" pile and reach for three more. However, before I can finish the first flourish, Janice stands up and circles the table. She leans over me, her forehead inches from mine. Then she reaches down and grabs my shoulders.

"Stop, Charlotte. Just stop. Breathe."

"Um, I'm . . . breathing, Deputy Marshal Stricker."

She locks gazes with me.

"Slow your head down, child."

"But we need to get all this done by—"

"No, *you* need to slow down. Look, I've never seen anyone work harder than you have this week, Charlotte. Not any kid, not any adult. You keep pushing yourself, you're going to make a mistake, and as your contact, I'm not going to let that happen."

"But the Trevors are relying on me to—"

She squeezes my shoulders a little harder. "You *are* a

Trevor, Charlotte. That's what you need to focus on. Not thanking me, or losing tails, or reviewing rules we already know you've memorized."

"I'm scared, Janice."

Well, that just sort of popped out. I meant to say *excited*, or maybe *ready*. . . . but *scared*? I almost take it back, but the more it hangs there, the more it seems true. Janice purses her lips and squints, like she's looking for something in the small space between us.

"Scared of the Cercatores?"

"No," I say quickly, but realize that's not quite right. "Well, yes. But that's, like, a faraway fear, like cancer or killer bees. I know they're dangerous, and I know they could be just around the corner, but I'm not obsessed with them, not fearing they're under my bed or behind that door. I'm worried that I'm not going to be able to do this."

Janice nods. "It was the same for me when I first joined the marshals. It wasn't the criminals out there. It wasn't the murderers, or the kidnappers, or the mob bosses. What made my skin crawl, turned my dreams into nightmares, made me work myself to exhaustion, was the fear of failure. That's what you're feeling now."

"Are you saying we're kind of . . . alike?"

She draws back, exhaling sharply. "I wouldn't go that far, Charlotte. But I do think you're starting to appreciate the responsibility we've asked you to accept, and that's a step in the right direction. It's . . . encouraging."

"Thank you, Deputy Marshal."

"It makes me feel a little less uneasy about giving you this."

I watch as she reaches down into the black duffel beneath her chair. She pulls out a package wrapped in plain brown paper.

"Did you buy me a present?" I ask skeptically.

"No. Got it from the supply room. But from what I saw this week, what I'm hearing now, I think you deserve it. Being standoffish, mouthy, and unruly does not inspire confidence, but hard work and well-placed fear does. So take it. Hide it. You don't have a permit for it in North Carolina, so keep it at home and understand it is only for the direst emergency."

I gasp. "Janice, you didn't . . ."

"Actually, Charlotte, I did."

I peel the paper away carefully, just enough to reveal the box art for an official U.S. marshal's Taser. I nearly drop it, I'm shaking so badly. Janice has turned her attention back to the paperwork, but she says over her shoulder, "No thank-yous. No ridiculousness. Just promise me you'll never, ever use it, unless absolutely necessary."

"I promise, Deputy Marshal," I spout. "Thank you! Er, I mean, no thank you. Or . . . wait . . ."

"You leave for North Carolina in three days, which gives us enough time for only a few training sessions. Three days to prove you can handle it."

"I will," I say quietly. Popping open the box, I see the black-and-yellow plastic of the barrel. The whole thing is incredibly light, and only about ten inches long. Whispering down into the box reverently, I murmur, "I shall call you Glamdring, Foe-hammer that the king of Gondol—"

"Charlotte! Don't name your Taser."

"But . . ."

"No!"

"Yes, Deputy Marshal," I say, chastened.

We get back to signing, and I'm on my thirty-fifth form or so, the Taser tucked beneath my seat, when I have an epiphany. I put down my pen and look at Janice.

"What, Charlotte?"

I smile and just keep staring.

"No, seriously, what is it, Charlotte? We don't have time for games."

I give it a few more seconds and then whisper, "You watched the videos, didn't you? You did! Did you see the one of all the police and army guys taking it right between the shoulder blades? They all make these hilarious pinchy faces. . . ."

She rolls her eyes, but as she turns away, she makes a little noise in her throat.

"Was that . . . was that a laugh?"

"Mind your own business, Charlotte."

"You laughed! You totally laughed!"

Janice grabs the stack of forms, pulling them into a pile and bouncing them ruthlessly on the tabletop to force them to fall in line. Then her eyes snap back to me.

"Don't make me regret giving you that."

I put my hands up, surrendering. "Yes, Deputy Marshal."

Janice makes good on the Taser training, even though I never actually get to fire one. Halfway through, I think she's trying to punish me for the YouTube clips, because for every one of those I've seen, it seems like Janice finds a technical video that's eye-wateringly, soul-crushingly boring: The history of the Taser. The proper way to grip a Taser. How to reset and reload a Taser. A virtual tour of a Taser factory. I swear, I've had substitute social studies teachers who have shown fewer videos.

By the time the training is over, I'm glad I hid Glamdring away, just so I don't have to read the safety warnings again. It gets packed with the rest of our things as Janice and I load box after box onto our moving truck. When we're through, we shove the ramp underneath the truck and close the rear door. Just as we slam it into place, the rest of my new family arrives, all wheeling small blue suitcases behind them. It's a warm day even for Georgia, and Harriet is wearing a broad sun hat and stylish sunglasses. My eyes widen as I see that she's now a blonde, her hair the color of honey. It makes me wonder why the marshals didn't ask me to dye my hair. Maybe because the Cercatores don't know me anyway. Or maybe because they sensed I'd fight them on it tooth and nail.

Jonathan has a newspaper rolled up under his left arm and his phone against his ear. From the sound of it, he's talking to his new employer—"Starting next week," "A corner cubicle will be fine," "Yeah, I'll fax it over as soon as we arrive"—that sort of thing. Jackson is looking at the pavement, little headphone buds shoved so far into his ear canals that I think he might have tied them into a knot right where his cerebellum should be.

I give Harriet a hug, and Jonathan offers me a wave with his newspaper—he's picked up on the no-handshakes thing. I force a smile at Jackson, but he doesn't respond. I think his strategy is to deny my existence. That's good. I can have a lot of fun with that one.

"Hey, Jackson!" I shout, interposing myself between him and the truck. "Whatcha listening to?"

"None of your business!"

"Now, now, Jackson. Rule five!" I tease. I grab at the cord for one of his earbuds and manage to yank it from his ear. As he reaches up to try to stop me, my left hand flashes and pulls the other one free.

"Why are you being such an annoying tweak, Charlotte?" he huffs. Not sure what a tweak is, but he says it with enough venom that I'm pretty sure it isn't good.

"I'm your older sister now, Jackson! This is what older sisters do, especially if their younger brothers just ignore them and sulk around on what's supposed to be a big, new day. We're moving to North Carolina, man. Your mom is, like, Wonder Woman, your dad is cool, and you've got me now! Lighten up!"

I totally realize I'm being mean—"lighten up" was a low

blow. Jackson has earned two or three months of moping cred at least, given what he's had to leave behind because of his mom's decision. Still, I'm too excited to stop, and how else will I know if light teasing cheers him up? It's worked with other foster brothers I've had, and I've been pulled out of a funk or two when Emmy pointed out my drama-queening.

Unlike Jackson, apparently.

He crams the earbuds back in, shoots me a look, and shoves his way toward the car.

We've been given a used Prius by the marshals, a nondescript four-door. It's silver and so terribly usual that I don't think they could have designed better urban camouflage. It's got Ohio plates with the words *Beautiful Birthplace of Aviation* stenciled across the top, along with a cute little biplane hanging in the sky over an aw-shucks farmstead.

I point to the back bumper. "Isn't that the Wright Flyer? I thought our new state was where the first flight happened."

"That *is* the Wright Flyer, Charlotte," Jonathan explains. "And you're right. The Wright brothers tested their plane at Kill Devil Hills in North Carolina. But they lived and worked in Ohio. I guess both states can claim to be first in flight, or the birthplace of aviation."

"North Carolina's not jealous, is it? Nobody's going to freak out if we say we're from Ohio?"

"I don't anticipate so. They're far more likely to freak out if you say you're a North Carolina Tar Heels fan. Duke University and UNC are huge rivals."

"And we're moving to the Dukey part of North Carolina?"

That came out wrong. Jonathan seems not to notice.

"Yes. Maybe when you and Harriet go clothes shopping—"

"I should pick up a Duke sweatshirt or two?" I ask, and he nods.

Janice hands Harriet and me new phones. She tries to give Jackson one, too, but it's clearly not as fancy as his other one, and he turns his shoulder away without even saying "thanks but no thanks." I do a quick check on mine. It's got Jonathan's, Harriet's, and Janice's numbers preprogrammed in, but that's about it. Still, it's nice to have, and I squirrel it away into my bag while Janice uploads the directions to Harriet's and Jonathan's phones.

We decide that Jonathan and Jackson will take the truck while Harriet and I lead the way in the Prius. Jackson actually suggests the arrangement, and he makes no attempt to hide his reasoning; he simply refuses to ride with his mom. Harriet sighs, and Jonathan opens his mouth like he's going to say something, but then shakes his head and offers Harriet a kiss on the cheek. Whatever he was going to say has probably already been said, and screamed, and begged, and threatened. I try to lighten the mood by clapping excitedly, and I scurry over to the car, calling out, "You can pick the first song, Harriet!"

In the rearview, I watch Jonathan kiss Harriet again, this time on the forehead. Harriet seizes Jackson before he can slink off, and she gives him a long hug, his own arms dangling limply at his sides. Finally, he squirms away, stalking toward the truck and straightening his shirt.

"He'll get over it," I offer as Harriet slips into the driver's seat.

She takes a long time to respond, instead fiddling with her seat belt, the height of the steering wheel, and the AC. Once she finally does, she just says, "He's young."

"Yeah," I agree. "I know what that's like."

I manage to coax a smile out of Harriet, and that gets her talking. I learn a lot about the real Harriet—that is, Elena—in that first hour of driving. Both her family and Pietro's came over from Italy about a hundred years ago; they are both third-generation Italian-Americans. That background is why her grand-uncle, the head of the Cercatore family, consented to the marriage. The way she describes it, it sounds like some sort of arranged deal, but she makes sure to mention repeatedly that she is in love with Jonathan, and deeply: She never would have had the conviction to testify against her family without his support. It makes total sense to me, and I wonder what I could do with someone caring about me like that.

After we cross into South Carolina, the subject turns to me. Harriet asks about where my actual (former? real? I'm not sure what to call it) name comes from, and all about what I like and don't like. She pointedly avoids questions about my birth parents or my foster experiences. Mostly, it's just silly little questions. It's fun, and it turns into a kind of game.

"Cats or dogs?" she asks midway through our rapid-fire round.

"Cats. I can't stand dogs."

"Why not?"

"Slobbery."

"Agreed."

"Dark or milk?" I shoot back.

"You're talking to an Italian woman here, Charlotte. It's not that simple for us. Chocolate is an art form. Making it that cut-and-dry is like asking Michelangelo whether he liked blue or red better. He'd reply, 'Which shades?' and 'For what purpose?' and 'In what light?' Do you see?"

I hold up my hands. "I see, I see! But let's say you just had a terrible day, and your choice is a Hershey bar or dark chocolate. What then?"

"You're kidding, right?" she responds wryly. "I actually thought you were going to ask me a legitimate question."

I giggle. "Yeah, I'm kidding."

"Then that one doesn't count. Ask a new one."

"Favorite color?"

She thinks for a moment. "I wonder if I should change it. . . . It's emerald green, but I've always been partial to royal blue, too." She wistfully holds out her left hand, fingers extended. At first, I think she's trying to block a bit of glare from the windshield, but then I realize she's looking at her engagement ring. When she speaks again, there's a touch of melancholy in her voice. "They gave me a new one, you know. My actual engagement ring is in my jewelry box,

96

buried in the truck. A tiny marquise surrounded by emeralds. Pietro . . . that is, Jonathan . . . he knew they were my favorites. Now I have these. . . ." She flicks at the new rings with the curled tip of her pinkie.

"Lemme guess," I say, "rhinestones?"

"To tell you the truth, I'm not sure."

I hold out my hand. "Can I see? I'll let you know."

She manages to work the engagement ring off her finger while keeping a hand on the steering wheel, and she drops it into my palm. I can tell she's watching out of the corner of her eye.

"Hmm," I murmur. "Not plastic, at least."

Bringing the ring up to my lips, I slowly exhale across the gemstones. Then I hold it to the light. Swirls of wispy fog dull the glimmer of the stones, and I pass the ring back to Harriet with a click of my tongue.

"Yep, rhinestones."

As she slips the ring back on and switches lanes to let a motorcycle pass, she says, "I won't ask where you learned how to do that."

I look at her. "You don't know?"

"I didn't read your file. They gave us one, of course, but Jonathan and I decided we didn't want to know. We wanted to accept you for who you are, not for what you've been through."

This is a revelation. On the one hand, it's a little like a fresh start. On the other hand, what I've been through kind of *is* who I am. . . .

"But I'm supposed to keep you safe. . . ."

"No, Charlotte. I'm your mom now. I'm supposed to keep *you* safe. And get to know you—naturally. Your file might have told me your favorite color, but I'd rather hear it from you."

"You know red plums?"

Harriet smiles. "Yes. The skin is a very deep purple."

"Well, it's not that color—not exactly. It's the bloodish-reddish-crimsonish-purplish inside of the plum, right after you take that first bite. I like it because it's a color, and a taste, and a memory. It just takes a while to explain. I usually just say purple."

She nods as I speak. "See? I'm so glad I found that out by road tripping with you, rather than by reading it on some sheet of paper. You're a fascinating girl, Charlotte. No file necessary."

"Thanks. I appreciate that. And your trust."

"Why," she says with a mischievous grin, "is there something mysterious in your past I should know about? Are you secretly the daughter of the head of the U.S. marshals or something?"

Immediately a weird image of my dad wearing a marshals T-shirt pops into my head, and a surge of anger wells up in me. My face must be doing a pretty good impression of my favorite color, because Harriet notices immediately.

"I . . . I'm sorry, Charlotte. That was silly of me. Insensitive."

"It's okay," I reply quietly. I close my eyes, aggressively

trying to kick my dad out of my mind. If he had wanted to have these conversations with me . . . well, he had two years to figure that out. He doesn't get to be here now, not even as a ghost in my thoughts.

"Maybe I should have read your file, Charlotte," Harriet says after a while.

"No, no. I'm glad you didn't. If you knew who my dad actually was, you probably wouldn't like me very much."

Harriet laughs. "Oh, Charlotte! I'm hardly in a position to judge people on their family background!"

Fair point. Still . . .

"I'd just rather not talk about him, if that's okay."

Fortunately, Harriet manages to change the subject, declaring that she needs a lavatory break. I actually like that she calls it a lavatory. She's got a gentle, almost regal voice, and she moves that way, too, gesturing gracefully when she speaks. Even though her hands are slender and her fingers long like mine, they move in very different ways. Mine dart and weave like the heads of cobras. Hers move like silk scarves trailing behind a ballerina. Take the combination of the two, and she makes even a bathroom stop sound elegant.

"I could stretch my legs, too," I add, and she points at the new phone sitting in the cupholder between us.

"Call the truck. Let them know we're stopping, and see if they want to as well."

I swipe over to her address book and find Jonathan's number. I click it twice, and after three rings Jackson picks up.

"What?" he says gruffly.

"How's your drive going, Sunshine?" I ask sweetly. Harriet smiles.

"Boring and pointless. Like you," he mumbles, and I can hear Jonathan snap at him in the background. I line up a vicious retort, but I sneak a glance at Harriet first. She shakes her head to warn against it, and I tuck the comeback away for a rainy day.

"Cute," I reply. "So, hey, I'm calling because your mom and I are going to stop at the next gas station. Do you or Jonathan need to fill up or anything?"

Though it's hard to make out, I think Jonathan says, "We're fine on gas, but it would be nice to get out and walk around a—"

"No," Jackson insists. "We're gonna keep going."

And then he hangs up.

"Did you hear that?" I ask as I slip the phone back into the cupholder.

"Every word," Harriet replies, shaking her head in exasperation.

"Maybe we woke him up when we called?" I offer.

"Don't make excuses for your brother," she says as she veers onto the exit ramp.

"Yes, Mom. Mother. Mama. Mom," I fumble, trying on each name to see which one fits my tongue best. We're about to make our debut in public, after all.

"I think *Mom* works."

"Same," I say.

We pull into the first gas station off the exit, our tires

crunching on the gravel. Our northward journey hasn't done much to dispel the heat, and both of us toss our jackets behind us onto our seats. Harriet keeps her hat and glasses on.

The screen door squeaks to announce our arrival. A scruffy man wearing a backward Atlanta Falcons hat waves a hand at us without taking his eyes off the TV mounted in the corner. Harriet finds the bathroom and asks for the key, which the man hands to her. It's got a huge keychain on it, a rectangle covered in plastic that features a slogan: *Yarn's fer knittin', a chair's fer sittin', tobacco's fer spittin', and this key is fer the restroom.* Harriet rolls her eyes and says, "Classy keychain."

"Heh. Thanks," the man grunts.

"Indeed," Harriet replies as she walks away. Once the attendant notices that the woman who just spoke to him is a pretty blonde, he smiles and rips his gaze from the television. He rubs his stubbly cheek as he watches her walk past the magazines and candy bars. I cough, and when he sees me, he hurriedly looks up at the TV screen. I give myself a little pat on the back and slip over to the magazines.

I'm checking out my horoscope—apparently, Venus and Mars are in opposition, so I should avoid impulse shopping—when the guy at the counter turns up the volume on the TV.

"And now more news out of New York City, where four bodies were found in the Hudson River overnight. Police believe the victims, all men between the ages of thirty and fifty, are linked to the investigation into the Cercatore crime syndicate. The chief of police also confirms that the bodies bear what he calls 'significant markers' suggesting connections to previous hits attributed to the Cercatore operation. Before being sent to prison, second-in-command Martin Cercatore infamously shouted in court that 'a winter of retribution' was coming. Whether these deaths were ordered by the Cercatores is as of yet unclear, but the NYPD is taking no chances."

The anchor continues to offer some of the backstory of the trial. Over her right shoulder, the station is flashing pictures of the arrested Cercatores. I wince at several of them—they look just like Harriet . . . and more than a little like me. Midway through the report, Harriet emerges from the bathroom. She sees me staring at the television, and she glances upward, too. Soon she is paralyzed, left hand at her lips and the key dangling from her right. The attendant's eyes are back on Harriet, so I act before he can start putting anything together.

"Mom," I whine, "I really got to go. . . . Can I have the key?"

Harriet does a double take, as though she's momentarily forgotten who I am. Then, though, she takes a deep breath, shakes her head to clear the cobwebs, and nods. "Yes, Char . . . sorry. Got distracted. Here."

Char? Cute touch. I grab the key from her and indicate the drink coolers with a tilt of my head. She walks with me, out of sight and earshot of the attendant. The newscast

drones on, the anchor talking now about the local contro-
versy surrounding the decision to move trick-or-treating to
four in the afternoon.

"I don't think he noticed anything, Charlotte," Harriet
whispers. "They'd never show my picture, and we're a long
way from New York."

"Yeah, but you know what that story means, Mom. The
Cercatores are still in business."

"We figured that was the case. We wouldn't be in
WITSEC if there wasn't a threat."

She has a point. Still, it's quite a shock to hear about
them in a random gas station in South Carolina.

"So you're not worried?" I ask.

"I'll admit, I'm not thrilled to hear any news about my
family, but I'm okay."

I nod, though I do notice Harriet's hands trembling as
she opens the cooler and reaches for a bottle of water. My
hands aren't faring much better.

"I'll be right back, Mom," I assure her, and head for the
bathroom.

I do what I have to do, but the smell of the place, the
flickering light above the sink, and the paper towels strewn
all over the floor aren't settling my nerves. I hurriedly wash
my hands, my skin prickling from the ice-cold shock, and I
shake off the water droplets before pushing the door open
with my foot.

When I come out, Harriet has grabbed a few other
things and has them on the counter. I put the key back near

the register and stand beside her. As the attendant is ringing us up, he says, "Any lotto tickets today?"

"No thank you," Harriet replies.

He looks up at her and smiles, but then his eyes narrow.

"Hey!" he says suddenly. "Hey, have I seen you before?"

Harriet blanches, and I feel her right hand grab my arm. She squeezes tightly.

"No," I hurriedly reply. "I really, really doubt it."

"Yeah!" he exclaims, slapping the countertop. "Yeah, I just saw you on TV! I should call this in to the newspaper!"

I feel Harriet tug on my arm, as though she's going to swoon. I can't think of anything to say, though my feet slide slowly apart, into a runner's stance.

"Yeah! You're a ringer for that actress chick! News said she just separated from her husband. You could, like, do body doublin' for her or some such!"

Both of us exhale sharply, not aware that we had been holding our breath the entire time. Harriet glances down at me, mouthing the word *Sorry!* as she pulls her fingers off my arm.

"And don't worry, honey," he says as he directs his attention to me. "You're every bit as pretty as your mom here."

"Thanks," I reply. "I'll be sure to tell my dad you said so."

He sniffles and clears his throat. "Yeah, well . . . yeah. That'll be fourteen twenty-two. Cash or credit?"

Harriet pays with cash and quickly snatches her change from the counter. The attendant murmurs, "But really, though. Spittin' image."

I offer a halfhearted smile as I grab our purchases. "Yeah, we get that a lot," I say.

"Bye now!" he shouts after us. We don't reply as we scurry to the car, shoes crunching on the gravel, dust clouds kicking up behind us, our hands clutched tightly around bags of dark chocolate.

CHAPTER NINE

The Old Homestead

We pass the North Carolina welcome signs around two in the afternoon; no more gas station stops for us. Despite our nerve-rattling interlude, we still manage to catch up with the truck. It turns out Harriet has a lead foot when she's spooked.

North Carolina is beautiful; the leaves are starting to turn, and it's still warm enough for us to roll the windows down. I'm letting my fingers swim through the air, playing the game where I pretend my fingertips are ever-extending lasers that can cut anything in two. Harriet has taken her hat off, and our hair is whipping around madly. With a piece of chocolate still pillowed on my tongue, the sun just behind us, and the road clear ahead, I think to myself that this isn't a bad way to greet our new home.

We pass a bunch of exits: Gray's Creek, South View,

Dunn, Smithfield. There's the odd Fuquay-Varina or Lillington thrown in there, but most of it sounds quiet and rural. I'm imagining general stores, old men playing cribbage, and county fairs. As we get closer to Raleigh, the signs get bigger, the billboards for Cracker Barrel and Fred Anderson Toyota come more frequently, and the traffic gets heavier. Route 95 turns into 40, which turns into 147, and like that, we're there. I spend the last twenty minutes tinkering with the radio, reprogramming all the presets with anything that doesn't sound like country music, gospel, sports, or news radio.

Twenty minutes, and I find two stations.

Not that Durham is a country town. Sure, it's no New York City, but it's a city, with a decent skyline and everything. We veer off the highway at the exit for Swift Avenue, and we're almost immediately deposited on the campus of Duke University. I notice the trees first. They're huge, sprawling, and so colorful that they'd give Mr. Jordanson's considerable crayon collection a run for its money.

Harriet suggests we drive around a bit before getting to the house—"Jackson can just stew in the truck for a while," she explains with a grin. Since it's still early afternoon, I'm all for checking out the neighborhood. The more I see, the more confused this little city seems. They have a Whole Foods and little bodegas, massive plantation-style houses and paint-peeling housing projects, a glorious Gothic cathedral, a tobacco museum, and a gourmet popsicle place all within a couple of miles of one another. In a way, it kind of reminds me of me, the wholesome Ohio girl and the daughter of a criminal, the U.S. marshal and the New York pickpocket all in one.

We swing by Whole Foods to get a few necessaries, and I'm happy that Harriet agrees that mangoes and peanut butter are essential. She also picks up a bottle of shampoo, some toothpaste, and a holistic-medicine magazine. The guy who checks us out is wearing a rainbow-hued knit hat over a head full of dreadlocks. When he leans in to speak, his lip ring glints, and I'm expecting some sort of surfer drone to tickle our eardrums.

Nope.

"Y'all gun' need a bag?"

Harriet nods, and the clerk—Vincent, according to the name tag—offers her a choice of a sack made of hemp or the old standby paper.

"What do you think, Charlotte?"

"Paper's fine, Mom," I reply, watching Vincent to see if he reacts to my calling Harriet my mother. He doesn't. I suppose if he can pull off hippie-banjo chic, we can pass the mommy-daughter eye test; even with Harriet's new hair color, we still look quite a bit alike. "We can use them as trash bags until we can get out to do a proper grocery run."

"Reusin'. Purty good i-dee-ar. Paper it is," Vincent remarks as he shakes open a brown bag. "Companies could save millions a year by reusin' trash bags 'n' such." He holds up a book on the impact of the green movement on modern business. It's got one of those yellow *USED* stickers on the spine.

"Oh, are you a student at Duke?" Harriet asks.

"Yes, ma'am. Econ major. Graduatin' next year."

Harriet and I both smile and thank him. As we walk away, Harriet says, "That's a college town for you. All types."

"This might be a pretty good place for us, then. We're at least two types, and I'm sure I've got at least three more bouncing around in my head."

Harriet laughs a little. "I've no doubt, Char."

We load the groceries into the backseat and navigate out of the crowded parking lot. It takes us only three minutes to get to the house, and I make a mental note of the way.

"Here we go," Harriet says excitedly. "This is our street!"

The trunks of the trees that line our avenue are twisted and thick, with impressive, knobby knots. It's a sunny day, but the light pours through the trees in scattered streams, running along parked cars, little lawns, and uneven sidewalks steepled by stubborn roots. The houses seem as old as the trees and just as large. Weathered, greening pillars lead to shady porch swings and mildewed shutters, and nests of leaves sprout from gutters like bristly eyebrows on wise old men.

I watch the houses roll by. When we slow down, I see the truck pulled into a driveway ahead. We ease to a stop just behind it, and I leap out, ready to get my first look at home.

It's not the biggest place we've seen, but it's still larger than any I've ever lived in. Two of those old oak trees flank the walk leading up to the porch, shading the front yard, and a sugar maple runs right up along the side of the house, forming a sort of trellis with its branches. It's easily twice the size of the scrawny one we had in the playground at the Center. Chrissy would just die to see it: She absolutely adored playing with the little whirligiggish seedpods. I bet this one drops them by the thousands when the time is right, like a fleet of helicopters hovering around our new home.

Plenty of windows, all shuttered, sit behind that wraparound porch, darkened by the overhang of the second floor. The shingles are green, and the rest of the house is painted gray. On the whole, it looks pretty plain, with one very noteworthy exception: It has a turret. On the right front side of the house, where the porch curves around the corner, the roof tapers to a perfect point, atop which sits a polished brass weather vane, fashioned to look like a squirrel. Beneath that is a hexagon of windows, like the teetering top of an old wizard's tower: something Hogwartsy, or Rapunzelesque. The sun breaks through the dwindling red leaves of the maple in just such a way that it hits those windows flush.

"It's beautiful," I whisper to Harriet when she joins me on the sidewalk.

"I suppose," she replies, her eyes cast downward at all the leaves. "How are you at yard work?"

"Never lived anywhere that actually had a yard."

"Neither have we."

I nod, and together we stride up the porch steps. The U.S. marshals have trained me well, because I notice that the third step creaks, and my first thought is that it'll be handy in case someone is sneaking up to the house.

Harriet pushes the door open and immediately says, "Ooh. Real hardwood floors! I love these!" Sure enough, there's nary a carpet to be seen. The walls are painted a pleasant, soft yellow, and the entrance leads directly into a huge living room. There's a fireplace, a big, open doorway into the kitchen, and a short hallway off to our left, which I peek down. At the end is a bedroom, I think, and a bathroom next door. There's also a staircase heading up to the second story. Right by the door, embedded in the wall, is a fancy keypad, the controls to our state-of-the-art alarm system. The marshals thought of everything, it seems.

Jonathan emerges from the kitchen, wiping sweat from his cheek. "Jackson and I checked out the backyard. Nice chunk of property overall. We got the storm doors to the basement open. The spiders didn't like that so much. How was your drive?"

Jackson comes in behind him, not sweating at all— I guess when Jonathan said *we* got the storm doors open, he used the term loosely. He's fussing over his phone again, and he doesn't look up when Harriet says hello, or when she tells her husband about our encounter at the gas station.

"That must have been scary," Jonathan remarks.

"It was," Harriet agrees, shuddering. "Which reminds me—we need to make a deal. Right here, right now. To make all this work, we have to trust one another. We have to look out for one another. So I promise all of you that if you see something strange, or you hear something that

111

concerns you, even a little, that I will take it seriously. I want all of you to promise me, too."

Jonathan nods. "Needed to be said, dear. I promise."

"Me too," I add.

We all stare at Jackson, who remains riveted to the little screen in his hands.

"Jackson, honey, did you hear—" Harriet begins, but Jackson cuts her off.

"Yeah. Fine. I promise. Can I go to my room now?"

Jonathan scratches his head, then grins.

"I checked out the marshals' write-up of this place. It's a four bedroom, three bath. The master bedroom is down here, and that's where your mother and I are sleeping. That leaves three bedrooms, and they're all upstairs. Now, honey," he says to Harriet, "you're a lawyer, remind me . . . what do they say about possession?"

Harriet grins wickedly. "It's nine-tenths of the law. . . ."

Jackson, I notice, is already slipping his phone into his pocket, and as soon as his mom finishes talking, he bolts past me toward the staircase in the little hallway. I gasp—the turret room!

I launch myself after Jackson. As I skid around the corner, Jackson's waiting at the staircase, chuckling maliciously. He's got both arms spread, blocking the way up.

"Think I'll take my time getting upstairs. No need to rush. Not like anyone else in *this* family needs to pick a bedroom."

I stalk toward him. The staircase is narrow, the steps

made from the same dark wood as the floor, and the only light is what trickles down from above. Still, I can see at the top that the brightest rays come from the right. That must be it. I'm one skinny staircase away from hexagonal heaven. I just have to get around Jackson.

His cloying boy-cologne stench fills the entire passage, and he's taking each step with exaggerated slowness, his legs bowed and arms low to prevent me from getting around. I might be his older sister, but Jackson's as big as me, and short of grabbing him and jerking him back down the stairs, I'm not breaking through. The thought does cross my mind, but dang it . . . Rule five: happy family. I'll need to take a different tack.

"Hey, Jackson. What kind of room do you want? Maybe we can just figure it out from—"

"What's that noise? Is someone talking? Can't hear over the sound of my feet."

He starts stomping a step at a time.

Mature, buddy.

I get up right behind him with eight steps to go. "C'mon, Jackson! Let me have the room to the left," I whine. "I like sleeping on the left side of a house. You can have either of the other two. Just give me the one on the left, please?"

"Oh sure!" he says snarkily. "You go left. I'm just going to go take the room that's in that awesome-looking castle part."

I growl, and he laughs. So no reverse psychology.

With three steps to go, I get desperate. This is warranted, though. That's *so* my room up there.

"Let me pass!" I shout, and I grab his left shoulder. He instinctively leans his body that way, thinking I'm trying to sneak under his arm. I whimper pathetically, and while he's distracted by the sound, the contact on his shoulder, and keeping his body flush with the wall, I slip my right hand into his pocket. The phone slides out easily.

"Oh no!" I exclaim. "Jackson, your phone!"

I let it fall from my fingers right before he turns around, and he makes this throaty, Gollumy noise as he watches it bounce down the steps. Without a thought for me, he lunges downward, arms outstretched, and I gracefully spin to allow him to pass. Then I casually skip my way up the last few steps and into the turret room.

It's small, bright, and perfect. The entry into the upstairs hallway is one of three doors. All are ajar, and I can see that the first to my left is a walk-in closet. The second is a little bathroom with a toilet, sink, and shower stall. The room retains the shape I saw from outside, and I can already imagine my bed under one window, a desk up against another. Maybe a thick, toe-tickling rug in the center of it all. Definitely curtains—a pale sky blue, perhaps. And crystals! I want crystals: different colors, different shapes, different sizes. I want to hang them in front of the windowpanes so they dangle down in the sunlight, casting rainbows around my happy little hexagon. When I open my windows, the breeze will swirl around my space, setting my crystals to spin, and it will be a fairy disco. I'll lie on my carpet, look up at my crystal constellation, and I'll . . .

"You!" Jackson screams from behind me. I turn to face him, and I have to take a step back. He's panting, and his cheeks are red. His phone is in his left hand, the screen cracked. Before he can charge in, I let out a little "Eep!" and slam the door. I jam the toe of my sneaker against the bottom, and sure enough, he shoulders the door, which rattles but doesn't give. A jolt of pain shoots up my leg.

Possession. This room is mine.

"Jackson, what on earth are you doing?" Harriet yells from downstairs.

"My phone!" he rages, and he barrels into the door again.

I can hear heavy steps stomping up the stairs, and then Jonathan's voice. "Calm down, Jackson. There are two other rooms. Why don't you go cool off in one?"

I can't resist.

"I hear the one on the left is nice!" I call.

Jackson growls something indecipherable, and then there's a knock. Hesitantly, I slip my foot away and turn the knob. When I peek out, Jonathan is standing there, hands in his pockets.

"Sorry about that," he says. "Jackson's going through a lot, as you know, and . . ."

I shake my head as I open the door fully. "No," I explain. "This one is on me. I made him mad."

"Actually, it's on us," he says, his voice warm. "We shouldn't have put you two in competition like that. What were we expecting? You're brother and sister now, and you go and act like brother and sister. I even told Elena that the

115

hullabaloo you two created made it seem like you'd been getting on each other's nerves all your lives. The marshals would be proud. Way to sell it!"

"Nobody says *hullabaloo* anymore," I say with a grin.

He chuckles and replies, "Oh, we do, Charlotte. We do. So you better get used to it. In fact, we take it as one of our solemn duties to embarrass our new daughter as much as humanly possible. It's a parental right."

"You . . . you're not one of those dads who takes his kids to the movies and . . . and . . ." I shudder. "*Dances* during the end credits music, are you?"

"With the 3-D glasses still on, Charlotte. With. The. Glasses. Still. On. . . ." He closes the door slowly behind him as he does his best megalomaniacal laugh. I'm still smiling as I plant my back against the door. I sink down, hug my knees, and close my eyes. I inhale the smell of this new, old house. It smells like wood and like fall. It smells like maybe it got just cold enough for the heat to kick on last night: a little bit musty, a little bit smoky, and a little bit sweet. When I open my eyes again, my little hexagonal room is still here, the redheaded maple tree waving just outside. Not Jackson Trevor, not the Cercatores, not the five rules, nothing is going to rip me from this space, because for the first time in my life, I feel like I might just be in control of what happens here.

CHAPTER TEN

Santa-Proof

The rest of the day we move stuff in, breaking only for a dinner of mangoes and pretzels dipped in peanut butter. The whole time I'm trying to apologize to Jackson, but he's not speaking to anyone; he's got his headphones in, his hair over his eyes, and his hood up. He does cuss every time his finger runs over the cracked screen of his phone. The only time he acknowledges me is to laugh when I delicately swaddle Fancypaws in a blanket before carrying her upstairs. I carefully raise one of her paws for her so she can shoot him a rude gesture in reply.

On about the third day of training at Glynco, I asked Janice whether our house was going to have one of those massive banks of video monitors, a real honest-to-goodness basement lair. Maybe a panic room we could lock ourselves in. She said no. Well, okay, she told me to "drop the nonsense," but same difference. Then I inquired about setting up trip wires and deadfalls, or if I could dig pits. And no, she hadn't seen *Home Alone*; I asked about that, too. When I did, she handed me a fifty-eight-item list of things to check. I even had to memorize it.

"Number nineteen is windows, Jackson. Gotta make sure they're all latched at night."

"Get out of my room!"

"Oh, you already put up your angsty posters! *A* for effort! 'Cept, if you want, I could rip that one in half.... That'd knock you down to a B-minus, and you'd be within the safety limits."

I duck a black sneaker and skitter down the hallway, testing the latches and seals on the windows there, too. After that, it's making sure the emergency supply kit has batteries and bandages, looking outside before it gets dark to see if there are any suspicious cars or loiterers, and triple-setting the alarm system. It's stressful work, actually, since every time I touch something, I imagine exactly how the Cercatores might take advantage of a slipup to exploit the mistake.

My last thing to check is the fireplace—yes, apparently hit men have been known to Santa their way in—and once I've confirmed that the flue is closed, I pause to look at the pictures Harriet arranged above the mantel. It's amazing, really, the job the techs did. They're all nicely framed, and they portray Harriet with blond hair and a much younger face, Jackson seeming happy (so *that's* what it looks like!), and all four of us posing, arms around one another. My fingers drift over these pictures, touching my own face, my smile. I recognize the angle of my posture. I was talking to Erin and A.J. one day just like this, making that gesture with my hand. The marshals must have taken the image off a security feed and Photoshopped it in. But even I had trouble telling at first.

Harriet catches me staring at one such picture, and she steps up next to me. "Did you see this?" she asks. In her hand is a small portrait. Harriet's there, her face radiant, looking like it was born to be framed by blond layers. She's waving at the camera, and in her right arm, sitting perfectly in the crook between her elbow and breast, is a little girl, dark-haired and giggling. Her own small, slender fingers are outstretched in a pantomime of Harriet's wave. This image I've seen as well, complete with this little girl sitting in another woman's arms. It resided on my grammy's piano for years, until she died and I was swept into the foster system. I guess Janice must have gotten it from Wainwright.

"It seems so real, doesn't it?" Harriet asks softly.

"I guess so, yeah."

"Look, I don't know where this picture came from, but you're clearly happy, and I'd never dream of trying to replace—"

"You can't," I say abruptly. That's not how I wanted it to come out; I meant to say that she didn't need to. But it hangs there anyway, and something stops me from correcting myself.

"Still, it's a nice picture," Harriet concludes after a few moments. "With your blessing, I'd like to put it up there next to the others."

I nod, and she nestles it in between the one of all of us and a wedding photo of her and Jonathan. I point to that last one by way of asking, and she shakes her head with a smile.

"Fake, too. As fake as my engagement ring."

Wistfully, she holds up her hand, tilting her fingers to try to get the rhinestone to catch the light. It's halfhearted, though, and with a sigh she slips the ring off and puts it on the mantel.

"Think tonight I'll put my real ring back on. It'll be our secret. Promise I'll switch them tomorrow before we go out."

"Go out?" I ask.

"Oh, we didn't tell you? Janice called while you were upstairs checking the windows for the tenth time. You and Jackson are all set to start school on Monday."

I gasp, and my brain sends freak-out signals to the rest of my body. "Monday? But that gives us only three days!"

"Exactly, which is why, young lady, we are going shopping tomorrow! Now upstairs and brush your teeth. It's been a long day."

I should be excited. No, I *am* excited—I have a list of three dozen things I need for my room alone, along with clothes and school supplies. And who doesn't dream of a shopping spree? But the notion of starting school so soon hadn't occurred to me. Even though I've jumped into several schools midyear, bounced around more than my fair share of first days, none has been quite like this. I manage a nervous smile for Harriet's benefit, and I dutifully scurry up the steps after she heads back into the kitchen.

Once I'm inside my room, I open my left hand.

There, in my palm, is Harriet's rhinestone ring.

I panic when I see it, and I drop it to the floor, where it attempts to roll away before coming to rest at my feet. It has left a little round imprint in my skin, already fading but still traceable. I rub at that circle with my fingertips, then sit down in front of the ring. I think about going downstairs and replacing it, but what if Harriet or Jonathan see me? Or worse, Jackson? I'm less than a day in and I've already broken at least one of the rules. Trying to return it seems like a good way to start a bad fight. Instead, I pick it up and slip it into the top drawer of my dresser, hidden between two white socks. I brush my teeth, position Fancypaws just *so* on the bedside table, and jump into bed. Then I close my eyes.

Nope. Nothing doing.

You know what will keep you awake longer than a triple shot of espresso?

Guilt, mixed with all the weird scrapes, clangs, trickles, and snuffles of an old house. After about two hours of lying there, I've got most of the noises cataloged. *Ktchick-scrizzle?* That's the maple outside my window saying hello. *Vurr-puthocka-puthocka?* The baseboard heaters firing up. *Click-sliv-tipply-tipple?* The tank of the toilet in my bathroom topping itself off. There's even a cadence of sorts to them, and it's finally enough to calm my nerves, to help me settle in and fall asleep.

Or would have been, if a sudden, strange rhythm hadn't just sliced through the melody.

I sit bolt upright, my heart beating so hard I can see it beneath my T-shirt. My brain tries to account for a *creak-pause-creak* with a subtle, swishing bass line.

I stop breathing, stop everything, and focus on the door to my room, as if I could somehow push through the wood to see what lurks beyond. The eerie sound obliges me by repeating itself, only louder. I try to rationalize it: new, wonky heater sound? Downstairs refrigerator practicing ventriloquism? Mice . . . the size of mastiffs? Absurd, I know, but imagining the ridiculous is way better than going to the most logical conclusion: a person, slowly and secretively dragging something along the hallway. Something soft but heavy. Something like a body.

It's ultimately the flicker of the tiny hallway light coming through my keyhole that forces me into action; someone is definitely out there, definitely sneaking. Daring to sip only the thinnest of breaths through my clenched teeth, I will myself to move. Every shred of my intention goes into being silent: my foot eases off my bed so slowly I can feel it moving the molecules of the air out of the way. My hands follow, and I crawl my way to the keyhole to peer out.

There *is* someone there, creeping toward the staircase. He's carrying something so strangely shaped that it's hard to discern. It's blobby, and part of it drags behind him like a thick, lazy tail. Only when he reaches the stairs and actually starts tripping his way down do I understand: Jackson's got all his pillows, his blanket, and his comforter from his bed, and he's clinging to them like a guy who's just been handed a parachute and told to jump.

I wait until he's seven thumps down the stairs before I ease my door open to follow.

When I get downstairs, I peek around the corner and see Jackson. He's standing at the door to Harriet and Jonathan's room, silhouetted by the moonlight that seeps through the blinds—blinds that I closed as part of security protocol number twenty-nine. He's still got his pillows and blankets in a headlock with his left arm, but his right is free, and it's the only part of him that moves. I watch as he slowly reaches up for the knob. Just as his fingertips extend, but before he actually makes contact, he stops, and his hand retracts like he just got burned.

After mumbling something, Jackson starts anew, his fingers actually closing around the knob this time. Again, though, he pulls away. He presses his hand to his temple, and he quietly bangs his fist there several times before running those fingers through his dark, greasy cowlick. He takes a deep, ragged breath—a sob, perhaps?—and turns back toward the staircase. Stifling a gasp, I spider my way up a few steps, just to be safe.

Seconds pass, but I don't hear any movement, so I inch my way back down for another peek.

He's still staring at the door, though he's giving me a bit

more of a profile to work with. He looks exhausted, paler than the moonlight that dapples his pajamas. His eyes are red, cheeks swollen, and he's wearing a grimace that seems locked somewhere between fury and despair. I exhale softly, a chill gliding its way along my arms, telling me to get myself back up in bed, mummify myself with my blankets, and make peace with my little symphony of sounds. Before I do, though, Jackson sighs heavily. His eyes flit from his parents' door to the floor and back. Finally, he just drops his stuff and sinks down, curling there amid his comforter and pillows.

I tiptoe my way back to my hexagon. It takes me another hour to drift off, and when I finally do, I sleep fitfully, my dreams full of Nazgûls, broken phones, and creaky porch steps.

SHOPPING LIST

- Low bookshelves for underneath the windows
- A good winter jacket
- Tennis balls
- Comfy socks
- At least ten shirts to mix 'n' match
- Five skirts
- Two nice dresses
- A better toothbrush
- Floss
- New phone for Jackson
- ChapStick
- More underwear
- Three pairs of jeans
- Hair ties
- Sweatshirts with big pockets (NO GLOVES!)
- Backpack for school
- Rug for room
- New earrings
- Crystals (arts and crafts store?)
- Shorts
- A funky belt
- Pajamas (silk?)
- Pillow
- Sheets
- Notebooks
- A binder
- Pencils, pens
- The Chronicles of Narnia
- Can I afford a Kindle?
- Sunglasses
- SHOES
- More wishes
- Decent shampoo
- Slippers
- Hairbrush
- Other stuff?

CHAPTER ELEVEN

Oh, Who Are the People in Your Neighborhood?

I wake in the morning earlier than I should, the noises of the house drowned out by the rumbling in my stomach. Despite my hunger, I stay in bed for a while longer, trying to suss out whether anyone else is awake. Unfortunately, all I can hear is my burbly belly, so I decide to risk it. I have no idea what will be waiting for me at the bottom of the stairs. Will it be Jackson? Will I have to sneak around his sleeping form like he's a bear in a cave? Or will it be Harriet, angrily shouting at Janice over the phone, blaming her for saddling her family with a no-good, ring-stealing pickpocket? One thing's for sure: When I leave the safe haven of my room, I'll be clocking in for my first full day as Charlotte Trevor. I only hope it's less nerve-racking than last night.

It starts out smoothly enough; Jackson apparently migrated from the hallway back to his bedroom, and Harriet and Jonathan's door is still closed when I reach the first floor. From there, I have a straight shot into the kitchen, and I know exactly what my target's going to be.

As soon as I've made sure the coast is clear, I grab the bowl of fruit from the fridge. I don't know where the knives are, so I pick a mango and go at it with my fingers, tearing off the skin like I'm a primal huntress. I'm making a ridiculous mess, cold juice running slippery along my knuckles as I bring flaps of mango up to my mouth and piranha the flesh away. It's just as I'm getting ready to tackle the seed that I look up. There at our back door, peeking in at me, is a woman.

I almost swallow the whole seed, which would have been both miraculous and deadly if I had pulled it off. Instead, I fire it down into the sink, where it ricochets around noisily before clogging the drain. Running my arm along my lips and chin, I slide away from the island at the center of the kitchen. Briefly, I consider going to get Harriet and Jonathan, or maybe running upstairs to find Fancypaws. However, a voice—Janice's—stops me, saying, "Normal, Charlotte. Be normal."

The woman smiles and waves. She's got a broad pouf of curly brown hair, heavy eye makeup, and those tattoo eyebrows. She's wearing a dark blue nurse's uniform, and she's got an ID tag clipped to the breast pocket. In a moment of inspiration, she remembers she has it and presses her entire body against the mesh of the screen door as if to show it to me. I still can't see it, but she seems to think it's helping. Then she steps aside, and behind her is a kid—a girl about my age.

I hold up my finger, and then I frantically hose off my face with the spray attachment from the sink. One deep breath later, and I'm swinging the door open. The screen's still there and hook-locked closed in case they try something, but we can talk . . .

. . . which the lady starts doing immediately.

"Hey there! You must be our new neighbors! I'm Nancie Guthrie, from next door—blue house, green shutters, the big brass knocker on the front door—can't miss us. This is my daughter, Brit. It's Britney, like the singer. . . . Britney Spears? You know her. Kids your age love her. What's your name, honey?"

I cast a glance at Brit, and she shakes her head, mouthing a silent "Sorry." I offer her a little smile in return. She's got her mom's brown hair, but it's perfectly straight, long bangs down to just above her completely real eyebrows and rimless glasses. She's wearing a pretty white peasant blouse with flower embroidery along the neckline and a gorgeous Navajo-patterned crinkle skirt. I'll have to ask her where she shops for clothes. They're great, in a sort of boho-chic way.

Turning my attention back to Nancie, I say, "I'm Charlotte."

"Oh, like the city?" she asks, beaming.

"Like the spider," I reply, and her look turns to one of puzzlement. After a moment, she scratches a pockmarked cheek and smiles again, shrugging.

"Well, that's nice. Say, Charlotte, your parents wouldn't happen to be home, would they? I saw the car and the truck out front, and—full disclosure—Brit and I were watching y'all as you moved in yesterday. Not busybody-like, but just curious. Always nice to see someone movin' in. It's a great neighborhood; you'll love it. This used to be the Werners' house. Nice old couple, but they had to head off to the retirement community when Mr. Werner's hip went. You know how it goes. Speaking of Mr. Werner, you should check out the garden box along the side of the house. He raised heirloom tomatoes. That's also where they buried their old German shepherd, Trudy. That old dog . . . come to think of it, she passed on the floor near the sink, right where you were standing. I tell you—"

"Mom," Brit interrupts. "You asked her a question. Maybe let her answer?"

I'd been told repeatedly at Glynco that southern folks speak more slowly than us northerners, but I'm betting none of my trainers had met Nancie Guthrie.

"Yes, but they're still asleep," I say, glancing over my shoulder. "I'm . . . eating mangoes."

"Goodness gracious! Well, we can certainly see that, can't we, Brit?" Nancie says loudly, guffawing and pointing at the place on my shirt where I dried my hands. Brit offers me another silent "Sorry," but I just shrug and try to change the subject.

"Where do you go to school, Brit?" I ask.

"Oh, she goes to Loblolly Middle School," Nancie trumpets before Brit can even part her lips. "It's the best school in the district. You should see their test scores! My pretty Britty takes the bus every morning, picks up just down the street. I wonder if—"

"That's where I'm going, too," I say, though I'm still looking at Brit, rather than her mother. "Seventh grade."

Brit's whole face lights up, just for an instant, before she resumes hiding behind her bangs. She starts shifting uncomfortably from foot to foot. Either she has to go to the bathroom really badly, or she's desperate to get her mom away from me. I know if it were me, I'd have been gone the moment the words *pretty Britty* twanged into existence.

Nancie is beaming now. "What luck! Brit's in seventh, too! She and I were just talking about how she has trouble making friends—all those computer games she plays, never gets out. You'd think she'd start talking about boys, go to the mall every so often. She's a thirteen-year-old girl, for heaven's sake!"

I want to blush on Brit's behalf, but she's flaring up just fine on her own. I've got to do something here. . . .

"Hey, I'm going shopping for school later today, and I could really use some advice on what to get. Maybe Brit could come with me? I know you, like, just met me, but I'm kind of desperate, and that's a fabulous skirt. . . ."

Nancie claps. "I think that's a great idea! See, Brit? I told you it'd be great coming over here. We talk to this nice girl for just a few minutes, and already you're getting invited out to socialize. You're not saying no to this one. And speaking of not saying no, would you do me a great big old favor, Charlotte?"

Other than being your daughter's best friend? Um . . .

"Sure."

"When your parents do get up, give them this. We printed it this mornin', but we've—that is, me and some of the other neighbors, the Concords around the corner, the Richardsons, the Perezes, the Roysters two doors down—we've been planning a welcome party for y'all before we even knew you. When we heard the old folks were movin' out and a young family was headed in, well, we knew we wanted you to feel right at home. Southern hospitality: can't beat it!"

She's still talking as she pulls a card out of her purse and hands it to me. It's like a greeting card, only there's no colorful envelope. On the front is a picture of the perfect American house, all dog-in-the-yardy and picket-fency. There's a row of outsize tulips in the foreground, and the bloom of each one is a letter. Together they spell out *Welcome Home!*

I pop the card open, and written in a fancy scrawl is an invitation. It reads:

Howdy, neighbors!

Hope you like parties, because we're throwing one in your honor! Join us on Sunday, November 9, at 3 p.m., for a special down-home, welcome-home, new-home pig-pickin' party! We'll bring the food, you bring yourselves and your stories!

We can't wait to meet you and help you feel like stayin'!

Your neighbors and friends,
The Trinity Park
Neighborhood Association

Beneath the words is a picture of a cute little piglet prancing around in a patch of wildflowers. I close the card and smile. "Thanks. I'll pass it along."

"We forgot the address on there, but it's over at the Roysters' place. They have a good backyard. Just built the porch last summer, and the bugs ain't been bad for weeks now. How many of y'all are there?"

"The four of us. Mom, Dad, and my little brother, Jackson."

"Ohhh, a darlin' family! Perfect. Well, we'll see you then. And when you're all set to go shoppin', just swing by and knock on the door. Brit will be happy to help, won't you, dear?"

Brit has her fingers over her eyes at this point and only

drops her hand when she hears her name again. She nods swiftly, but it looks for all the world like she's going to get sick right there on our back steps. I can't blame her. So far, Nancie's display makes Jonathan's promise to dance during the credits music at a movie seem like a gesture of loving support.

It takes Brit and me five more minutes to finally dislodge Nancie. She's talking the entire time, but she keeps trying to peek past me. Trying to check out our kitchen, maybe? I know she's already been inside—she's said so about four times: The Werners kept their dog food in the pantry near the fridge; she knows because they'd ask her to watch their German shepherd when they went down to Tallahassee every spring; yes, it's the same one that died next to the sink; the Werners made a mean potato salad; and does my mom cook anything special?

I eventually say I have to go upstairs and take a shower, and I write down Nancie's phone number, promising that I'll tell Harriet and Jonathan to call her once they're up. I watch from the window above the sink as Nancie and Brit mosey their way back to their house, stopping frequently to allow Nancie to crane her neck and squint at every darkened pane they pass along the side of our home. I sigh once they're out of sight. Southern hospitality, indeed—Nancie doesn't even know us, and she's already volunteering her daughter as my personal shopper. Either she's the most trusting person I've ever met, or she's just that desperate to find friends for Brit. It makes me wonder whether Brit might have a few more if her mom would back off just a tad.

I scratch my arm and realize it's still coated with sticky mango juice, so I decide to make good on that shower. When I turn around, though, I gasp. Jackson is standing there in the shadow of the doorway leading to the living room.

"Um, mango?" I offer, picking up the last one from the bowl at the center of the granite island.

"Who was that?" he replies gruffly.

"Our neighbors. Nancie and Brit Guthrie. They came to welcome us to the neighborhood."

"At eight thirty on a Saturday?" he says, and he pointedly holds up his phone, cracked screen and all, to show me the time.

"Well, okay, it's more like they were snooping, noticed me noticing them, and took advantage. Brit seems nice. Nancie's a talker, for sure."

"Don't care."

I sigh, but given what I saw last night, I cut him some slack. "Yeah, maybe. You're probably just exhausted. You'll feel better after—"

He cuts me off. "What's that in your hand?"

"Um, a mango?" I say, holding it out for him to see. I keep the invitation behind my back.

"No, stupid. Your other hand."

My ladylike smile fades. Granted, it was fake, but still, I *was* trying.

Jackson smirks. "Yeah, that's what I thought. Got nothing smart to say now, do you, Charlotte?"

I still don't lash out, but if I were a rattlesnake, my tail would be going off right now.

"You know, Jackson, rule five doesn't apply in the confines of our own kitchen, I'm fairly sure. The 'world hates me and I'm gonna take it out on Charlotte' routine is getting real old, real fast. So the way I see it, either you cut it out, or I go all mango on you."

He actually backs up a step. I wait for the comeback, but he doesn't seem to have one—and for good reason. Just as he's about to slink off, Harriet comes around the corner, stretching and rubbing her eyes.

"Heya, kids. What's all the commotion?"

I mean to jump in first, but the sight of Harriet sends a guilty shiver down my spine. As a result, Jackson pounces.

"She was threatening me, Mom!"

Harriet looks at me incredulously, blinking. It's pretty clear she's not quite awake yet.

"I can't deal with this without coffee," she mutters, moving to a cabinet and opening it. It's empty, of course—the caffeine fairies didn't have a chance to visit last night.

"I did it," I admit. "He called me stupid, so I told him if he wasn't a little more respectful I'd chuck a mango at him."

"Can we not do this right now? Jackson, apologize to your sister, and for God's sake start treating her better. And Charlotte . . ." She covers her brow with her hand. "Just . . . stop brandishing breakfast at your brother."

"Fine. Sorry," Jackson says, though he doesn't look at me.

"I'm sorry, too," I reply, making sure to hit just the right note of sincerity. Poor Jackson—he's never had a sibling before. By comparison, he's my ninth brother, with three different sets of parents. This ain't my first rodeo, not by a long shot.

"Thank you both. Now, give me that mango," Harriet says flatly. "I'll see what I can do with it, and as soon as Jonathan's out of the shower, I'll send him out for coffee. And a better breakfast."

"I've already eaten, so Jackson can have it," I say demurely. "Oh, and I met our next-door neighbors! There's a girl my age, and the mom seemed . . . invested? She gave us this. It's an invitation to a pig-pickin' party, whatever that is."

"A pig-pickin'? Sounds like some weird farm thing," Jackson murmurs.

"Maybe it's a bit of southern hospitality," I offer. "What if they give you a pig to welcome you to the community? You get to pick one for your backyard? Hey—people keep potbellied pigs as pets. They're so cute!"

Harriet shakes her head. "We're not bringing a pig into this house, free or not."

I get the sense that it's not just the lack of coffee talking there.

"Then maybe we get to adopt a cute little piggy at a farm. You know—pay for its food, visit it, get a picture of it.

Or maybe they have pigs, and we just get to name one. I'd name mine Wilbur, or Snortensia if she was a girl."

Jackson rolls his eyes.

"Eh," I say, "probably just a pig-shaped piñata or something. Pin-the-tail-on-the-piggy. Hmmm . . . maybe a football thing, like pigskin? Tomorrow's Sunday. Do they like football down here?"

"Carolina Panthers," Jackson mumbles.

"Huh?"

"Carolina Panthers. It's the NFL team down here. Don't you know anything?"

Again, I smile. "Yep! I know the NFL team in North Carolina is the Carolina Panthers. Why do you ask?"

"Because I just told you!"

"Told me what?"

"That the Panthers are Carolina's team!"

"No, you just asked me, and I told you," I say sweetly, resting my chin upon my latticed fingers and leaning over the counter.

"Ugh!" Harriet shouts. Or at least I think it's a shout. It's the loudest I've heard her, but I've had teachers whose normal speaking voices delivered more decibels. I glance over at her, and she throws her hands up and stomps out of the room. As she's leaving, Jonathan comes in, the collar of his gray T-shirt still wet. He's rubbing at his head with a little hand towel.

"Everything okay, darling?" he asks.

"You deal with this. And get coffee," she mutters.

He watches her go, then turns around, shrugging. "Couldn't find the bath towels. How are you this morning, Charlotte?"

"I'm good. Met our neighbors. Here," I say, handing him the card.

"A pig-pickin'? What's that?" he asks as he flips the card around. "Some sort of football thing?"

"That was my guess!" I say proudly.

Jonathan nods, and then looks at the lonely little mango sitting in the bowl. That, plus his wife's crystal-clear message about coffee, has him slipping on his shoes and grabbing his wallet.

"Want to come to the store?" he asks both of us. Jackson shakes his head, and I decline as well.

"Gonna get dressed, then talk to our neighbor. I think she'll help us go shopping later."

"Don't go too far!" Jonathan calls as he heads out the back door. A few minutes later, and I'm gone, too.

It's colder than yesterday, a fine mist dewing on my skin almost immediately. I shiver and cross my arms in front of me, pining for that winter jacket I'm going to buy today. The air smells sort of like fall—chestnut carts in Midtown, dusty heating ducts, the pumpkin-spice candles Grammy and I liked to light—only there's something thinner about it, like I can't get enough to latch on to any one memory. I make my way to the street, watching a couple of joggers dutifully pounding their way around the trail that runs inside the stone wall across the street. Sniffling, I blink the mist from my eyelashes, and I set off. The next house over is Brit's, and she's outside rummaging through a trash bag, separating different recyclables into colored containers. Nancie is nowhere in sight.

"Hey," I call from the edge of her driveway. She jumps nervously, clutching the half-empty bag to her chest. When she sees that it's me, she exhales, sets down the bag, and walks over to talk to me.

"I . . . um . . . I'm sorry about my mom earlier. She can be . . ."

"Hyper-welcoming?"

Brit smiles. "That's a . . . way to put it, I guess."

"It was nice of your mom to volunteer you to come shopping with me, and I'd love the company and the help, but you don't have to if you don't want to."

"No, I'm happy to," she says, slipping her fingers through her mist-soaked bangs. "I don't know how much help I'll be, though—it's not like you need much for school."

I arch an eyebrow. "What, is Loblolly a nudist colony?"

She laughs, a nervous titter punctuated by the faintest of snorts. "No! But we do have to wear uniforms."

Well, that's a wrinkle. I pout, and Brit holds up her arms. "I know, I know!" she says. "But I don't make the rules!"

In truth, I'm relieved. Removing what to wear from the equation solves a big, big part of my "fit in but don't stand out" challenge. However, I'm also aware that I'm supposed to balk at such restrictions; if I'm going to perform normal girl, I've got to freak out at the notion of being forced into fashion conformity.

"What are our colors? And do we have to wear pants? What about makeup and earrings?"

Brit shakes her head. "You're not going to like this, either. Our school colors are green and gold."

My face scrunches up, and I stick out my tongue. She hurriedly waves her hands at me, trying to ward off my feigned hissy fit.

"But the dress code says girls have to wear navy blue, black, or dark green skirts or pants. No jeans, nothing above the knee—and they do nail you on it if you're even a finger's width too short. Shirts have to be white with a collar, for both girls and boys. Sneakers for everyone except on assembly days. You can wear earrings and makeup, but I'm . . . I'm not the best person to ask about those kinds of things."

"It's okay," I respond. "What about jackets or sweatshirts?"

"Yeah, you can wear a coat or sweatshirt, but make sure they don't advertise anything or have another school's name on there. You can't even wear a Duke hoodie."

"Well, that sucks, but I still wouldn't mind it if you came shopping with us today. That is, if you're cool with it."

"My mom won't let me say no. She's kind of . . ."

"I saw," I say as she trails off. "I'm just sorry she forced me on you. You probably have better things to do than babysit the new girl in town."

"No!" Brit says quickly, and perhaps louder than she

would have liked. She blushes and quickly adds, "I mean, it's fine. I'm glad to."

"Cool," I reply. "I hope everyone at Loblolly is as nice as you."

"A-heh, um, yeah . . ." she stammers, gazing down at her shoes and turning away. "Some are, I . . . I guess."

"Okay . . ." I say slowly, offering her a grin. "Anyway, I'm going to walk around a little more, but I'll call you when we're heading out."

As I wave good-bye and start heading up the street, I can hear her sigh behind me. At first, I don't know what to think about it, but I deftly slip behind a bush and peek back. She's still standing there, a hand over her heart and another up to her forehead. She's smiling, and as she walks back up her driveway, I think she whispers, "Yesss!"

Huh. I guess I made an impression.

CHAPTER TWELVE

It Takes Guts

So it turns out a thousand dollars doesn't go nearly as far as I thought. I spend two hundred on school-appropriate clothes alone. Another hundred disappears on a decent winter jacket. Then come shoes; a nicer outfit for assemblies, dinners, and whatnot; and the requisite stock-up on underwear, socks, and toiletries. After a rug for my room and a backpack for school, I'm left with less than a quarter of my card, and I haven't even looked at phones for Jackson. Brit says she's never seen anyone buy so much stuff, ever, and asks if we're rich.

"No—I wish!" I laugh. Hitting the halls of Loblolly tagged as a spoiled kid isn't the kind of attention I need. "When my dad got his job, he got a signing bonus on these cards, and he said we had to get ourselves ready for school with them."

Mental note—tell Jonathan about the signing bonus I just made up.

Brit volunteers to take my newest shopping bag, but she's already carrying four, so I decline. I do offer to buy her one of those cinnamon-sugary pretzels, though. Can't go to the mall without getting a pretzel. She whispers her agreement, and we drop off our bags with Harriet in front of Pier 1. If Brit notices that it's the fifth time we've checked in during the last hour, she doesn't mention it.

"I've . . . I've never had one, you know . . ." Brit says as we're standing in line.

"Never had a mall pretzel? Not a big shopping fan?"

"No . . . no, I guess not. I used to come sometimes when I needed to get a game, but now I just order them online or download them."

"I can see that being easier," I concede, and she exhales. I think she was relieved that I didn't say anything about her game playing.

"You come to malls, or . . . I mean, go to malls often?" Brit asks.

I nod. "Yeah. You could say that. I used to spend a lot of time with my grandma—I called her Grammy. She . . ." I pause, figuring out how to put this. "Worked at malls a lot. I'd go with her."

"Oh, did she run a store?"

"Sort of," I admit, but that's as far as I'm going to go. I'm not about to explain that malls are a surefire score; everyone there has money, and there are usually a bunch of

143

restaurants, which are prime territory. Just figure out when the waiters and waitresses change shifts, do a bump-and-grab as they're hurrying outside to smoke, and you've got a fistful of untraceable cash. I can still clearly remember how proud my grammy was whenever I'd show her what I nicked after an hour at the mall. She'd even let me throw a few of the coins into the fountain. It didn't occur to me at the time to feel badly for what I was doing.

Now, of course, I'm wishing as Charlotte Trevor, and she just wants to keep things calm . . . which, apparently, is easier said than done.

"Is that BritGut?" a shrill voice twangs.

I saw this documentary once about octopi changing colors in the blink of an eye, and even they couldn't go green as fast as Brit does. She closes her eyes and swallows hard, refusing to turn around.

Again, the voice rings out, emanating from the direction of the dELiA*s across the way.

"It is! BritGut! Ohmygod! Of anyone from school, you're, like, the last person I'd ever expect to see here! And you're actually, like, buying new things! Time to replace that sweatshirt finally? I'm totally going to blog about this later! BritGut, shopping! In public!"

I pry my gaze off Brit's stricken face and trace the voice. It belongs to a girl our age, shorter than us, with an almost perfectly round face highlighted by half the makeup counter at Macy's. Her hair is in a braided updo, a huge white bow-scrunchie keeping it back. She has perfect teeth, a dance-studio windbreaker, and yoga pants that don't flatter her nearly as much as she thinks they do. Her fingers, French-manicured nails impeccable, clutch at her purse—a Gucci GG Plus top-handle bag, if I know my stuff. My mind instantly stats it out—zip closure, hand-sewn leather handles, room for about a hand and a half from the back. Looks to be three-quarters full, likely holding nothing even remotely as valuable as the bag itself. Of course, there are three other girls just behind this Gucci-wielder, tittering at everything she says. She flits her way right up to Brit, ignoring me for now, though her trailers give me a serious once-over.

"Can we cut you, BritGut? Thanks!" the girl says as she sidles in front of us.

Brit doesn't offer any resistance. She just mumbles, "Oh, okay, sure, I guess, Deidre."

It's like this girl found the tiny valve behind Brit's smile, twisted it, and completely deflated her. The other girls chirp, "Yeah, thanks, Gut!" and they fall into formation behind Deidre.

"Gut?" I mouth, looking at Brit. She blinks like she's fighting off tears, and her fingers are clenched into balls at her side.

Apparently, Deidre was sneaking a peek back at us, because she catches my question and turns around.

"Yeah, Gut! Like Guthrie. It's her last name."

"I'm aware," I say.

"Hi, by the way. I'm Deidre. Brit goes to our school. Are you Brit's friend?"

There's a twinge of something in the way she says *Brit's friend,* maybe the little snap she puts in the *t* and the *d* that makes it seem like she's painting the tips of her words with poison. Given that each time her mouth opens, Brit goes a little greener, I'm guessing that Deidre can get a whole lot nastier than this.

Before I can reply, Brit murmurs, "She's . . . she's not my friend. Just my new neighbor. She . . . yesterday . . . moved in next door. I'm helping . . . helping her shop . . ."

Not your friend? That's fair, I guess.

Deidre laughs, a high, staccato titter that bounces through her posse.

I brush a lock of hair behind my ear and smile. "I'm Charlotte Trevor."

"What, like the city?"

"Like the queen," I reply.

"Sure," Deidre says, looking back at her friends, who dutifully laugh again. I'm still smiling. Funny what being hunted by killers does for your sense of perspective—it makes Deidre seem a lot less menacing. There's been a girl like her at every school I've ever attended. There was bound to be one at Loblolly.

"Well," I say to Brit, though I'm speaking loudly enough for all to hear, "you've been the nicest person I've met since

I got here, and it's cool if you don't think of me as a friend yet. As far as I'm concerned, you're mine."

Brit swallows slowly, her eyes darting from girl to girl.

"That's awful nice of you, Charlotte," Deidre says. "Brit probably doesn't know what a friend looks like, anyway. She doesn't get many. Good luck with it!" Then she turns to her girlfriends and says, "Blogging this one for sure!"

Okay. That's actually a little menacing. Unless I do something, Brit and I are going to be front and center on the latest post. Granted, I doubt the Cercatores are perusing the blogs of preppy public schoolers in the Tar Heel state, but at the very least I'll get a vicious talking-to from Janice if WITSEC finds Charlotte Trevor on this girl's website. Time to take matters into my own hands.

There's an elderly couple in front of Deidre; the man is counting out exact change from his pocket, pushing a penny at a time toward the utterly bored pretzel boy. I time my positioning just as a family of four tries to squeeze through the line, situating myself so that the stroller they're pushing will have to go between the old folks and Deidre's group. The girls step back, and when they do, I'm inches behind them. Two of the girls bump into me. I apologize as they roll their eyes.

Sure, rule one says no stealing. And I still feel terrible about taking Harriet's ring. Heck, I'm feeling pangs of guilt for swiping from those servers five years ago. However, I'm not stealing the two credit cards and the rolled-up

147

twenty-dollar bill I just slipped out of the girls' jacket pockets. I'm just relocating them.

"Actually, Brit," I say loudly, "I'm not much in the mood for a pretzel right now. Let's head down to meet my mom."

Brit stammers, "O-okay . . ."

I lean forward, tapping Deidre on the shoulder. As she swivels, my index and thumb are on the zipper of her Gucci bag. Her twist unzips it for me, and it's easy to slide the credit cards and cash into her purse.

"It was nice meeting you, Deidre. I'll see you at school on Monday!" I say cheerfully.

"Yeah, k. Whatever," she replies, and she steps up to the counter as the elderly couple shuffles off with their coffee. Her own forward motion rezips her bag, and I let go before she can feel any tension. Then I grab Brit by the sleeve and tug her away. She gamely follows behind me until we reach the airbrushed T-shirt kiosk, where I pretend to look at a Hello Kitty shirt. I whisper to Brit, "Watch this," and tilt my head back toward Deidre and company.

We can't hear what they're saying, but we do get to see the look of utter embarrassment on one girl's face as she tries to pay for her pretzel, only to fumble around in her pocket for her credit card. It's easy enough to guess what her friend is saying when she steps up and volunteers to pay for it. Then the same look of sickened shock paints its way across her brow as she rummages through her pockets, coming up empty each time. Cue the exasperated sigh from Deidre, who proudly plops her Gucci on the countertop, unzips it with all the flourish of a magician reaching into a bag of tricks, and pulls out her precious little leather clutch. Spilling out with it, of course, are her friends' cards and cash. I'm not sure exactly how the argument goes after that, but it's intense.

Puzzled, Brit asks, "What . . . what happened?"

"Let's just say Deidre has something else to blog about now instead of your sojourn to the mall with your nonfriend."

Brit blushes, pushing up her glasses. "I didn't mean it, Charlotte. About you not being my friend. I'm . . . I'm sorry I had to say that. But . . ."

I wave my hand. "Don't worry about it. I get it. Attention from girls like Deidre isn't exactly a plus."

She shakes her head, and I have to lean in close just to hear what she's saying. "No, Charlotte. That's not it. I mean, yeah, I'm scared of Deidre. I'll admit it. But I wasn't saying that to save myself—I was trying to save you. I— I don't have many friends . . . at least, not at school. And Deidre . . . her and some others . . . might make it harder for you if they thought you were my friend. I'm not . . ." She pauses, lower lip trembling, eyes closed. "I'm not popular."

My first thought is to hug Brit, and my second is to walk over to Deidre and give her the U.S. marshal–issue chop to the larynx. I don't know what kind of torture Brit's undergone, but the stoop of her shoulders and the tremble in her voice suggest that life hasn't been easy for her. She should be tall and willow-graceful, but she's gotten so good at shrinking herself that I haven't been able to shake the notion that she's somehow smaller than me. And the idea that she was protecting me by distancing herself? After knowing me for less than a day?

Brit, you're already a better friend than you give yourself credit for.

In the end, hugging wins out, and I wrap my arms around her. She sighs once, trembles, and then pulls away.

"Thanks," she says. As Brit and I make our way to the rendezvous point with Harriet, all I can think about is how familiar this seems—Brit, Deidre, her friends, the tension, all of it—and yet how strange. I wonder if Nicki Demere would have dealt with the situation differently than Charlotte Trevor. Would I have felt so comfortable sticking with Brit in Deidre's face if I didn't have a greater mission? And why is it that it didn't seem weird to pretend to be someone I'm not? Have I been doing that at every school I've ever gone to? With everyone I've ever known?

Heck, is there anyone who *isn't* doing that?

CHAPTER THIRTEEN

Pickin' Pigs and Pockets

I wouldn't call Harriet frantic, but there's definitely some desperation percolating as we're getting ready to head across the street for our pig-pickin' party. She's got her blond hair tied back, sunglasses high on her head, and bangle bracelets bouncing as she rolls from room to room.

"I swear I did not have it yesterday. And I didn't go out. I was just working here, putting up pictures that aren't ours and rearranging furniture that I'm supposed to say has been in the family for three generations," she says to Jonathan, casting her hand about the living room. She points at the sofa with poised fury. "I've gone under this thing's cushions for my ring five times now. Nobody would keep this couch in their family for three minutes, let alone three generations. Now it's ours, and we can't get rid of it, because it's part of our 'backstory.'"

She slumps down by the front door as Jonathan searches the corners, picking up pictures, turning over pillows, and scooting chairs around. It's all I can do not to rush upstairs, get the ring, fall to my knees, and ask for forgiveness. I would, too, except Jackson's here, and I don't want him seeing me like that. He'd probably take a picture and e-mail it to Janice. So instead I stew right along with my fauxmily. The longer we wait, the more nervous I get. I have to do something soon if I'm going to maintain my Charlottey composure.

My hands trembling, I drift over to Harriet and offer to help her up. She shakes her frown off and reaches out. I clasp her wrist and tug her to her feet, careful not to actually hold her hand.

"Thank you, Charlotte. I'm sorry I'm in such a mood."

"No problem," I say, my own nerves settling almost immediately. "Nobody will notice, I'll bet, and if they do, just tell them the truth—you spent all day yesterday moving boxes and unpacking, and in the craziness you misplaced your ring."

"You're right, Charlotte. Such a good girl. We really got lucky with you," she replies, and her whole face brightens. She gives my shoulder a squeeze and then goes to fret over Jackson. He's standing in the center of the room shaking his new phone and cursing under his breath about the number of bars he's getting. When I gave it to him, he just growled at me. I chose to interpret that as Jackson-speak for *thank you*.

"Put the phone away for two minutes, Jackson. We have

to seem neighborly. *E per amor del cielo*, fix your hair. It looks awful."

I watch him shoot her a look before he tromps off to the bathroom. Apparently, when Harriet breaks out the Italian, she means business. It makes me wonder what sort of Rosetta Stone she'd roll my way if she found out I stole one of her bracelets while I was helping her up. I've got it in my back pocket now, the ruffled hemline of my new shirt hiding the evidence. In my defense, it was getting really uncomfortable in here. Besides, when I'm stealing is the only time I've ever been able to stomach people touching my hands, so if I was going to help her up at all, I'd have to be stealing something, right? Right?

Yeah, I'm not even convincing myself. Guilt washes into its familiar place behind the ebbing anxiety, and as I run up to my room, I'm silently yelling at myself to return the circle of platinum I just swiped. Heck, I even manage to sit down on my bed and gaze at the bracelet before stashing it in my sock drawer next to the ring. But again, something stops me from doing what I know I should. Instead, I do what Charlotte Trevor has gotten pretty good at already: I slide a bunch of socks over the purloined pieces and push the drawer closed, hiding Nicki Demere away for another afternoon.

When I march downstairs, everyone else is ready to go—even Jackson. We take a collective breath, and Jonathan opens the front door. The music from the party twangs its way in, accompanied by the smell of charcoal. We head out,

153

the whole Trevor family ready to appear in public together for the first time. Here's hoping I pick pigs better than I police myself.

We follow the music two doors down to a sturdy brick home ringed by pine trees. There's enough space between the houses for gardens, side yards, and tire swings. If this was New York, we could have built two whole other houses in there, but here in suburban North Carolina, they like their homes to have a bit of elbow room. Nancie Guthrie is in the driveway, and as soon as she sees us, she waggles her hands in the air and shouts like a bee just flew up her dress.

"Ohmyohmyohmy!" she screeches. "You're here! Hey, y'all, the Trevors are here! C'mon, everybody, and meet the Trinity Park Neighborhood Association!"

She bounds down the driveway, and she grabs me by the shoulders. "Goodness me, but you have better taste than my Brit. Lovely new shirt! What fun!" Then she turns to Harriet and Jonathan. "You must be Charlotte's parents. Sweet girl you've raised there. Welcome, welcome to y'all! Get yourselves on back there and say hello to Jeff Royster, host of this shindig."

Jonathan nods and sets off with Jackson in tow. I aim to follow, but Nancie blocks my way. "Brit'll be along directly. Had some sort of event going on with her computer. But let me tell you, Charlotte, you made an impression on her. She came home smiling. Still panicky like she always is, but smiling, too. You're gonna be good for her. Anyways, you ready for a party?"

154

"Yes, ma'am," I reply once my mind has replayed Nancie's words at a normal speed. "I'll go find Brit, if that's okay. Then I'll be ready to pick my pig."

Nancie arches one of her painted-on eyebrows at me, but only for a second. Then she swoops toward Harriet like a hawk spotting a wounded rabbit. "And you, Mama—Harriet, was it? I'm Nancie! Charlotte probably told you all about me, and that's fine, but I've gotta say, the ladies and I have been swapping speculation about you and yours faster than green grass through a goose. Not that I'm a rumor-monger, mind you, but I do like to have things right, and if you don't mind my saying, there's a certain degree of respect afforded to the girl who gets the gossip first, if you get my drift. So, pretty neighbor lady, do tell—where're you from, exactly, and what's brought you to Durham, North Carolina, here in the southern U.S. of A.?"

Wrapping her considerable arm around Harriet's shoulders, Nancie pulls her down a few inches and leads her into the backyard. I'm left standing in the driveway. I shrug and head over to Brit's house.

Nancie wasn't lying when she talked about her brass knocker. It's the head of a bull, with the ring dangling from its nostrils serving as the business end of the device. I knock gingerly, unsure of how much noise this thing actually makes, and I'm half expecting it to come alive and snort at me.

After a few seconds, I try the door. It's unlocked—yay, the South!—and I push it open.

"Brit? Hello? It's Charlotte!" I yell. I don't actually know if any other people might be here. Or vicious guard dogs, now that I think about it. In all our time yesterday, Brit didn't mention her dad, or siblings. So I yell again. Fortunately, or maybe not, there's no reply.

Inside, it looks like a craft store exploded all over Brit's living room. There's an impressive TV in an entertainment unit, but where you'd expect there to be pictures, or maybe a DVD collection, there are instead big skeins of yarn in all colors and patterns piled up and shoved in every nook and cranny. Still more yarn overflows from a basket on the floor near the couch. Long, red needles stick out from the tangle, as if the Guthries just brutally and efficiently put down a yarn insurrection, leaving the rebels where they lay as a warning to other fabrics that might have ideas. Several stands along the wall hold crocheted blankets, and a huge quilt has been hung like a tapestry behind the couch. Its colors are vibrant, almost garish, all purples and pinks and turquoises. They remind me of Nancie's eye shadow.

From above me comes a creak, like somebody moving around. The stairs are to my left, much broader and more inviting than those in our house, except that there're piles of yarn festooning every step like sleeping Technicolor cats. I hop my way up carefully. When I get halfway, I can hear a voice—Brit's, I think—from behind the closed door just off the second landing.

"Fremo, this is why I told you we don't play pugs! God, you're acting like a Silver Five out there!"

That's Brit's voice all right. Playing pugs? Silver Five? And who's Fremo? I press my ear to the door and hear more.

"You get all weird and try to ninja them. . . . No, no, you do. Don't argue with me. I'll just loop the demo of you doing exactly that, post it on Twitch, and let the world laugh at you. No, I'm serious! They're just camping the bomb. You run in there like you're the Batman or something, and we all have to Leeroy to save you. There's a reason I'm the caller and you're not. Deco round? Are you serious? You're not good enough for a deco round."

Again, Brit's voice, but there's nobody responding. She's either on the phone or talking to herself. What's more, she's speaking effortlessly—no stammer, no hiccups, none of the shy Brit I've heard before. I push open the door just in time to see Brit swivel around in her chair. She's got an exasperated look on her face, and she's wearing a headset, complete with a mic attached.

"Eaack!" she screams, rocketing backward in her chair so hard it bangs the desk behind her. The computer screens—two of them, both bigger than some TVs I've seen—jiggle and sway on their stands, and she wrenches around to steady them.

"Sorry!" I exclaim, holding up my hands. "I didn't mean to scare you!"

With eyes wide, Brit scrambles to pick up various little objects on her desk: figurines, toys, wrappers, and pens. She dumps them all in a drawer so quickly that I can't tell what's trash and what's treasure. Then she squeaks into her mic, "No. No, Ashea, I'm okay. My neighbor just showed up, IRL. Gotta go. Yeah, see you tonight for the tournament. Tell Fremo to cut that junk out, or we're gonna lose."

So that's it—she's talking to people online. On the screens are images of what looks like a Middle Eastern city, all dusty and derelict. There's a score tracker at the top, and it shows the counterterrorists beating the terrorists three to two.

"It's . . . it's not what . . . I mean, I was just . . . how . . . how did you know I was here, Charlotte?"

"Your mom told me. The doors were unlocked. Um . . ." I pause. She's still panting, her face so pale I can make out the blue of the veins in her forehead. "So . . . you're a gamer. That's cool."

"What? Oh," she mumbles, immediately looking down at her feet and pulling her shoulders in. "Yeah."

I regard her setup—the double screens, the futuristic computer tower to their left that glows red like some alien's body armor, and her impressive headset. My attention is drawn back to the right-hand screen, where there's a list of what I can only assume are other players. At the top of the list is the name BR1TN3YSP34RGUN. I puzzle it out for a second, then ask, "Britney Speargun?"

"Um, yeah." Brit laughs nervously. "That's me. It's like, you know . . . like, when I kill someone, it says on their screen, 'randomguy has been killed by BR1TN3Y-SP34RGUN.' And then they hear my voice, or see my live stream of a game, and they realize that I'm actually a girl, and it's . . . it's just for fun. I figure if I'm stuck with this name, I might as well use it."

"It seems like you're really good at this, Brit. You're at the top of the leaderboard!"

"Yeah, well, yeah. It's Counter Strike, so I'm pretty good. I'm not as good at some others. But if we win tonight, I might get an invite to join a pro team."

She's blushing with embarrassment and pride. I'm betting Brit is truly awesome at this game stuff, which explains a lot: Brit has a thing. Sure, some people might label her a geek, but this just makes Brit that much more valuable a friend. I'm betting she *knows* computers, same way I *know* pick-pocketing. So we have something in common, even though I can't really tell her about it.

"It does seem kind of violent. Does your mom know you're so good at it?"

"My mom?" Brit whispers, her words almost dying in her throat. "N-no. Not really. Well, I mean, she knows I play games. I do summer work, at camps and stuff, to pay for it . . . but I use the headphones so she . . . so she doesn't really hear. She's at work a lot of the time anyway."

"Can I see you play a round?" I ask.

"Wh-what?" Brit whispers. Her eyes are narrowed, like she thinks I'm setting some sort of trap.

"Hey, it's not every day you get a chance to see BR1T-N3YSP34RGUN in action. I want to say that I saw you owning scrubs online before you get famous."

There's just a hint of a tic at the corner of her mouth, and she adjusts her glasses. Then she cracks her knuckles. "Well, okay. I can play one really quick."

"Awesome!" I say, and I cast around for someplace to sit. There's a ridiculously poufy beanbag chair in the corner, and I toss myself down. It takes about a minute for the thing to stop making Rice Krispies noises. I can't help but sigh happily, and I wriggle my way as deeply into the bag as I can.

"Here goes," Brit murmurs after a moment of loading.

I can barely follow what's going on, Brit is flying around so fast. She dodges explosions and bullets, leaps off buildings, and issues orders through her mic, using so many acronyms she'd give WITSEC a run for its money. With her attention so squarely on her screens, I can kick back, watch Brit do her thing, and take a break from Charlotte Trevor. It feels good. It feels a whole lot easier than the pig-pickin' is going to be, or school tomorrow.

It feels, for this brief little window of time, normal.

On the screen to Brit's right, there's a score counter. BR1TN3YSP34RGUN leaps to the top of the list and stays there the entire match. When the pixel dust settles, Brit has logged forty-three kills and is named the game MVP. She takes off her headset, shakes her hair out, and turns around.

"That's . . . that's about all there is to it," she says.

"That was incredible! You shredded them!" I exclaim.

It's only now that I realize I'm standing up, having leaped to my feet after her thirty-fifth kill or so.

"I guess . . . I guess I did all right. It was fun having an audience."

I laugh. "Any time! Wow . . . Do the kids at school know about this?"

Brit gasps. "No! And please, please don't tell them! Can it . . . can it be our secret? If Deidre found out—"

I wave my hands rapidly to cut her off. If there's one thing I can sympathize with, it's having a secret to keep.

"No worries, Brit. I won't tell, I promise. And hey, speaking of Deidre, can we check her blog? I want to make sure we're not in it."

"Oh!" Brit smiles—an honest, unhidden grin. "That's no problem. Anything you need computer-wise, or on the 'net, I can do!"

Within seconds, I'm looking at Deidre's blog. Appropriately, it's titled *Because Y'all Love Me—a Blog by Deidre, about Deidre, and for Fans of Deidre.* The font is some hideous alphabet soup of puffy *D*s, heart-dotted *i*'s, and *o*'s with smiley faces inside. At least the actual entries aren't in the same type. I watch as Brit scrolls down to the most recent one.

LIFE IS UNFAIR!!!

Hello, blogfans! Big news! You know how I sometimes blog about a certain someone and her totally forgetful streak? Well, this unnamed girl, whose nails, BTW, are conveniently identical to my most recent mani, finally took it to a whole new level today at the mall. Like, freak-level stuff! So we're coming out of dELiA*s (shoutout—thanx for the awesome boots! Très cute!), where we all bought something, and unnamed paranoid girl says she wants to get a pretzel. So, being an awesome friend, I agree! We get over there, she goes to pay for her 'zel, and BOOM, her credit card is missing. Same with last week's BFF, who has now been demoted to just F (that's what you get!). Of course, because I'm nice, I offer to pay for both of them. I open my bag, and there are their cards!!! They immediately accuse me, ME, of stealing them! I totally didn't! I don't even know how they got in there! Probably they forgot them on the counter at dELiA*s and I picked them up for them by accident. It's amazing what people will accuse you of, even when you're doing nice things without knowing about it. God! How unfair is that? Of course I gave them their stuff back. But if you're reading this, you two, you have a lot of apologizing and explaining to do. And try not to be so forgetful next time!

Deidre OUT!!!

I hum appreciatively when I finish reading it. "See? No mention of us. It's too bad she sells out her friends, but I get the feeling that they'll just come yapping back at her heels on Monday."

"You're not wrong," Brit confesses. "I wish . . ."

I wait, but she seems to have packed that thought away in the drawer with the rest of her knickknacks. Instead, she sighs and smiles at me.

"Well, at least you won't have any trouble making friends, Charlotte. You'll have a ton of them. Girls like you always do."

Girls like me? Ones that need governmental intervention just to get adopted? Who steal from their fake mothers? Girls on the run from vicious killers? Girls who can't even share their own names?

"Girls like me?"

"Yeah, you know. Pretty. New. Good with makeup. Funny. Smart. Nice."

I blush. "Thanks for all that. But I don't really know what's going to happen. I've got a few plans, but I'd like to concentrate on just getting settled first. Besides, I've already got one friend, and that's more than good enough for now. Especially since she kicks butt with virtual assault rifles."

It's Brit's turn to blush, and she turns her face away. Closing the webpage and setting her computer to sleep mode, she says, "Do you maybe wanna go to the party now?"

"Sure," I reply. "I'm as ready to pick a pig as I'll ever be. When you moved in, did you get to pick a pig?"

Brit shakes her head, arching her eyebrow warily like her mom did. "No . . . I was born here. We didn't have a pig-pickin' for me. But I've been to a few."

"Are they cute? Or is it a football thing?"

Brit wrings her hands nervously. "I think you'd better just see for yourself."

I shrug. "If I get a little runty one, I'm naming it Wilbur. Wouldn't that be funny? Charlotte and Wilbur? Or maybe I'll name it something elaborate. What do you think of Ivan Totrufflehunt?"

"It's . . . um . . ." Brit stammers. She's a step and a half behind me now, and I just keep chatting all the way up to the Roysters' backyard.

"If I'm feeling spiteful when I get there, and it looks at me crosswise, I might name the little guy Jackson. Or Deidre if it's a girl, especially if it pushes the other pigs around with its snout and grunts orders at them. And hey, what smells so good? It's like a mixture of barbecue and Italian dressing and somethi . . . Ohmygodwhatisthat?!"

I freeze, and so does everyone else. A gaggle of neighbors and parents, mine included, stares at me, which is appropriate, I suppose, given that I just screamed. I continue to point, even as Jackson brays with laughter nearby.

"Your face!" he cries, the red cup in his hand sloshing lemonade all over the place. "Your face is hilarious! You should see yourself, Charlotte!"

I'd find a mirror and look if I wasn't paralyzed by the sight before me. Yawning open is a coal-black steel drum, laid on its side and propped open like a coffin. Tendrils of shimmering heat warp the air, but I can still see clearly enough. There, spitting and hissing over a steel grate, is an entire pig, its head brown and shriveled and its hairless legs left to dangle over the edge. Where its body should be, no . . . where its body *was*, is shredded meat, piled like grass mulched out the side of a lawn mower.

"Wh-wha?" I stammer. Jonathan shuffles up and tosses an arm around my shoulder.

"Charlotte," he says sheepishly, "welcome to your first pig-pickin'. Everyone, this is my daughter, Charlotte."

I think they all say their nice-to-meetchas, and I think I dodge a bunch of handshakes. I hope I'm smiling at everyone. I'm not sure, though, because I keep staring back at that pig. Eventually, Jonathan leads me to a picnic table. Brit scoots in next to me, and Jackson joins us a few moments later, carrying two paper plates piled high with meat and things of other colors. He slides one in front of me, and he crows, "Enjoy your lunch, sis!"

"I tried to tell you, Charlotte," Brit murmurs apologetically. "It can be a bit shocking at first."

My stomach growls. The sight of that pig still has me shaking, but the smell screams, "Dig in!" Jackson catches my eye and shovels a forkful of the meat into his mouth. Smiling, he starts chewing with his mouth open, working the shreds of meat around like laundry in the dryer.

"Mmm!" he says, spitting pieces of pig as he talks. "Tasty!"

It's all to freak me out, I know, but something happens.

"Wait a sec," he says, and takes another bite. "Actually, this is the best thing I've ever eaten. I'm not kidding. The best . . ."

We watch as he takes his phone out and snaps a picture of his plate. Then he resumes shoveling.

"We often lose northerners to pulled pork," Brit whispers.

I pitchfork my meat around a bit but don't take a bite.

"Are you a vegetarian?"

I shake my head. "No, but . . ."

Jackson jumps in. "But she tried last year, to impress some guy. It didn't last, though. I caught her up in the middle of the night eating leftover bacon. Just shoveling it into her mouth. She had a piece hanging out like a lizard's tongue or something."

My head snaps up, and I narrow my eyes. Jackson is still talking—with his mouth full, no less—but he's grinning mischievously all the while.

"Uh-huh! Big bowl full of bacon. You should have seen her. She looked so stupid!"

Brit seems incredibly confused, and I grit my teeth. Two can play at this game. I think about bringing up his little evening excursion from a couple of nights ago, but my conscience wins out . . . kind of.

"Yeah. My vegetarian days—back in Ohio, where we lived—didn't last so long. But my adorable little brother here wouldn't have caught me if he hadn't been up looking for someone to help him change his sheets. He still, you know, has bladder issues every now and again. Speaking of which, you might want to take it easy with that lemonade, buddy."

Jackson makes some sort of awful choking sound, coughs, and spits a wad of corn and collard greens back onto his plate. Brit murmurs, "Ewww . . ." and we both watch as he sweeps up his plate, growls angrily at me, and stomps away.

The next hour is spent schmoozing with people and casually laughing off my shock and horror at seeing the poor pig on the barbecue. Jackson mopes by himself, Jonathan hovers around the grill, and Harriet alternates between chatting with Nancie and fretting over Jackson and his bad attitude.

Eventually, I do try the pig. Jackson was right. It's delicious. I'm just glad nobody told me its name.

Hey Jackson . . . Are you there?

I h8 U. Leev me alone

I see your new phone works. You're welcome!

Hold on
Let me check sumthin
Ya I still h8 U

Joy. You're like my rock of stability. Life gets tough, I can always say, "Hey, at least Jackson still hates me." There's comfort in that, you know? Sun rises. Dog barks. Jackson mopes.

Shut up

Anyways, I'm not writing to make you mad. I just wanted to see if you're okay about school tomorrow. I've been to lots of schools, and I've done 6th before, so if you wanted to know stuff . . .

I dot wanna kno U
*don't

Maybe not. But it might be nice to have someone to talk to. Someone who knows who you really are. So you've got me if you need me.

[USER HAS EXITED CHAT]

K.
Good night, little brother.

CHAPTER FOURTEEN

Battlefield: School

The first time I crashed a new school midyear was a disaster. The second time was . . . well, okay, that was a disaster, too. By the third time, though, I started getting the hang of it. I guess that's one of the reasons the marshals picked me—I've done this sort of thing before. Granted, not as Charlotte Trevor, and not with people's lives at stake, but I know enough by now to have a plan of attack.

I take a shower as soon as my alarm goes off. The clothes are easy—dark-green-and-black-plaid skirt, white collared shirt with three-quarter sleeves that I roll up just above my elbow. I had Brit preapprove it as school-worthy. My makeup is light as usual, hair in a quick updo, and my new gold studs in place of the Swarovskis. It's all just enough to show that I care without drawing attention to myself. But the smell? The smell is something I fret over. I know I'm going to be the new girl; I just don't want to be the *pungent* new girl. So I go with one shot of body mist—a gentle hint of violet, vanilla, and sandalwood right at the nape of my neck, and that's it. If it's still too heavy, I can rely on Jackson to make fun of me for it before we even walk out the door. Obnoxious little brothers make great early-detection systems for embarrassing moments.

After breakfast, Jonathan gathers us for a pep talk. Jackson, dressed in black cargo pants, his new black skate shoes, and a white undershirt, is already seated on the couch. He is glaring at Harriet, who just tossed him a button-down shirt and demanded he put it on, pronto. I sit right next to him, even though there's a full cushion-length to my left. He turns that glare on me but says nothing, even when I hold my chin high and expose my neck.

Good. No odor issues.

"Good morning, children. Son. Daughter."

Jonathan takes a moment to look at each of us. He nods like a captain inspecting his troops. "Your mother and I know what a leap this has been for both of you and understand the gravity of what we're asking you to do here. Lucas . . . Jackson, my boy, we cannot tell you how much we appreciate your sacrifice. You gave up your friends. You gave up your family—cousins, aunts, uncles—to help us do the right thing, and years from now you'll be able to look back on this with pride, knowing that you played a part in justice being served. For now, though, we have to ask you to give a little more. Can you do that for us today? Be good. Be kind. Listen. Make friends, but don't make waves. Deal?"

Jackson just turns his head and pouts.

"Deal, son?"

"Deal. Fine. Deal," Jackson murmurs.

"Thank you. And you, Charlotte. We're relying on you. Watch out for Jackson. He's new to this, and we're depending on your support. Keep him and yourself under the radar. Make sure things go smoothly. God, but we're glad to have two pairs of eyes at that school, looking after each other. We're so grateful for the peace of mind that brings us."

"And you," I reply. "The same goes for you and Mom at work."

"Don't call her Mom. She's not your mom," Jackson grumbles.

I reply nonchalantly, "As soon as we get to school, she is. Same as I'm your sister, whether you like it or not."

"Not," he says.

I shrug. He's nervous, and layered on top of his usual grumpy, it makes him even more displeasing. But I've got bigger pimples to pop today.

The drive to school takes us through the Duke Forest, and it's a bit otherworldly, to be honest. Though the pines are packed close together, they have no lower branches—all their needles, some still green, some brown, are bunched up in the canopy. It looks like a never-ending army of upended brooms swaying gently with the breeze. The ground is carpeted with needles. It's both dark and peaceful at the same time, and I decide I like it.

Loblolly Middle School, it turns out, is named after all these pine trees—they're loblolly pines. Jackson announces as much from the backseat; it's the first thing he's said all drive. Jonathan hums appreciatively at that little nugget of knowledge, but then scopes out his son in the rearview mirror and starts harping on him to put away his phone. I'm not really paying attention. My mind is way too loud right now. I've got a jumble of questions popcorning around in there, and they only multiply when we join the line of minivans waiting to pull into the school parking lot. Our car slows to a crawl, giving me a chance to check out the school grounds.

Loblolly is a lot like the facility in Glynco. It's spread out, different buildings nestled between stands of pines. Kids are running along needle-covered walkways while teachers patrol the grassy patches, pointing at classrooms and shooing students along. The closest building has one of those signs that lets you pull the letters off and replace them, kind of like they have on the poles out in front of McDonald's. This one says *Welcome to Loblolly Middle School! School of excellence, 10 years running. Serving 403 students and supporting 84 faculty members. Go, Fightin' Pinecones!*

We're the Fightin' Pinecones? I suddenly get this vision of a giant mascot, all spiky and terrible, chasing little kids around and trying to hug them.

"Gotta take you into the main office. We meet with the

vice principal, who will give us a little tour and tell you where your homerooms are," Jonathan explains once we're parked.

I grab my backpack and hop out. The smells of pinesap and coffee are light in the air, and a chilly breeze whips around the car. I zip up my jacket and fold my arms across my chest, tugging at the straps of my bag. Jackson's hair, which he finally washed last night, frames his face as he scans the buildings.

"Come on, brother. Let's make this happen," I say, and with a deep breath I follow Jonathan up the hill toward the main office. Jackson slings his backpack over one shoulder, mutters something, and scuffles along behind, kicking up piles of needles with his shoes.

I check out the other girls. How do my clothes compare? Am I taller than they are? Do I walk differently? Will they be able to tell I'm a northern, skyscrapers-and-subways City girl?

From what I can see, I've done just fine with the uniform. It seems I've actually taken a bit more care than most of the other students, but that's easy enough to explain away. Any new kid at any school would want to look her best at first, even halfway through the fall. The boys try to be as sloppy as they possibly can—shirts untucked, pants sagging low, and buttons skipped. I silently give Jackson his props. His style actually seems to fit.

Double doors open onto a reception area. A cold draft sneaks in with us, fluttering bunches of announcements and sign-up forms on a bulletin board. Thick carpet stretches down the center of the room, the image of a huge pine tree sewn in. Underneath are the words *Commitment, Achievement, Respect, Excellence, Scholarship—Loblolly CARES*. A long hallway to our right bristles with doors, and I assume they lead to classrooms. To the left, an open doorway is flanked by four padded chairs on one side and a table on the other. The table features a green cloth stitched with the same slogan as the carpet, and atop this sits a woven basket filled with pinecones. The whole place smells, appropriately, like Pine-Sol.

"Can I help y'all?" a cheerful voice chirrups from the room to our left. Jonathan follows the voice, and we, in turn, follow him.

"Yes, ma'am," Jonathan says to the woman behind the long desk. "We're the Trevor family. This is Jackson—he's twelve, enrolling in sixth grade—and this is Charlotte, thirteen, going into seventh."

"Oh!" the curly-haired lady replies. She grabs a pair of reading glasses from where they dangle on her chest and lifts them to her eyes without actually slipping them on. Shuffling through stacks of paper, she says, "Here y'all are. Trevors. Right on time. You must be Jonathan Trevor, the father?"

"Yes, ma'am, that'd be me," Jonathan says congenially. "I've got some paperwork here for the kids."

"Good!" the secretary replies, and she hands him a clipboard. "I have to chase most new families all over God's creation for those things. Glad you're on top of your game, Mr. Trevor. Medical forms can be stapled to the blue sheet in there. If they still need physicals, just have the pediatrician mail us the info." She turns her attention to us, letting the glasses fall back down to bump against her white sweater. "Y'all don't have any allergies, do you? 'Cause we're not a peanut-free campus."

"No, ma'am," I say politely. I wait for Jackson, but he's busy reading a pamphlet he grabbed from her desktop. I sigh. "Same with my brother."

"Good. That's good. Tell you what—Mr. Jessup's waitin' for you in his office. You two can head in while your dad here fills in the necessaries. Go on. He's a nice man. Don't bite hardly at all!"

She chuckles at her own joke, and she's so cheerful that I can't help but smile, too. It's obvious from a scan of her desk that she's got a system down. A thick stack of pink attendance sheets are impaled on a long spike, and she's got four colors of Sharpies neatly arranged near her computer keyboard. A glass jar shaped like an apple holds mints, and a smaller matching one has paper clips inside. All of this sits atop a panel of thick, clear glass, underneath which she's collaged pictures of the same seven or eight kids. I'm guessing grandchildren. The topmost row on her phone says *Front Desk—Mrs. Childers*.

"Thanks, Mrs. Childers," I say, and I nudge Jackson toward Mr. Jessup's office.

"How did you . . ." Mrs. Childers begins, but then she picks up on the evidence and chuckles again. "Oh, clever girl! I like you!"

Thanks, Mrs. Childers. I like you, too.

I'm still smiling as I lead Jackson down the little hallway. I only hope the vice principal is as welcoming as the secretary.

Our knock seems to be swallowed by the carpet and ceiling tiles, but the door swings wide. Standing there is a tall, strikingly handsome man in a decent suit (Perry Ellis Portfolio, side vents, four-inch-deep front pockets and button-closed back ones). He looks like Denzel Washington, if Denzel was a little younger and completely bald.

"Welcome, welcome. You must be the Trevors," he says. His voice is gentle—reedy and reassuring. "I'm Mr. Jessup. I've been waiting to meet you all for weeks now, ever since we heard you were coming!"

"Thanks," I say. "It's good to be welcomed."

"She talks!" He chuckles to himself. "Sorry. Most new kids are so scared I can barely hear them. Your response, Charlotte . . . it is Charlotte, right?"

I nod.

"Well, Charlotte, your response speaks highly of your confidence. And this is . . ."

"Jackson. I'm Jackson," he murmurs, averting his eyes. At least, I think that's what he says—his lips moved, but no sound really came out.

Mr. Jessup shoots me a knowing wink. "That's more like it."

The vice principal indicates a couple of chairs across from his desk. I plop down my backpack and sit. Jackson hugs his bag to his chest. The shades are drawn, but the lamp in the corner casts a comfortable glow on the bookshelves all around us.

Mr. Jessup takes a seat in his squeaky leather chair and folds his hands in front of him. "Know why I'm so excited to meet you both?"

At first, I think it's a rhetorical question, but he's staring at us with intense brown eyes, and the silence lasts too long. He wants an answer.

"You both?" I echo, my brow furrowing. I tap my lip with my index finger and repeat, "You both . . . you both . . . Not y'all. You're not from here, Mr. Jessup. I'm guessing you're . . ."

I peek at his desk for clues, and my gaze settles on a blue-and-white Xavier University mug. I remember the name of the place from our training. I remember where it is, too. Of course. We just got here, and they fire this cannonball for us to dodge. Well, here we go. . . . "You're from Cincinnati."

He beams, sitting back in his leather chair and clapping his hands once. "Montgomery, to be more precise. Moved here about fifteen years ago. Tell me a little about the Queen City these days. How's she holding up?"

Jackson actually squeaks. Mr. Jessup says, "Yes, Jackson?"

"N-nothing."

"It's like nothing?"

"No. I mean, I dunno." Jackson shrugs. I believe if he could unzip his backpack and crawl in there, he'd do it, like one of those little dogs rich people tote around.

I frantically try to think through all the information that the marshals taught us, but for some reason it's just not coming up—at least nothing relevant anyway. I could spew out our fake street address, the name of the school I never actually attended, and the county we're supposedly from, but I don't think, "Hurr durr . . . Osage Road, Indian Hill Middle School, Hamilton!" is quite what he's looking for.

The seconds stretch out like gum between a hot sidewalk and a shoe. Fortunately, before my shaky left hand shoots out to swipe the calculator off Mr. Jessup's desk, something comes to me. It's not from the marshals' training, though, or from any file. Rather, it's from an old book I read at the Center. Thank goodness for books.

"Well," I finally say, "you know. It's like Twain said. If the end of the world is coming, I want to be in Cincinnati, because—"

Mr. Jessup jumps in. "Because Cincinnati is always twenty years behind the times!" He laughs and smacks his desk. "I love that saying. So darn true. It's probably about the same—you're right, you're right. Well, anyway, it's great to meet two students from my hometown. Don't worry. You'll like it down here. Durham's actually not that much different from Cincy, except maybe in how we handle ribs. Still can't beat the Montgomery Inn, for my money."

I smile and nod, then elbow Jackson, who sits up abruptly and bobs his head up and down crazily. If Jessup notices, I can't tell—it seems he's already moved on.

"Let me tell you a little about Loblolly, and then we'll go on a campus tour. I'll try to have you to your homerooms in about fifteen minutes. That'll give you a few minutes to say hello before you head off to your first classes. Here are your schedules, by the way."

I look over the color-coded chart carefully, and Jackson does the same. Homeroom, math, language arts, gym, lunch, Latin, science/history, and something called *flex* for the last forty-five minutes of the day. It all seems pretty standard to me, and with my B-minus target average, I'm worried less about what I'm taking and more about who's in there with me. Hopefully, Brit will be in at least one of my classes.

"I'll show you where to go, and we're assigning each of you a buddy from your classes to help you out this first week. Any questions so far?"

"Um, how do we sign up for clubs or sports?"

"So you're an athlete, Charlotte? What's your game?"

Other than legerdemain and sneak-thiefing?

There's a case of trophies behind him, and though I'm too far away to read the plaques, I can at least see the little bronzy figures frozen atop each one. They might be school trophies, or his own personal ones. It doesn't matter, though, because I only want what isn't there. I see a football guy, a swimmer, a soccer player, and either a tennis or racquetball person.

"Basketball," I say. Jackson coughs.

Mr. Jessup rubs his hairless head. "Well, that's good, Charlotte. You might just be the piece our team needs. We're not exactly known for our basketball prowess here at Loblolly, and as you can imagine down here in the Triangle, the schools we play take their hoops seriously. We haven't won a game in three years, but who knows? Maybe you'll be part of turning that corner. And there are three practices next week, so your timing couldn't be better."

"I'm sure it'll be fun," I lie, throwing enough syrup into it to suggest sincerity. "I'm just looking forward to being part of something."

Okay, so that second part's not a lie.

"Well, you're already part of something here, Charlotte. Loblolly Middle School prides itself on academic achievement, and you're a member of that team now. Our students study hard, love to learn, and take their work seriously. We fully expect you to do the same."

I nod. "We saw the sign outside. A school of excellence for ten years—that's great!"

He smiles broadly. "It means our test scores consistently exceed the state standards. We've fostered a culture of success here, and I think you'll find that at Loblolly, it's cool to like school."

I offer a courtesy giggle, then lead Jackson out to the

reception area. Jonathan is waiting for us. He says good-bye, kissing each of us on the cheek before wishing us luck. I dutifully wipe it away, even though I've never had a dad's good-luck kiss before. Since Charlotte Trevor would have had plenty in her time, Nicki Demere will just have to enjoy the memory of it.

We head outside, navigating the paths between buildings. Jackson is the first to get dropped off, and as we stand at the doorway, I give him a quick hug.

"Good luck, Jackson. I'll see you this afternoon," I say, smiling. He's so nervous he forgets he hates me for just a second.

"Yeah, you too," he mumbles, and he slips in behind Mr. Jessup. I lean against a locker while I wait for them to finish, and then it's just the vice principal and me.

After a few more twists and turns on the breezeways, Mr. Jessup comes to a halt in front of a green-painted door. On the door is a laminated poster, markered up to look like the Declaration of Independence. It's a set of classroom expectations—*We hold these truths to be self-evident, that all students should come prepared to learn, to respect one another's ideas, and to do their best*. Hmmm. Nothing about cruelty and perfidy scarcely paralleled in the most barbarous ages. That's good, I guess.

At the bottom of the poster, inked in a flowery hand right where John Hancock's name should be, is *Ms. Zelda Millar*. Surrounding it are kids' names—some printed, some signed. In the bottom-right corner, there's a yellow sticky note haphazardly flapping in the wind. Upon it, in the same cursive as Ms. Millar's name, is *Charlotte Trevor.*

I wrinkle my nose. This means they know I'm coming.

Mr. Jessup knocks at the hollow aluminum door, and a mousy, jittery sort of woman opens it. She squints momentarily as she sizes me up.

"Ms. Millar, meet Charlotte Trevor. Charlotte, this is Ms. Millar. She's your teacher for homeroom and history. Be prepared to learn about colonial America this semester. Or, as the kids call it, the Pirate Year. Arrrrr!"

There are a few giggles from inside the room, and I lean in to look. Sure enough, there are two dozen kids, all craning to see me. Once they get a glimpse, they quickly sink back into their seats, whispering furiously to one another.

"Hi, Ms. Millar," I say.

She looks down at her pink attendance pad and drawls, "Oh, he—"

"Hello, Charlotte! It's *so* nice to meet you!"

The interruption is so abrupt that I jump. Ms. Millar rolls her eyes but makes room for the bubbly girl, who practically throws herself into the doorway.

"My name is Holly Fiellera! I'm the head of the Student Welcome Committee, the Community Outreach Committee, the Environmental Club, the Hispanic Heritage Club, the Choir Student Board, the Service Club, and, in the spring, the Student Graduation Ceremony Honorary Advisor. I run the Academic Progress Club as well. Also, I volunteered to be your buddy this week!"

Of course you did, Holly.

"Wow," I remark, which sets Holly to bouncing like a puppy. "Harvard called. You're accepted."

She grins, exposing the most perfect set of teeth I've ever seen. They match her thick but impeccably sculpted eyebrows, olive skin, and her immaculate hair. I can imagine reaching up there and breaking off a piece like a jet-black icicle. I'm impressed—pulling off this look and volunteering for everything ever has to be exhausting.

"You're so sweet!" she replies, taking my arm and tugging me into the room. I hear Mr. Jessup say, "Whelp, looks like she's all set," and Ms. Millar closes the door behind us. Now I'm center stage, and I slip my hands behind me so nobody can see them. I know this is a necessary moment, but all-eyes-on-me is exactly where I'm not supposed to be.

"Ladies and gentlemen, this is Charlotte Trevor," Holly announces. "She's new. Make her feel welcome!"

The class just stares. I stare back, keeping a smile shellacked onto my face. Eventually, a familiar voice murmurs from the back, "It's . . . it's nice to meet you, Charlotte. Um, again."

There's a tidal shift of focus from me to the back, where Brit's face peeks out from behind the bookbag on her desk. I replace my fake smile with a real one and wave. The rest of the class keeps staring at Brit until she sinks so low that her bottom slides off the seat.

A few more seconds of awkwardness ensue, like those moments after you pour pop into a glass filled with ice, and you're wondering if it's going to fizz over. That ends when Holly tips over the whole darn glass, both figuratively and literally.

"Charlotte, do tell us a little about yourself! We've been gossiping, of course, but we want to hear it straight from the horse's mouth!" she exclaims as she tries to squeeze between me and Ms. Millar's desk. There's a mug of pencils there, though, and she smacks it with her elbow as she passes. Before I can think, or stop myself, or anything, my right hand darts down to grab the mug, and I invert it beneath the pencils, catching most of them before they hit the floor. My left hand is moving, too, and I nimbly snatch three more out of the air. Then I cram them into the mug and slam it back onto the desk. When I straighten myself, my backpack hasn't even shifted on my shoulders.

If kids were staring before, well, they're fixated now.

"Whoa," one boy says, and the rest of the class echoes, "Whoaaa!"

Slowly, Holly asks, "How . . . how did you . . . ?"

"Do people still say that?" I reply innocently, trying to change the subject. "'From the horse's mouth,' I mean. I, like, haven't heard that in forever!" Some kids snicker, and one boy near the back hee-haws like a donkey before turning Coke-can red and joining Brit in the seat-slide. Most are still locked on me, though.

Holly is as impervious as her hair. "Well, I do. . . . But seriously, how?"

"Oh, nerves, adrenaline, something like that, I guess?"

I lie. "Anyway, I'm Charlotte. Everyone knows that already, I suppose. I'm from Ohio. Just moved. My brother also goes here. He's in sixth grade. I think your campus is beautiful, and I'm looking forward to—"

Some boy shouts, "Do it again! The thing with the pencils!"

I zero in on the speaker, a guy in the first row with big hands and a sweaty forehead. Holly levels a formidable frown at him. He makes a face back. Ms. Millar senses a situation brewing, and she heads it off at the pass.

"Charlotte, your seat is next to Holly, over there. Ladies and gentlemen, continue discussing your projects. The bell will ring in about five minutes."

The class breaks out into a dozen conversations, and I slip into my seat, placing my backpack down beside me and spreading my schedule on the desk. I try to crane around to see Brit, but Holly scoots her desk next to mine and smiles at me until I look at her instead.

"So how long have you been here?" she asks.

"Since Friday."

"Are you in any clubs yet?"

I fold my hands over my desk, glancing at the rest of the class. Some seem to be talking about their projects, but more are murmuring and sneaking peeks at me.

"No, not yet, but I'd like to be. Got any openings?"

Holly looks like I've just told her she won the lottery.

"Oh, Charlotte, you're speaking to the right girl! There are openings all over the place, and even in the clubs that don't have them, I can probably get you in. What are your interests?"

My interests? This is a topic Charlotte's file wasn't particularly clear about. I try to think of something else besides books and burglary.

Before I can, though, the boy to our left leans in and brushes a lock of blond hair from his eyes. "Hey," he says, his voice as smooth as honey on dark bread. "Slow down, Holly. Charlotte, you said? That was unreal, how fast your hands moved there. Tell me your secret. You have a superpower?"

"Yes," I reply, smirking. "It's not interrupting other people's conversations. If you want, I can teach it to you sometime."

He laughs and holds out his hand. "My name is—"

"Archer. Archer Brantley," Holly finishes, and she smacks away his hand. Her tone is still upbeat, but there's a hint of a hiss there. "And we'll take it slowly if you will. She just got here, for heaven's sakes." Leaning in to me, she whispers, *"Tenga cuidado de él. . . ."*

Though I don't know Spanish well, I've heard enough to recognize when I'm being warned. I nod almost imperceptibly.

"You know I love it when you speak Spanish, Holly," Archer says with a Cheshire grin. "Someday, I'm going to learn it, just for you." He turns to me. "And what language are you in, Charlotte?"

I look down at my schedule. Holly peers over my shoulder. "Room 402. That's the Latin room. You're taking Latin. So am I!"

"Too bad," muses Archer. "I'm in French. When's your lunch period?"

"I'll look later," I say. Archer shrugs, but I can still feel his eyes on me as Holly clasps my shoulder and turns me away.

"Now, about clubs. You should think about—"

I hold up my hand. "I will, I will. But Ms. Millar mentioned a project? Am I stepping into the middle of something major?"

"Kind of. Group report on North Carolina in the Revolutionary War. I already volunteered you to be in our group. We're doing the Edenton Tea Party. You totally don't need to worry; we're basically done. You'll just stand up there with us while we present!"

"Thanks," I say, hiding my irritation. Granted, tea parties aren't my thing, but I like doing my own work, and if Holly is as overachieving as she sounds, being lassoed into this isn't likely to help me keep my grade in the B-minus range. Before I can say any more, though, a loud buzz fills the air, and all the kids explode from their desks at once.

"That's the bell!" Holly exclaims.

"Thanks for everything this morning. I'll see you in Latin?"

"Oh, before that, girlfriend. I'll find you, don't worry!"

As she skips off, Holly actually kisses her fingers and

wiggles a wave at me. I sigh and wave back. Then I join Brit near the door, where she's skulking.

"Well, she's exhausting," I whisper.

"Holly?" Brit asks, blinking, like she didn't expect me to talk to her.

"Yes, my welcome wagon."

"Oh, she's . . . she's not so bad."

"She seems fake," I observe.

"Yeah, but that's the weird thing," Brit notes. "She's kind of not. Deidre hates her, of course, but even she doesn't bother making fun of Holly—it just kind of rolls off her back, and she keeps going, and going, and going. She's like the Energizer Bunny of Loblolly Middle School."

"I bet the teachers love her."

"I guess. Mr. Alcontera tells her to stop raising her hand for every question in math."

I take out my schedule.

"I have math now."

"Me too!" Brit says, her smile the first truly sincere one I think I've seen all day. "Oh, and I made something for you!"

I watch as she rummages through her bag and produces a piece of graph paper.

"I . . . I know it can be tough getting around this place sometimes. I get lost, and I've been here since sixth grade. So here. I drew this for you."

It's a map of campus, painstakingly drawn and color coded. So Brit can add cartography to her list of talents.

"Wow!" I say softly. "When did you find time to do this? It's amazing."

"Right after my game last night. I . . . I stay up late most of the time."

I gasp. "That's right! Your game! How did you do?"

She bites her lower lip and glances around. Satisfied that we're out of other kids' earshot, she whispers, "We won! They said they wanted to see me play a few more, but I'm at the top of their list for the team!"

I clap as quietly as I can. "Can I come over again sometime to watch? That beanbag chair totally had my name on it."

"Sure!" Brit says, and she beams. It's hard to believe that BR1TN3YSP34RGUN is somewhere in there, but it's reassuring to have a friend who knows a thing or two about hiding in plain sight. If Brit can pull it off, maybe Charlotte Trevor has a shot, too.

As we leave homeroom, I ask Brit to tell me about the teachers—who's nice, who's uptight, who the favorite is, who will bore me to tears. She says the same thing about all of them—they're intense.

"They all really want you to do your best, especially on the EOG."

"EOG?" I ask, pronouncing it like the name of a particularly loathsome under-the-bridge troll.

"End of Grade test," she clarifies. "It's big around here."

"So I've heard. Why?"

"You'll see when you get to the cafeteria, or the computer

lab. They're awesome, and it's because we get money for our great test scores . . . at least, I think. I know the teachers get bonuses and stuff. But it's cool, because they still want us to learn."

"EOGs are a big deal. Got it."

"What's a big deal, Charlotte?"

Brit and I are suddenly separated, with Archer and two of his friends sliding between us.

"Um, we were . . . we were just saying . . ." Brit begins, but Archer waves his hand by his ear like he's shooing a fly, and she stops talking. He stares expectantly at me, keeping up with us step for step.

"Really, Archer? It's my first day," I scold. "Aren't you supposed to wait a few weeks before pouncing?"

He laughs, shaking his head. "And aren't you supposed to be all quiet and shy?"

Dang. I thought I *was* being quiet and shy.

I speed up, but he matches us stride for stride again. "It's weird. You don't have that new-girl vibe."

"Whereas you definitely have that old-dog vibe."

He laughs again and playfully makes a grab for my map. "C'mon, let me see where you're going!"

It's a decent attempt, but against my hands, he's painfully slow, and in the time it takes for him to try to paw at the paper, I've creased it twice, palmed it, and thrust it behind me into an open side pocket of my backpack.

"Still not sharing, Charlotte? You're a girl of mystery," he says, nodding appreciatively. "I like mysteries. And you know what? You're a mystery I'm going to solve. Don't worry, I don't mean in a creepy way. I just think we'll end up being friends. Watch and see!"

His friends snicker, and all three peel away, headed in the opposite direction.

"He's the most popular boy in the seventh grade, you know," Brit remarks. "You're way lucky."

"Way lucky? I'd settle for fitting in."

Brit nods. "But you've got to admit, there is something about you. I mean, you're nice to me."

I sigh. "Don't start that again. You're my friend, I like you, and that's that."

"Okay," Brit says, and I swear she skips, just once, as she walks. She's quiet for the rest of the way, except for the occasional mumbled "Excuse me" or "Sorry" as we bump and shuffle our way through the crowds of kids cramming into classrooms. When we finally reach the door to math class, I shake my head. I've been here less than a half hour, and I've already got Holly signing me up for anything with a bake sale and a cause, Mr. Jessup wanting to reminisce about the old neighborhood, the entire homeroom thinking I'm Houdini, and Archer's bull's-eye on my back. I can see why Brit prefers her virtual war zones; Loblolly is more than enough minefield for me. I'm just glad I've got a map.

Dear Deputy Marshal Harkness,

What a terribly pleasant surprise it was to see you and your beautiful son playing in Central Park yesterday! It warms my heart, Eddie, to see a man so invested in his job show the same dedication to his family. In fact, it led me to wonder: To which is this man more dedicated? If asked to choose, would he favor his government's responsibilities, or his precious son's safety? An intriguing question, don't you think?

Very soon an opportunity will arise, Mr. Harkness, which will allow us to answer the conundrums above. A representative from my family will be in touch and will have a few questions for you. You may choose to answer them, or you may choose not to. I believe your son would urge you to answer the questions—perhaps he'd do so just after getting home from his pee-wee football practice, on Tuesday afternoons at 3:45 p.m., or maybe upon returning to New York after visiting his beloved granddad in his apartment on Communipaw Avenue in Jersey City. Yes, I believe your son would very much like his loving father to answer those questions.

If you choose not to answer the questions, or if you share this letter with anyone, I would be forced to visit you myself. The outcome of that meeting, I fear, would be unpleasant.

Most sincerely,
A friend

CHAPTER FIFTEEN

The Eye of the Storm

Math goes about as well as math can, I suppose. Mr. Alcontera shouts a lot, but he's manageable. Turns out he declined getting a SMART Board or any other technology in his room—he's paranoid that kids will calculate with something other than their brains. So I watch as my classmates march up to an actual chalkboard and crumble, smudge, and squeak their way to algebraic answers. I quickly realize the best way to pass the time is by counting the number of times Mr. Alcontera says the word *algorithm*. It beats looking up at my classmates, only to see them staring back—the ones from my homeroom especially. The sweaty-forehead boy, it turns out, sits right next to me, and he spends half of the period poking his pencil with his finger, letting it tumble to the ground like I'm going to snap my hand out and be his savior. Eventually it gets so annoying that I whisper, "Hey, what's your name?"

"Cuss," he replies.

I glare at him, and he elaborates.

"It's a nickname. Short for Atticus."

I shrug. "I guess that beats Tic . . . or Attic." Thinking about it for a second, I shake my head. "Actually, no, it doesn't."

"Do the pencil thing!" he says eagerly, and flicks his to the ground.

"I don't do requests," I retort gravely, and then I tilt my head toward Mr. Alcontera, who is turning around again, adjusting his belt and scanning the classroom for his next volunteer. Cuss quiets down, but he doesn't stop letting his pencil dribble to the floor every two minutes. By the time the period is up, I'm feeling a powerful urge to steal every dang pencil in the place, just to keep people from bugging me with them.

My next class is language arts. It's always been my favorite subject, and the teacher has to be right. Now, I'm not asking for a storybook teacher like Miss Honey, Mrs. Jewls, or Ms. Frizzle—heck, I'd settle for a Lupescu, McGonagall, or Retzyl. But whoever it is has to let us read. I take a deep breath, swing the door open wide . . .

. . . and nearly get run over by a stampede of students headed out. Brit and I get swept up in the tide, and it's all I can do to ask her what's going on.

"Library day!" she mouths just before being backpack-battered away.

"Sweet," I whisper.

The teacher, Ms. Drummond, is as no-nonsense as the rest of them; she'd do a decent Defense Against the Dark Arts class. She brings up the rear, stomping along to keep the herd moving. There are a few stragglers, but as far as I'm concerned, she needn't bother. I'm scampering ahead to get to the library as fast as possible.

At first, I think I've accidentally entered an aquarium. There's a huge circular fish tank in the center of a sunlit atrium, and its base is surrounded by a velvet-cushioned bench. More benches line the walls of the entryway, and several kids are reclining on them, the books in their hands held skyward like an offering to the sun. Past the fish—and a turtle, all native to North Carolina, a plaque says—the library opens up into one of the finest marvels I've seen. It's two stories tall, with wooden spiral staircases in each corner. In the center is the circulation desk, and off to the right, a lushly carpeted reading corner. At the back, nuzzled between the shelves, are individual little carrels, each one boasting one of those bendable reading lamps, a flat-monitored computer, and a view out into the pine forest. And the shelves! There are dozens of them, each one labeled meticulously. It even smells like books—bindings, old dust, and new discoveries. I pause for a moment and just breathe.

By the time I'm done soaking it in, everyone else has already slipped silently into the stacks. No teacher gave instructions or groused about proper etiquette. They just did it on their own. Curious, I seek out Brit, who is trying to choose between two fantasy novels.

"Go with *The Last Unicorn*. It's awesome," I whisper.

Brit puts a finger to her lips, even though I was quiet. So softly that I have to turn my ear to her just to get anything, she replies, "What do you think?"

I take another look around. "This is like a church!"

"I told you we had awesome facilities. Wait 'til you see the computer lab."

"Not gonna," I say. "I'm never leaving this library."

Brit giggles, which earns a disapproving glance from Cuss at the end of the row. Wow. Even he takes this place seriously.

"So what are we doing?" I ask.

"Just browsing. Once a week, Ms. Drummond brings us here. We get the entire period to just read or check stuff out."

"Don't mind if I do!" I smile, and Brit stifles another giggle as she watches me skip down the first row.

I reach out with both hands, pressing my fingertips to the spines of the books to my left and right. As I walk, I trace their shapes, feel their textures, and inhale their scents. When I reach an old friend, I stop and mouth the title to myself, letting the memories of all those adventures echo in my mind. I whisper hello to Bud (not Buddy), Tarzan, Gilly Hopkins, and Hugo Cabret and proudly let them know that I'm finally not the only orphan in the library without a tale to tell.

A few minutes of wandering leads me to the reading corner, and I notice there's a bulletin board there. A couple of kids are looking at it, so I step in behind them to peek. In the top corner is a bubbled-lettered list of the "Academic Superstars" of the previous year; apparently, the students on the list got the top ten scores on last year's EOG. We had tests like these in New York, but I've never been to a place that took them so seriously before. I guess if it gets Loblolly the funding for a library like this, I can understand. Still, that's a lot of pressure. . . .

Farther along on the board, a familiar face beams at me. It's a picture of Holly, and she's holding up a pinecone in one hand and a miniature American flag in the other. The caption reads *Holly Fiellera—Isn't it time you had a friend on student council? Vote Holly, by golly!* Below that is a countdown to election day, which is next week. I turn to one of the girls looking at the board and ask, "Who is Holly running against?"

The pigtailed girl smiles. "Oh, right. You're new. Have you met Holly yet?"

I nod.

"Let me guess—she baked you cookies and threw a party to welcome you?"

Smiling, I say, "Cookies? There were supposed to be cookies? I think I got hosed. . . . She just volunteered to be my buddy."

"Yep. That's Holly. She's running against a lot of people, only most don't campaign like she does."

"I'll bet."

"Yeah. Anyway, there are six student council members. It's supposed to be two from each grade, but everyone can vote for anyone, and you get two votes. The student with the highest total overall becomes student council president for that year."

Hmmm. Holly didn't list that one on her verbal résumé.

"Who else is running?" I ask.

"Why? You want to run?"

I laugh—I'm sure Janice would love that.

"No thanks," I reply. "I'm Charlotte, by the way."

"Like the city?"

"No, like the skating move."

"Oh . . ." she says, perplexed. "Well, nice to meet you. I'm MZ. It's short for Mary-Elizabeth, but everyone just calls me MZ."

"Nice to meet you, too. Gonna keep checking out this sweet library."

"I know, right?" she says, and we go our separate ways.

I use the rest of the time to commit the layout of the library to memory. I have a feeling this is going to be my happy place here at school, and I want to stake out which carrel will be my go-to spot, where my favorite authors live, and which seat is the comfiest. I also make note of the exits, and I decide this is a good place for Jackson and me to meet if something goes haywire. I wouldn't have thought of these things last month, but in Charlotte's reality, knowing where to hide is a thing.

In the end, I settle on a quiet little carrel nestled between L'Engle and McGraw. I've got C. S. Lewis and Lois Lowry in easy reach, the view out the window is peaceful, and nobody's carved any inappropriate pictures into the surface of the desk. On the whole, I couldn't ask for more. It almost makes me forget about the rocky start to my morning. Between my room at home, Brit's comfy beanbag, and the library, I might just be able to make something of this place.

Welcome back, Mr. Cercatore! Congratulations on your victory!

-Must all our conversations take place with that device on?

Come now, Mr. Cercatore. You know anything said here is protected by attorney-client privilege. And besides, I'd think a man of your talents and extremely impressive list of accomplishments would take it as an insult if his lawyer didn't go to at least some lengths to protect himself. Consider it a compliment.

-I suppose you know why I am here.

I suppose I do. Your family has loose ends to secure, and nothing does that better than a button, am I right?

-Amusing.

I do try, Mr. Cercatore.

-. . .-

Yes, well...ahem. As per usual, I'm guessing you want as much plausible deniability as possible, Mr. Cercatore.

-Naturally.

That will be exceedingly difficult in this case. She is your sister, after all.

-They are my family, yes.

And are you sure you want to go through with this? That's got to be tough–your own flesh and blood.

-. . .-

Right. Yes. Sorry I asked, Mr. Cercatore. Tell me, though: Have you found them yet? I suppose you're calling house by house, if you have to. And what about when you do find them? Surely you know the trail will lead straight back to you.

-No. We have not found them. But we will. And when we do, I am certain that options will present themselves. All in due time.

CHAPTER SIXTEEN

The Lunchroom

Entering the Loblolly cafeteria at lunchtime is a bit like stepping from a primeval forest into the New York Stock Exchange during a sell-off. In the corner, there's one of those traffic signal noise monitors, the kind that switches from green to yellow and eventually to red when the decibel count reaches earsplitting. When I walk in, it's as crimson as a tomato. Of course, that only makes it worse when above the din, a single sentence rings clarion-clear.

"Hey, it's pencil girl!"

I watch as the traffic signal flickers for a second, then shifts to yellow, and then settles at green. When I look back at the tables, I see the eyes of every seventh grader at Loblolly Middle School locked on me. I can feel the blush in my cheeks firing up as fast as the signal winds down, and now

I'm the one glowing red. I clutch at my skirt pleats and scan the crowd.

Thanks a million, Cuss.

I have only a fraction of a second to respond, and so I fall back on that old standby: I level a soul-crushing stare at Cuss, then roll my eyes and click my tongue disapprovingly. As I turn away, I brush an errant strand of hair behind my ear and shake my head. This is universal girl-speak for "Ugh. Boys are stupid." When the cafeteria explodes into frenetic noise once more, I know it's worked.

Once I've collected my green beans, grits, and . . . something else—stew? I think it's stew?—I slip back into the lunchroom. I know that I should keep my cool, especially given my unique situation, but I can't help it—my eyes dart frantically about the cafeteria for someone to sit with. Here, I'm grateful for my tray of whatsit, because if I wasn't holding it I know I'd be tempted to nick the forks off the plates of everyone who walked by. After a couple of tense seconds, though, I spot Brit sitting alone at a circular table near the back windows. I breathe a huge sigh of relief.

As I'm dodging through tables and skirting around chairs, Brit sees me, too. She puts her spoon down, sweeps her hair from her eyes, and smiles. I return her grin, but then feel a tug at my sleeve. I can tell it's going to be trouble before I even look down; Brit's smile disappears instantly, and she practically buries her face in her food.

"Hey, you're that girl from the mall, aren't you?" a familiar voice says.

"Yeah, the one with BritGut!" another adds.

I grit my teeth, but at least manage to wipe the frown from my face before looking to my left.

"Oh, hi. Deidre, wasn't it? And . . . friends. Nice to see you again."

Deidre sizes me up quickly. Her eyes flick from my shoes to my lips to my hair to my earrings and back to my skirt before she decides I've passed the eyeball test. When she's finished, she says, "Sit down and tell Bethanny here that there's no way I stole her credit card at the mall. You were there. You saw us."

God, Deidre is a pro. . . . She doesn't even glance at Brit; I have to figure out the game from one of her other friends at the table, who hides her knowing, evil little smile behind her straw. If I sit down next to Brit's mortal enemy, she has to watch as Deidre spends the next thirty minutes buttering me up, and I become one of her little Deidrettes. That, of course, isn't happening.

"Actually, Deidre, I wouldn't be surprised if you were a thief. I mean, to afford that incredible Gucci bag you had? I was, like, totally jealous. You have great taste!"

Deidre beams, unable to avoid being pulled in by the irresistible magnetism of herself.

"So, yeah, I'm going to let you guys work out the who-stole-what thing," I continue, "but enjoy your lunches!"

When I sit down across from Brit, she gasps. She was actually shaking a little, and it takes her a couple of seconds to pull her arms away from the hug she was giving herself.

"Hi," she says.

"Hi," I reply.

She exhales sharply and her whole face brightens. "I thought for a second there you were going to sit with Deidre."

"We still can," I joke, picking up my tray. "C'mon. We'll see if she'll let us lick her boots for dessert. . . . That is, if there's anything left after her friends are done."

Brit laughs, and we tuck into our lunches.

About midway through my green beans, a shadow falls over our table. Before I can swallow, the other six seats around us are filled, and there's Holly, her yellow-and-blue lunch bag unzipped and handmade tortillas unrolled. Five other girls join her.

"Like, hey, Charlotte! I'm glad I found you! And hey, Britney!"

Brit glances nervously at all the sudden company but doesn't say anything.

"Hey, Holly. Wow," I say, "lots of people."

She grins. "They're my campaign managers. I'm running for student council this year. Elections are next week; we're totally busy, but I'm your volunteer welcome buddy, so I wanted to make sure you were having a super day!"

"So far, so good," I reply. "And I heard about the election. Good luck!"

"Why, thank you so very much!" she exclaims, putting her hand atop mine. I pull back quickly, but she doesn't seem to mind. "I was thinking, Charlotte. You said you wanted to join a club, and I have just the thing! After elections, there's a group that forms. It's called the student advisory committee. Basically, they help the student council by bringing stuff to our attention that we should talk to school administrators or the PTA about. Wouldn't that just be perfect? There's no pressure, and we'd get to work together!"

"Wait, why does there need to be a student advisory committee to tell the council about stuff when the council is made of students anyway?"

One of the girls, her hair in the most elaborate cornrows I've ever seen, says, "It's one of those clubs kids form just so they can say they're in a club. Holly started it last year when she didn't win."

"Tanika!" Holly gasps.

"What? It's the truth. Anyway, it's not a bad thing. I joined, and I had fun."

Appeased somewhat, Holly says, "Anyway, Tanika is right. It's a lot of fun. And if I win the election, there will be a vacancy. I could nominate you to fill it!"

"Sounds intriguing," I admit. "But I'm kind of looking for something behind the scenes."

"Oh, this is totally behind the scenes," Holly assures me.

Tanika nods. "Yeah, trust me. Holly and the rest of the student council will be the ones front and center. She's basically an attention sponge."

Rather than seem insulted, Holly beams and nods. "Yep! It's just . . . I need to win first. . . ."

She punctuates that last statement by reaching into her lunch bag and pulling out a paper plate wrapped in cellophane. She sets it down in front of me and peels off the plastic.

"By the way, I plumb almost forgot. I made you cookies to welcome you to Loblolly!"

"Whoa," I mutter. "Good call, MZ. . . ."

"Huh?"

"Nothing," I say. "Just said thank you. For the cookies, and for letting me know about the student advisory committee. It sounds like a great opportunity."

"Yep! Sure is! Let's just hope I win! I mean, I can count on your vote next week, right, Charlotte?"

I take a smiley-face-frosted sugar cookie from the plate and salute with it. "Sure thing, Holly," I reply.

"Great! Well, it was awesome chatting with you. I have another club meeting now, but I'll see you in Latin class. Take care!"

Holly's entourage leaves with her, and Brit and I watch her go. We finish the rest of our lunches in relative peace—it was actually chili, not stew—and toss our trays. Brit heads out toward the classrooms on the other side of campus, and I pause to check my map. When I look up, I'm surprised to see Deidre and company in front of me.

"That was, like, super charitable of you, sitting with Gut at lunch today."

"Um, thanks?" I reply, and I casually start walking toward . . . well, somewhere. I figure I'll get away and reorient myself from there. Unfortunately, Deidre matches my pace, her perfect bun bobbing as she walks.

"So anyway, Charlotte, was that Holly I saw you talking to over there?"

"Sure was."

"What about, if you don't mind my asking?"

I arch an eyebrow. "The student council election. Why?"

"Ugh!" She groans, and her posse shares it around. Once the chorus quiets, Deidre continues, "I knew it. You know she's only being nice to you to get your vote."

I shrug. "She seems sincere to me. And hey, I got cookies, so, bonus!"

"Well, anyway, *friend*," she says, teasing that word out as she glances back at the other girls, "you know you can sit with us any time you want. And by the way, I'm running for student council, too. Holly's not the only one who controls things around here."

"I can . . . see that?" I murmur.

Deidre nods. "Science, right? That's where we're going, too. It's over here."

Having no other choice, I walk with Deidre, and after the requisite Hi-I'm-Charlottes, the teacher plunks me down next to her. I spend the rest of the afternoon listening to Deidre whisper about Holly, about the election, and about how she is so totally and for sure not a thief. That one, at least, I'll give her—we thieves are generally less devious and manipulative.

CHAPTER SEVENTEEN

How Do I Kill Thee? Let Me Count the Ways.

By the time we meet Harriet in the parking lot after school, I'm ready to fall asleep with the window down, just listening to the car speed past the trees. Jackson seems similarly beat; he's dragging his backpack along behind him, leaving a sluglike path through the pine needles. Harriet, on the other hand, is twitching with excitement.

"So, how was it? First day of school!"

"Fine," we both say in unison. I don't even have the energy to call jinx.

"Just fine? Come on! How were classes? Are your teachers nice? Did you make friends? Are you going to be happy there?"

"Just drive, Mom," Jackson mutters, his head lolling back.

Harriet inhales sharply and starts the car. As we pull out, her fingers start drumming on the wheel.

"Seriously?" she presses. "That's it? Come on! Each of you tell me one awesome thing about today."

I yawn. "The library is really cool," I manage.

"Thank you, Charlotte! What about it is cool?"

"I dunno. Stuff."

That's really all my brain can manufacture right now, though this conversation is familiar. Other "parents" have asked me these questions before, and I've answered in the same way. I think sometimes they forget that kids are putting on performances all day, just acting like the people we think we are until, like, ten years from now, when we figure out who that actually is. At least I had my personality handed to me in a file.

"Well, maybe this will brighten your spirits. The cable company came, and we're all hooked up for TV and internet."

"That's . . . yeah . . . that's good," I reply as my cheek slides down the seat belt. Next thing I know I'm blinking prickles of sunlight out of my eyes and staring up at my maple tree. Harriet has already opened the passenger door and grabbed my backpack. With limbs like lead, I crawl out of the car, trudging my way up the steps.

It takes a snack, six splashes of cold water to the face, and nearly falling over in my chair to get through my homework, but I manage. The math in particular takes twice as long as it otherwise would—I have to answer all the questions correctly, then go back through and change just enough of them to get a B-minus. What's worse, we have to show

209

our work, so I can't just erase a two in my answer and replace it with a seven. I've got to get under the hood of the problem and mess with the wiring. I will admit that by the end, I think I've learned the quadratic equation better than I would have if I was just blitzing through the worksheets.

A quick call downstairs reveals that dinner's not quite ready yet, so I finally have some time for me. I arrange a few things in my room, pick out my outfit for tomorrow (more black and green. Yay!), and carefully take Harriet's jewelry from my top drawer. I look at the ring in particular as I lie on my covers. The rhinestone catches the light from the window. It's technically not a diamond, but it still sparkles like one: Little motes of light, each one a spectrum, dance around on my arms, on my pillow, on me. It would look good on Harriet's finger.

A wave of guilt rolls over me. It feels just like getting carsick.

I glance over at Fancypaws, who gives me the old button-eye stare. She still doesn't seem too happy with her perch on the bedside table. Next to her is my new tennis ball, and I grab it. Holding the jewelry in one hand and the ball in the other, I start my routine. It's harder, since my bed isn't nearly as close to the ceiling as my bunk back at the Center, but I still get a pretty good rhythm going.

Well, at least until Jackson bangs on my door.

"Stop it with that noise!" he yells. "I'm trying to do my homework!"

"What noise?" I ask just before I fire the tennis ball at the ceiling again.

"That one! That bouncing noise! It's like a jackhammer!"

"Ohhhhh," I go on, "you mean this one?"

I give it five more good throws.

"Yes!"

"Okay!" I shout, and I replace the ball, the ring, and the bracelet, making sure the two stolen items are well hidden. Another surge of guilt wells up, but I suppress it. When I open the door, Jackson is still there, his face scrunched like that of a bulldog trying to get the last bit of peanut butter out of a jar.

"What were you doing, anyway?"

"Practicing."

"Practicing what?"

"Is dinner ready?" I ask, ignoring his question. The smell coming from downstairs is quite intriguing—something rich and spicy. My unease is swiftly overruled by hunger. I slip past and race downstairs, with Jackson tromping after me.

Harriet is putting plates on the big coffee table in front of the TV, and Jonathan scoops lasagna onto each one. They both smile when they see me. Harriet looks so happy, and Jonathan, too, that I banish any last wisp of a thought about bringing up my secret; whatever good I might do for my own conscience surely wouldn't be worth ruining this moment. At least, that's what I tell myself.

"This is a family specialty," Jonathan explains. "There are four kinds of meat in here!"

I nod appreciatively—it looks delicious, and I'd settle for anything that wasn't mango, uncertain stew, or sacrificial pig.

"I hope you don't mind—we watch the news while we eat dinner," Harriet says.

Jonathan continues, "Yes . . . it's not that we're trying to be antisocial, but we've been a little obsessed with the news ever since this whole ordeal started."

I shrug, find a spot on the big blue recliner, and pull up my legs to sit crisscross. Harriet hands me a bowl of salad, and I dig in.

"How'd homework go?" Jonathan asks, balancing his plate and bowl on the arm of the couch.

I twist a forkful of spinach around. "So-so. We'll see if I actually pulled off a B-minus."

"About that . . ." Harriet says ominously. "Jonathan and I have been talking, and we've come to a decision."

Jackson freezes, a steaming dollop of lasagna poised inches from his mouth. I hear him whisper, "Oh no . . ."

"Oh no?" I echo. "What's 'oh no'? Is something wrong?"

"Nothing's wrong, Char," Jonathan says. He's smiling like a doctor trying to hide a tetanus needle. "Your mother and I have decided that we'd like you to show us all the homework and tests you get back from your teachers at school."

I nod congenially. "No sweat. I'll just give you my folder when—"

Jonathan cuts me off. "So we can have you redo them properly afterward."

"I knew it!" Jackson growls. "I knew you'd do something like this!"

"You know how important school is to your father and me," Harriet says, her voice as soothing as she can make it.

"Char, you understand, right?" Jonathan asks hopefully.

I put down my fork. "Not gonna lie, Dad. That sucks a little."

"It sucks a lot!" Jackson yells. "And he's not your dad!"

"Oooh, hey!" I say. "Jackson and I agreed on something! Not, you know, the dad thing . . . but about the sucking of your plan! We should celebrate by not having to redo all our schoolwork!"

"It's not a discussion, kids. You'll do it, and we'll check it. It's a time commitment for us, too."

Waving my spinach wand for emphasis, I counter with, "Yeah, but if we double down on our homework, we're likely to get significantly smarter. And if we do that, it'll be twice as hard to hide our brilliance at school. Soon enough we'll be making honor roll, winning geography bees, giving valedictorian speeches, and facing the eternal, hell-fiery wrath of Deputy Marshall Stricker."

"Charlotte!"

I shrug. "Just sayin'."

"Well, you can stop sayin'. It's final."

"Wait, just so we're clear, does this family go with the 'ask again in two weeks' version of 'final,' or the final 'final'? It's helpful to know in advance."

"Final-final . . ." Jackson mutters, and it's clear from the angle of his eyebrows that he means it.

"Fine," I add, mollifying myself with some lasagna.

Jonathan fiddles with the new TV for a few minutes before he figures out which of our five hundred channels broadcasts local New York news. My ears perk at the mentions of traffic on the Tappan Zee, rescheduled Moon Festival activities in Chinatown, and the shellfish situation in the Sound. It's comforting, in a way, to have that connection back to the City, but I'm not holding out hope that a picture of Emmy or Wainwright will flash on the screen.

Really, it's just as interesting to watch my family as it is to watch the TV. Every time a story switches, every time a new headline flashes on-screen, they lean in, unblinking. When they find out it's not about the Cercatores, they slouch, allowing forks to find food again. They keep up this rhythm until the anchor says, "And turning to legal news, an apparent prosecutorial error in the ongoing Cercatore case has led to a significant development. . . ."

Utensils clatter to plates. Harriet puts hers down entirely and scoots out from under Jonathan's arm. In fact, she's so tense that I'm not sure she's sitting on the couch at all anymore; it's like she's hovering just above it, every muscle locked and eyes narrowed.

"While ADA Petersen has criticized the defense for hanging its strategy here on a technicality, Judge Lin sided with the defense in its motion to dismiss all charges. As a result, Arturo Cercatore, the man authorities have taken to calling 'The Bard,' has escaped conviction. Here he is on the courthouse steps. . . ."

"Damnit!" Harriet shouts, slamming her hand down on the ottoman in front of her. It shocks Jackson so badly he tosses his lasagna in the air. I watch it soar upward and then break apart like an asteroid hurtling through Earth's atmosphere on its way down. Jackson tries to maneuver his plate underneath to catch all of it, but little meteors of cheesy meat and pasta pepper his pants.

Jonathan hovers ineffectively between rubbing his wife's shoulder and paper-toweling his son's clothes. I'm paralyzed, just watching the spectacle. Arturo's face is still on the screen. He's a young man with a thick, shaggy mane of black hair. It's in weird opposition to the flamboyance of his suit, which features a purple silk scarf and matching pocket handkerchief. His strong chin and thick lips give him an air of power, but the gray of his eyes is the most startling. Whereas Harriet's eyes are tempestuous, Arturo's are all about distance. Even in the close-up shot, it seems like he doesn't care about anything.

Or anyone.

We watch the rest of the news in silence, and after Jonathan has cleared the dishes and Jackson has stalked off to change his clothes, it's only Harriet and me. I start to stretch a foot toward the floor, thinking I'll slink away as well, but Harriet sits forward abruptly. With her head lowered, fingers rubbing at her temples, she says, "He's my brother."

"Jackson's uncle?" I ask, and she nods.

"Yes, though Arturo would never care about something like that."

"He knows you testified?"

"Oh yes," she confirms. "And if he's free, we're in greater danger than we ever were before."

"Why?" I dare to ask.

"Arturo is the head button for the family, and he loves it. Or, rather, I guess he doesn't hate it. Doesn't even think twice about it."

"Button?"

"Hit man. Assassin." She moves her fingers from her temples to her forehead and covers her face. "God, I was afraid of this."

"How could they let him go? I mean, you told them he was a killer, right?"

"Of course I told them," she laments. "Much good it did, though. He's The Bard. He's always got an answer."

"The Bard?" I ask. "Like Shakespeare?"

"He'd get a kick out of that, I'm sure. But no. It's a nickname the media gave him after his fourth acquittal. It's an acronym that stands for 'Beyond a Reasonable Doubt,' as in precisely what no prosecutor has ever been able to prove. He's as careful as he is ruthless, Charlotte, with an angle and an escape for every situation."

"Will he come after us?"

"I'm almost certain he'll try—if my family is going to send anyone, it'd be Arturo. In fact, if he's not on the trail already, it's only because he hasn't decided how he'll get away with it yet."

"But he's your brother! Maybe he'll ignore their commands and leave you alone?"

Harriet laughs, but it's not because she thinks my idea is funny.

"For Arturo, I'm afraid the promise of blood is more powerful than blood, if you follow my meaning," Harriet says, shuddering. "Of all my relatives, I fear Arturo the most. We all should."

It was one thing when the Cercatores were just an idea, were just the bogeymen up north. Now that they have a name, a face, and soulless eyes, it seems much more real.

"He'd kill us all, wouldn't he?" I whisper gravely.

"*In un baleno*," she replies. "In a heartbeat."

To: Stricker.Janice@usdoj.gov
From: Trevor.Charlotte@usdoj.gov
Subject: AC?????

Dear Deputy Marshal Stricker,

How are things in Georgia? We're settling in okay
in North Carolina. We got our internet up and working,
obviously, and today was our first day of school. It
went all right. I'm doing a decent job of making friends;
I think it's actually helping that I'm not trying too hard.
There's one girl who I think will be a really good friend,
and a few more who I met are nice. I've also got the
inside track on my sport and on my club. Classes will
be fine, too.

I wanted to let you know we saw a news report
tonight that really freaked us out. H's brother is free.
I'm sure you guys are up on the news, so no big
surprise, but just in case, I thought I'd send along the
information. Maybe y'all (see? I'm getting the hang of
this already!) could keep an extra-close eye on him?

Say hi to Eddie for me!

Also, if we promise not to tell each other where we
are, can I write to Erin or A.J.? It'd be cool to have
someone else to talk to about all this.

Anyways, I hear the phone ringing. Gotta go answer
it. Write back if you can.

Thanks,

N/C

To: Trevor.Charlotte@usdoj.gov
From: Stricker.Janice@usdoj.gov
Subject: Emergencies Only!!!!!!

Charlotte,

As you have already been informed, this e-mail address is for emergencies only. Do not write again unless you have identified a pressing threat to the Trevor family.

We are aware of the AC situation.

No, you may not write to Erin or A.J.

—JS

CHAPTER EIGHTEEN

Deidre for the Block, Charlotte for the Steal, Holly for the Win

It turns out Janice was spot-on about Loblolly's sports prowess; the girls' basketball team is so terrible that I don't even need to try out. I just walk into the gym teacher's office, ask about basketball, and they're handing me a uniform. Two days after that, and I'm in my first scrimmage. I score two points and do absolutely nothing worthy of any attention. The coaches are super impressed that I know how to dribble, though. Guess that tennis ball work helped.

Even in the slowest of weeks, the little I do on the basketball court wouldn't raise an eyebrow. These days, though? Well, with the election coming up, it's the perfect time to just blend in, especially with how things have been going at home. Everyone is on edge; we watch the news obsessively, Harriet is jumpy and drinks more coffee than she should, and Jackson . . . well, I'm not sure what he's up to. I only see him getting into and out of the car for school. Jonathan tries to keep everyone moving and upbeat, and we manage to do some decent bonding as the only two communicative people in the house. He even agrees to do a read-aloud at night for me, which nobody's done since my grammy. If there's one thing I love more than reading, it's having someone else read to me. We're starting with some *Mrs. Frisby and the Rats of NIMH*, and even though I've already read it a dozen times, it's still great to hear it in someone else's voice. With that to look forward to every evening, I sleep okay, despite recurring nightmares starring Arturo Cercatore.

At school, I hang out mostly with Brit, though I do shill for Holly when I can. I even put up a few posters for her. Her win, after all, means a spot on the student advisory committee for me, and you never know when having a friend on the student council will come in handy.

The morning of the election, Holly is perched on the curb. We drive up, Jonathan lets us out, and Holly waves us over.

"Wow!" she gasps. "Charlotte! Is this your brother? It's so nice to meet you!" She holds out her hand. Jackson just barrels past, nearly knocking her onto the pavement.

"It's not you," I explain when she looks at me nervously. She smiles and pretends to blow an errant lock of hair from her eyes. Of course, there wasn't one.

"Oh, here!" she says after a moment. "Vote Holly!"

She hands me a plastic bag. It's been tied closed with a green-and-gold ribbon, and inside are Hershey's Kisses. Behind her on the sidewalk sits her backpack, and it's overflowing with bags just like the one she gave me.

"Last-minute campaign bribes?" I ask.

"I prefer to think of it as a sweet little taste of the goodness to come if I'm on student council."

"In that case, I accept your gesture."

"And can I count on your vote?"

I sigh loudly. "On Monday I said yes. Tuesday I said sure. Wednesday I promised, and Thursday I made a solemn vow. Today? Eh. I heard the sixth-grade candidates are pretty strong."

"Charlotte!"

"Kidding. You've got my vote. Remember, I'm gonna swipe your committee spot once you win."

"Right. But . . . pinkie swear just in case?"

She holds out a well-manicured little finger and grins expectantly at me. I cringe, but manage—I think—to pass it off as a smirk. I hide my hands behind me and shake my head. "Yeah, right. Not without hand sanitizer. I can only guess how many hands you've shaken this morning."

Holly laughs. "Only about a bajillion."

I hold up my hands and scoot around her like she's got oozing sores, and she makes a decent zombie face back. By the time I've reached the doors, she's already charging toward the next carload of kids, flinging chocolate and shaking hands.

The actual voting doesn't take place until lunchtime. Brit's got her computer club, Holly's in freak-out mode in her "war room" (the picnic bench near her locker), and MZ is sitting at a full table when I come in, so I emerge from the line alone. As I scan the lunchroom, I feel a tug at my shirt.

"Hey, Charlotte, right?"

It's Bethanny Karstens, one of Deidre's posse. She's tiny; if I didn't know better, I would have guessed she was maybe a fifth grader. I have to tell myself not to talk to her like I did Halla and the other younger kids at the Center.

"Yeah. What's up?"

"So, like, Deidre was wondering if you'd sit with us today—you know, because Gut isn't here."

I sigh and stare at her until she figures it out.

"Oh yeah. I mean, since Britney Guthrie isn't here."

"Why doesn't Deidre ask me herself?"

"Well, I was already getting up to take her tray to the trash, so I said I'd ask for her."

"Let me ask you this, Bethanny—do you want me to sit with you?"

"Me?" she asks, looking around.

"Yeah. What do *you* want?"

"I . . . um . . . well, Deidre asked me to ask you."

I shake my head, but motion forward with my tray. "Lead on."

"Cool!" she replies, and flicks her blond bob as she spins.

223

There are five other girls at Deidre's table, with two free seats—one right next to Deidre, and one across the way. Bethanny pulls out the chair next to Deidre, but without even looking at her, Deidre says, "No. You're over there."

"But I already put my food down here." Bethanny pouts.

"You can move it, right?"

"Y-yeah, I can. Totally, Deidre."

Just like that, Bethanny picks up her tray and wanders over to the other side. The girls flanking her scoot away in unison, almost like robots.

As soon as I sit down, Deidre turns toward me. Her eyes are intense, though she's grinning.

"Hello, Charlotte! What did you think of gym today? Lacrosse better than croquet?"

I push a bit of applesauce around and reply, "It's all sticks and wickets to me. I guess I liked cr—"

She cuts me off. "So I heard you're voting for Holly. Is that true?"

Ah, here we go. I'm glad she got to the point before I started on my chicken.

"Haven't voted yet, Deidre. I will once I'm done with my lunch."

"Yeah, but you're voting for Holly?"

"I get two votes."

"And one of them is Holly?"

"Well, she is really driven, and smart, and goes out of her way to be friendly."

"You need to vote for me."

I blink. "I could vote for both of you."

"No, you really can't. We're, like, nothing alike."

Well, that's true.

"You do realize that one of you could be a panda bear and the other a bottle of ketchup, and I could still vote for both of you."

Deidre's brow knits. "What?"

"Pandas and ketchup . . . they're nothing alike. You said . . ." I pause, watching as her eyes start to glaze over. "Oh, never mind."

"So you'll vote for me?"

"Well, let me put it this way: I like pandas, but I'm sure as heck not putting them on my french fries."

"Um, yeah. Okay. Sure," she says, and I wink at her. I guess she takes that as a good sign, because she winks back, smiles knowingly, and gathers her pack to go. It leaves me alone, but half the cafeteria is empty by now, so I don't mind, and it beats having all those girls watch me eat. As they head toward the door, I sigh. I hope I was just weird enough to deflect Deidre's questions, and not enough to become a permanent blip on her radar.

I'm almost ready to tuck into my food—finally—when I notice that Deidre has pulled all of her Deidrettes into the shadowy corner just outside the cafeteria. She's unzipping that Gucci purse, and I watch as she hands each girl a rubber-banded stack of thin white strips of paper.

Let me guess, Deidre . . . you're thinking of stuffing the ballot boxes. Cheating to get ahead. Grumbling, I peer down at my lunch. Today's not going to be an eating day after all.

My initial instinct is to head to Mr. Jessup's office, or maybe to clue in Ms. Millar. However, that's a no-go. If I blow the whistle, that's all kinds of attention heaped on me. Playing election-day hero isn't exactly blending in. Still, I can't let Deidre sabotage Holly's chances—she's my friend, yes, but I also need that behind-the-scenes spot on the student advisory committee. So after dumping my lunch, I home in on the first of Deidre's minions.

I find the girl already in the voting line, and she couldn't look more uncomfortable. She rocks back and forth, plays with her hair every five seconds or so, and refuses to make eye contact with anyone. I watch as she fills out a ballot and folds it. She then steps to the side as the attendant helps the next kid.

With everyone else distracted by the newest voter, the girl reaches into her back pocket, takes out the other slips of paper Deidre gave her, and folds them in with her own ballot. She then dumps all of these into the lockbox.

Yup. Cheating.

Immediately I jump out of line and find one of the voting station maps Holly has been plastering up on the walls. I memorize the shortest routes between them and book it to the next closest, dodging kids, bushes, and pine trees on the way. Sure enough, when I arrive, there's Bethanny,

226

looking every bit as nervous as her partner in crime did a minute ago. I sidle up to her and say, "Heya, Bethanny! I guess you'll be voting for Deidre today!"

She's so startled she actually jumps, which is perfect—I've got my index finger and thumb pinched on the tip of the fake ballots sticking out of her jacket pocket. Her movement lets the stack of papers just fall into my waiting hand, and I've got them in my own pocket before she even manages to register what happened.

"Oh, hello again, Charlotte!" she sputters. "You . . . you ate quickly."

"I wasn't that hungry after all. Anyway, I think the line here is too long. I'm gonna go vote somewhere else. Good luck!"

I skip off to the next station, leaving Bethanny so spooked that she forgets to pat her pockets until well after I'm away. Poor girl probably thinks she dropped the evidence somewhere in the hall.

The other three are just as easy to fleece, and within a span of five minutes I've got all the bad ballots shoved into my big hoodie pocket, except those from the first box. I duck into a bathroom, close the stall door, and sift through the papers, expecting to see Deidre's name over and over and over again.

My eyes narrow as I cycle through each slip. Deidre's name isn't on any of them. In fact, it's Holly's name that appears on every ballot, written in the same fancy script.

"Huh?" I say aloud.

And then it hits me.

Bursting out of the stall and onto the breezeway, I careen toward the nearest bulletin board, ducking past Archer and his crew.

"Hey, Charlotte, why the rush? Not that you don't look good while you're running. You know, I run cross-country for—"

"No time. Be icky later, Archer," I pant as I speed past.

His friends laugh at him, and to his credit, he laughs, too. I round the corner, nearly bashing into the bulletin board on the adjacent wall.

I instantly spot what I'm looking for. It's a poster of Holly's smiling face, and beneath it the words *Dedicated to improving Loblolly Middle School—you have my word! Sincerely, Holly Fiellera.* Her name is signed exactly as it appears on the ballots I pilfered.

"Oh, Deidre, you malicious, clever little witch . . ." I mutter.

My next sprint takes me right over to Holly's home base. Fortunately, she's still there, looking so nervous that her campaign helpers are having to fan her just to keep her from passing out.

"Charlotte!" she says. "Did you vote?"

I pause, catching my breath. "Well, actually, no . . . not yet . . ."

"But . . ." she begins, eyes wide with panic.

"Guys, can I get a moment alone with Holly?" I say gravely.

"But . . ." she repeats, though she trails off when she sees the way I have my arms crossed.

"O-okay . . . let's go over by the water fountain."

I lead the way, a trembling Holly close behind. She's shaking so badly her bangs look like frosted porcupine quills in a stiff breeze.

"Holly, we've got a problem. It's Deidre. She's trying to fix the election."

"Fix the election!" she screams, but I shoot her such a vicious stare that she claps her hands over her mouth.

"Yes. But I managed to stop her for the most part. Here," I say, and I hand her the ballots I managed to collect.

"I . . . I don't get it. They're all for me. They're all for me *twice*. And it's my signature both times. How . . ."

"She copied it off your posters. But that doesn't matter. What does matter is what she's trying to do."

"Trying to get me to win the election? I don't understand . . . she's my biggest rival!"

"Think about it, Holly. Let's say you're the teacher counting the votes. You're going through the ballot boxes and you find a hundred slips, all identical, all for you, all in your handwriting. What do you think would happen?"

"I'd be disqualified, maybe even suspended!"

I nod, letting that sink in. Then I add, "If Deidre stacks the ballots for herself, she might win, but you could still very well come in second. You'd still be on student council, easily. Heck, you could come in sixth and still be on the council. But if you're accused of cheating . . ."

"Even if I'm just accused, there's no way I could be on the council. My reputation would be shot. . . ."

"Yep. It's Deidre's only way to make sure you're not on the council at all."

"God, she's always hated me. I don't know why!"

"Maybe it's because you're likable without having to bully your way into it?"

Holly blushes and puts a hand on my arm. I swat it away. "Save it. There will be plenty of time to thank me later. For now, there's still trouble. At least twenty of these things are in the box nearest the cafeteria. I couldn't get them in time, and I wasn't sure what was up anyway. I had to figure it out."

"Well, we just go to Mr. Jessup, and you tell him what you've found. He'll get the bad ballots out, Deidre will be punished, and . . ."

I shake my head emphatically. "No, that's no good. Deidre was extra-careful. As far as I can tell, she didn't try to plant any of these ballots herself. She had her friends do it for her. So if we tell, all we do is get Deidre's friends in trouble, and it's not really their fault."

Holly nods. "And even if one of her friends did turn her in, she'd deny it, and they'd have no proof. This is really wicked."

"Yup," I concede. "Brilliant, but wicked."

"So what do I do, Charlotte?"

I lean in closely. "Nothing. Absolutely nothing. Don't confront Deidre. Don't talk to a teacher. And whatever you do, don't mention my name. I'll take care of this."

"But how?"

Telling her I have no clue isn't going to be productive, so I go with the old standby:

"I've got a plan."

"Thanks, Charlotte!" she exclaims, and she throws her arms around me, squeezing me so hard I think I'm going to lose what little I had for lunch. "I'll find a way to repay you for this!"

"No need. We're friends, aren't we?" I ask.

"Good friends." She smiles. "Best friends."

"Slow down there, sister. I'll settle for friends."

She backs off, laughing. "Deal. But I still totally owe you!"

As I race back toward the cafeteria, I can't help but wonder if this is the way Janice envisioned me getting along at school. Something tells me it's not, but I also couldn't have guessed that so much would go into protecting my normal little niche. One thing's for sure: It's tougher to get on the student advisory committee than I thought.

I skid into the building awkwardly, and I have to grab the door frame just to slow myself down. There are only two kids in line waiting to vote, so I don't have much time before the attendant sweeps up the ballots and takes them to the counting room—wherever that is.

The attendant is hovering right over the box, and while I'm pretty sure I could distract him, the box itself is another matter entirely. It's metal, about the size of a shoe box, and hinged. It's kept closed by a combination lock, and there's a slit in the top where voters have been slipping their ballots. I might have long, slender, speedy fingers, but there's no way they're fitting in there. In fact, short of learning how to pick locks in the next ninety seconds, I'm not getting my hands inside. That leaves getting the ballots to come to me. . . .

I look around desperately, and my gaze settles on the trash can, of all things. It's heaped with lunchtime garbage: wrappers, chicken legs, and apple cores. I start casting around for another solution, but whether it's divine nudging or just the smell, my attention keeps drifting back to the trash. I decide to give it one more look, and there, wedged into the dead center of the mess, I spot salvation. It's a pristine, unopened chocolate milk carton.

I crack my knuckles and look around to make sure nobody's watching. Then I reach in. It's one thing working a wallet out of a businessman's back pocket. It's another matter entirely to wriggle something free from a tower of gross. There's a moment when my breath catches in my throat— a spatter of mustard hits the back of my hand, lolling off a quarter-chewed hot dog that hangs just above my fingers. I stifle a gag as I freeze; I can feel a panic attack coming on, almost as bad as when I try to wear gloves. Gritting my teeth, I exhale and refocus. Just two more taps to the right and a subtle tease to the left, and I've got it.

I want to run to the bathroom to wash off the mustard, but I know there's no time. There's only one kid left in line to vote, and the eighth grader in charge of the box is already cleaning up the pencils and blank ballots. I pop the milk open, and as casually as I can, I stroll up behind the last kid. I slip to his right and clear my throat. Both the kid and the attendant look at me, and as they do I perch the milk in place, its yawning chin jutting just over the opening of the box.

"Sorry to jump in, but am I too late to vote?" I ask sweetly, biting my lower lip softly at the eighth-grade boy presiding over the table.

He runs a hand along the back of his neck and blushes. "Well, obviously you'll have to wait for him, but you can vote after. What's your name?"

"Charlotte Trevor," I say, and he squints down at a laptop.

"Nope, you haven't voted yet. You're good to go."

Just as the attendant looks back up, the poor sixth grader in front of me finishes writing down his votes and turns to slip his ballot into the box. Of course, there wasn't a milk carton there a few seconds ago, so when he reaches out to drop his paper into the slit, he doesn't even think about it. His hand hits the carton, tips it, and chocolate milk glugs out over the top of the box. Some of it seeps through the slit.

The sixth grader stands there stammering, "But . . . but that wasn't mine! I didn't . . . didn't . . ."

I gasp innocently, my non-mustard hand over my mouth.

"Pick it up, kid!" the eighth grader yells as his gaze bounces from the accident to me and back to the accident.

The poor little kid fumbles around with the carton, and while he does get it off the ballot box, he ends up sploshing the rest of it on his shirt.

"Awwww, man . . ." he grumbles as he runs off to find the closest sink. "Not again!"

"Again?" I whisper, but I don't have time to ponder the boy's ill fortunes. The attendant is staring at the box, frozen, a hand pressed to his forehead.

"Whaddawedo? Whaddawedo?!?" he shouts.

"Quick!" I respond. "Open the box! Save the ballots!"

He grabs the lock, fiddles with the dial, and pops the thing off in one smooth rip. Milk cascades onto the table and the floor as he springs open the box. We both grab for the soggy ballots, but I let him nab the top ones; I figure the stack of forged slips has to be farther down. He takes ten or so; I grab about fifty.

"Check to see if they're still readable," I say, and I fly through each one, passing them back to the attendant after I make sure they're not Deidre's planted papers. He's shaking off the wettest of the ballots, trying to decipher the names. I figure I have at least another twenty seconds with my stack.

Fortunately, I need only five—the Holly/Holly ballots are still bunched together, and I count them all out before sticking them in my hoodie. I'll need to wash it later to get the chocolate milk out of my pockets, but a quick glance at the eighth grader shows me my ploy was successful.

"There," I say. "All these are still good."

I pass him a big spaghetti-tangle of ballots just as he

carefully replaces the last of his into the box. He breathes a sigh of relief, closes the box, and gives me a suave smile.

The results are announced during an assembly at flex time. We're all packed into the gym, and Miss Treadway, our business-suited, silver-haired principal, with Mr. Jessup to her right, reads off the names of the winners.

"Andrew Chissolm, sixth grade!"

A cheer erupts from the sixth-grade section.

"Megan Gillette, seventh grade!"

Our turn to applaud—Megan, from what I know, crushes math tests, captains the tennis team, and, if the rumors are true, has a boyfriend at another school. A perfectly reasonable choice.

"Deidre Mendelbaum, seventh grade!"

It's easy to spot Deidre, since everyone's head turns toward her at the exact same time. She waves and smiles, though it might also be a wince, since she didn't win president. I applaud just like everyone else. I don't think she bothers to look at me.

"Derrick Carver, eighth grade!"

This receives a thunderous ovation. Football player, maybe?

"Eduardo Perez, eighth grade!"

Another roar. Brit leans in and says, "He was Sky Masterson in *Guys and Dolls* last year," as if that explains everything.

"And your student council president for the upcoming year will be . . ."

We all lean forward, craning our necks as if getting physically closer will let the announcement hit our ears that much quicker.

"Holly Fiellera! Congratulations, Holly, and congratulations to all our council members. I look forward to working with you this year to uphold Loblolly's traditions of student pride and academic excellence! We'll dismiss by grade. . . ."

Cheering and relative chaos ensues. While most people are clamoring for a look at Holly's joyous, gracious celebrating, I'm zeroed in on Deidre. She's sitting cross-legged, clapping with just two fingers against her palm. Her mouth is pursed into a little bee-stung button, and she's glaring at her clique. I can't help but smile, and when I finally do catch a glimpse of Holly, she meets my gaze and mouths, "Thank you!"

I nod and wave in reply, my hands completely clean.

{INCOMING CALL – 5:47 pm}

Hello, Trevor residence. Hello? Hello? Is anyone there? Hellooooooo? Huh . . . **[Call Disconnected]**

{INCOMING CALL – 7:51 pm}

Hello, Trevor residence. Hello? Look, if you're talking, I can't hear you. Hello? Geez . . . **[Call Disconnected]**

{INCOMING CALL – 8:32 pm}

Okay, look. You really need to stop calling. Either your phone isn't working, or you're being intentionally creepy. Either way, we're not picking up the phone again. *{Who is it, Charlotte?}* I don't know. Probably some stupid machine. Maybe we should check in with . . . **[Call Disconnected]**

CHAPTER NINETEEN

Jackson's Dangerous

"Wow! That's a lot of B-minuses!"

I look up from my carrel, where I've got five tests splayed out. The last six weeks have been tense; in addition to scaring ourselves silly every night watching the news and dealing with these weird calls on our landline, we've run into the heart of our school schedules. Homework, projects, and essays have started piling up, leaving me with precious little patience to deal with other distractions.

Like, for instance, Archer Brantley.

"Shhh," I hiss, using my pencil to point at the books around us.

Archer puts two hands on the back of my chair and leans over me.

"Hey, you know, I could help you with this stuff. Like,

tutor you or something. I'm really good at lit exams and simplifying equations!"

I toss my hair back to tie in a ponytail, making sure most of it hits Archer in the chin.

"What?" he says, pulling a black strand from his mouth. "You don't want to get good grades?"

I swivel around. "Don't you have someplace to be?" I whisper.

"It's flex time. I can be wherever I want to be," Archer says casually, and he leans up against the edge of the carrel.

I decide to adopt a different approach. "And I'm flattered you've decided to spend it with me, Archer, but as you can see, I've got so much work to do. . . ."

"What about after school? I could help you out then. . . ."

"I have basketball practice," I fib.

"Skip it! You guys have lost, what, six straight?"

"Seven, which is exactly why we need to practice."

"I watched you in the games, you know. I'm the head photographer for the yearbook committee. I keep trying to get a picture of you in action, but, well, you're never in the action, so I have to just stare and wait."

I arch an eyebrow. "That's not creepy or anything."

He holds up his hands defensively. "I mean, I'm a fan is all. And you, well, you're fast, you move well, and you pass well, but you score two points every game. It's like you're only sort of trying."

"And does it look like I'm only sort of trying here?"

"No. You're in the library almost every day, studying or reading."

"Yes. I work hard. I'd like to be working hard right now."

Archer shrugs. "You could get better-than-average grades for all that work."

"It actually takes me a lot of work to get those B-minuses." Technically it's true, especially with the redos Harriet makes us hammer out.

"Well, you just gotta work smarter, not harder!"

I smirk. "Are you saying I'm not smart?"

"No, no!" He backtracks, laughing. "No! It's just that, you know, you seem better than this, more interesting, like you're hiding something. . . ."

"That's disdain. And I wasn't trying to hide it."

Archer actually is kind of cute when he's flustered, and he's got a pretty good blush going. It almost makes me want to tell him he's barking up the wrong tree. Between the Cercatores, the rules, and just being Charlotte Trevor, boy drama is the last thing I need. It'd be a different story if I had to be popular; then I'd have to cultivate crushes and get myself a boyfriend for a couple of weeks, at least until I could dump him, cry a little, and soak up the sympathy. That's a different kind of exhausting entirely.

"So you're saying . . . Okay, I don't get what you're saying."

"I'm saying thanks for the offer to help, but I'm going to do this on my own. I don't care how many hours in the library it takes."

"Well, all right. If you change your mind, let me know."

"Will do," I mutter, returning my attention to the papers in front of me. He lingers for a bit, but then wanders off, letting me pack up my stuff so I can go find Brit. Her last tryout game is tonight, and she's invited me over to cheer her on. I could definitely use the distraction.

The sharp smell of winter, accompanying a stinging-cold breeze, greets me as I step out onto the path outside the library. Brit is already there, hunkered over her laptop. Her face is obscured by the ring of fake fur surrounding her hood, but I can tell it's her—nobody else's fingers move across the keyboard that fast.

"Hey, Brit. You'll never believe the weird conversation I just had with Archer. He was all like—"

Brit holds up her hand. "When I told Erik Bemmelhaus I was meeting you, he told me something about your brother."

"Erik who?"

"He's a sixth grader in my programming class last period. He was like, 'Charlotte? She's Jackson's sister, right? Man, he keeps showing his butt on Facebook. It's hilarious.'"

I drop my backpack.

"He's . . . he's showing *what*? On *where*?" My voice reaches an octave I didn't think it could, and Brit scoots away a few inches, like she's scared I'm going to explode—which I just might.

"Butt. Facebook," she repeats, and squints down at her screen. "I'm trying to check on it."

"You've got to take it down right now! Brit, take it down!"

"I'm not on his page yet. It's Jackson, like, with a *C-K*, right?"

I'm panicking so badly I have to sit down, and I trap my hands between my knees as I peer over Brit's flying fingers. "Yeah, *C-K*."

She shakes her head. "Nope. I don't see a page for a Jackson Trevor that looks anything like him. There's a Trevor Jackson, a Jackson Five fan page, and a Trent Reznor page. Nothing about your brother."

I force myself to breathe. "Could Erik have been lying?"

She shakes her head. "No. He had it open on his laptop—at least, I think he did."

"We need to find that kid."

I dart up, leaving my backpack behind. Brit grabs it as she stumbles after me. "Wait, Charlotte! He might not even be in the lab anymore! There's only five minutes left before the dismissal bell rings!"

I barely hear her. "I'm gonna kill him. Wait. No. First I've got to get that Facebook page down. Then I'll kill him."

That is, if the Cercatores don't get him first. Or Janice.

"But why, Charlotte? What's wrong with Facebook?"

I gnash my teeth. "It's . . . it's against our parents' rules, that's what."

Yeah, we'll go with that.

When I reach the lab, I burst through the door. Programming class is clearly over, but there are still a few kids fiddling around with iPads and such.

"Which one of you is Erik Bemmelhaus?" I fume.

One kid is so shocked he almost drops his laptop. Another squeals in fright. The rest look at a round, waxy-faced kid in the corner. Brit pokes her head in behind me and points. "That's him."

I stalk up to the kid and plant my hand on the tabletop beside him.

"Jackson Trevor's Facebook page. Show it to me. Now!"

"But . . . but . . ."

"Yeah!" I rail. "That's the problem. Are you his friend? Did you encourage him to post pictures of his butt? Of all the stupid, immature, bizarre things to . . ."

"Wait . . . huh? Post pictures of his . . . his . . . like, eww!"

I lean in so close I can smell the Doritos on his breath. "You told Brit my brother was showing his butt."

"Yeah, you know . . . like, complaining and raging. Showing his butt!"

Brit gasps. "Oh . . . oh, I'm sorry, Charlotte! I thought you knew!"

I rub my temples. "Knew what?"

"Show his butt . . . it doesn't mean . . . Wow, I'm so sorry. . . . It doesn't mean to really, you know, *show* your *butt*. It's just something we say . . . like an expression. People don't say that in Ohio?"

"No, people don't say that in Ohio! Nobody says that!"

"We do," Brit responds sheepishly. "It's a southern colloquialism."

"Yeah! That!" Erik adds.

I think both of them are surprised when my mood doesn't change. Erik yelps when I snag his collar and turn his head back to the screen.

"Raging, mooning, I don't care. Show me his Facebook page."

"Okay, okay! Jeez! Just a sec!"

I watch, tapping my foot impatiently as he navigates to a page. Sure enough, there's Jackson's picture, though it's tricky to tell since his face is buried deeply behind the hood of his black sweatshirt.

"No wonder I couldn't find it," Brit says. "He's made up a fake name—'Luckson Siccurevor.'"

"That little moron!" I growl. Couldn't he at least have come up with something more clever? And using part of his old name, at that? I scan the rest of the page, my teeth bared and fingers balled into fists.

Smack dab in the middle of the page is what Erik and Brit must have meant by Jackson "showing his butt." There's a long column of rant, complete with extra punctuation and continuous capitalization:

Luckson Siccurevor

December 13

I H8 the SOUTH!!!!

School every day, no xcape from the STUPIDITY!
And Y do they talk so weird??? It's the same in
all my classes. Even my teachers! No wonder
I don't want 2B friends with any of these kids.
All the people here R backwards stupid country
hicks. If U R one of my friends from home, hit
me up here. I promise I'm still the same LS U
knew. METS 4EVA, older sisters NEVA!
PS J-E-T-S JETS JETS JETS!

"See? It's frickin' hilarious!" Erik says. When he sees my eyes, he adds, "I mean, to other people. Not to me. Nope. Very serious to me. I . . . hey!"

I grab the laptop from him, ignoring his protests. Quickly I click Jackson's profile. The page has only been up for a day. He's got nine friends so far, but there's no way to tell if any of them are from New York, or from his Cercatore family. I click on the list of friends and shove the screen back in Erik's face.

"Tell me who these people are. All kids from Loblolly?"

"Man, are all the Trevors ragebeasts?"

"Just look!"

He runs a finger down the screen. "I . . . I think most of them are, yeah. Not sure about a couple."

I rip the laptop away from him again and push it into Brit's arms.

"Please, Brit! Take it down."

"I can't! I'd have to have his password!"

We spend the next five minutes entering everything I can think of. While Jackson is dumb enough to create a Facebook page, dumb enough to risk everything, he's apparently too savvy to use *password* as his password.

"There's got to be another way," I grumble.

"There isn't," Brit concedes. "Not unless you managed to get onto his page after he signed in."

"Wait," I say, "can you stay signed in even if you're not on Facebook?"

"Yeah. A lot of people do that with their phones."

I breathe, maybe for the first time since the library. "So if I can get his phone, and he's autosigned in, I can take the page down?"

"Yeah, you can do that."

I nod grimly, but Brit isn't satisfied.

"But Charlotte, why can't you say that your parents will be upset? Maybe he'll take it down himself!"

Part of me just wants to tell her, to explain that right now, Jackson's little internet tirade is basically a blinking beacon to gangsters. She's certainly earned my trust, but without knowing if my wrecking ball of a brother has actually done any damage, I certainly can't risk blowing our cover. Instead, I just murmur, "He won't."

"Okay. If you say so," she says, and she hands me my backpack.

"Thanks. Oh, and regardless of how this goes, I'm going to need some serious beanbag time tonight."

"Deal," she says, and we split up. I make a beeline for the parking lot.

I watch Jackson in the rearview mirror of the car all the way home. He's got his phone cradled in his lap, and he's smiling as he swipes the screen. I want to announce to Harriet what he's done, but he'd deny it and probably lock his phone, too, ruining my chance to reverse the damage. So I wait, and I stew. There's no way I'm giving up my friends, my room, my spot in the library, and my life for Luckson Siccurevor's butt-showing. Why can't he cope with good old-fashioned screaming, stubbornness, and petty larceny like the rest of us?

When we're out of the car, I hit Jackson with a bump-and-switch, leaving my calculator in his pocket where his phone should be.

"Gonna go check the locks on the cellar and back gate!" I yell, and before Harriet can protest, I'm sprinting around the side of the house. I hunker down just behind my maple tree and take my own phone out of my backpack. The first order of business is to see if Janice knows.

I've got eleven new text messages, all from Janice, all within the last two hours.

Yup, she knows.

I replace my phone with Jackson's and flicker my fingers across the screen. Sure enough, he's still signed in to Facebook, and I'm able to delete his page in a matter of moments. I do try to check who else has looked at it, but I can't find a way, and I'm not about to go ask Jackson to show me how. When I'm done, I briefly consider digging a nice, deep hole and burying the phone next to the remains of good ol' Trudy. I manage to restrain myself, though, and my step is a billion pounds lighter as I skip into our kitchen.

"You took my phone!"

Jackson is there, my calculator in his hand. He's holding it like he's going to throw it at me. I look around quickly for Harriet.

"She ran to the store, *Nicki*," he spits, adding as much venom to my real name as possible. "Give me my phone."

I inhale sharply and set my jaw. Then I stride right up to him. "Not only did I take your phone—I deleted your stupid Facebook account. What the hell were you thinking, Jackson? You could get us all killed!"

He snaps; there's no other way to describe it. His eyes jerk wide, his jaw drops, and he swings the calculator at me. I duck, and it hits the kitchen island, exploding into bits of plastic and circuitry. Before I can regain my balance, he pushes me down to the floor. I roll under the table near the bay window, narrowly avoiding a kick.

"I don't care anymore!" he says, half screaming and half crying. "I want my old friends back. I want my grandma, and my aunts, and uncles, and cousins! I want my old house,

248

and my old school, and most of all I want you gone! You've destroyed my life!"

I back into the corner and pull a chair in front of me; pieces of broken calculator and fruit from the bowl on the island crash and spatter onto my makeshift shield.

"I didn't destroy your life! I'm trying to save it!" I retort.

"Shut up! Shut up!" he cries, his voice breaking.

"And your mom didn't destroy it, either! Your mom is the hero here, not the villain!"

All I get in reply is a bunch of bananas nailing the wall near my head.

"I know, Jackson! Believe me, I know! Here!"

I slide his phone across the floor, where it glances off his foot. He picks it up, and for a second I think he's going to throw it, too. However, he instead goes into a frenzy of fingerwork.

"You . . . you really did it . . . you deleted my page!"

"For your own good, Jackson. Think about it, please!"

"You destroyed the one thing that I had. . . ."

"Let's talk to our parents. Talk to Janice. We'll find something else for you!"

He kicks the table, and I wince.

"They're not *your* parents! They're *mine*! It was always us. Now you're here, destroying that, too!"

"Jackson . . ."

"That's it! I'm gonna show you how it feels! I'm going to destroy something precious to you!"

I flinch again, thinking he means something like, oh, maybe my skull, but instead I hear him tear out of the kitchen and up the stairs. I hear his footsteps above me, right where the door to my room sits. I hear him kick the door open.

Oh God . . .

Fancypaws . . .

"Jackson, no!" I screech as I throw the chair aside. Slipping on pieces of apple and banana, I hurtle into the hallway. Just as I reach the stairs, I hear a terrifying, short gurgle of pain, followed by a sickening thump. I use my hands and feet to scramble up the steps like a desperate dog. When I skid to a stop at my room, I gasp.

There, in the center of the hexagon, sitting just as primly as you please, is Fancypaws. She seems utterly unfazed. However, trailing from under her right armpit are two wires, the insulated cords of the marshal-issue Taser I hid in her well-stuffed torso. It's where I had always hidden my treasures, ever since Grammy first taught me to steal. It's been home to wallets, to billfolds, to diamonds, and to dog tags. I couldn't think of a more perfect place to hide Janice's gift, even when I was desperate for a place to stash Harriet's ring and bracelet. I felt safe with Fancypaws by my bedside, always within easy reach. . . .

Quickly, I follow the path of those wires around my bed. Jackson is on the floor, stiff as a board, his shoulders and legs still twitching. His head is turned to the side and his jaw is locked tight. I check to make sure the wires aren't live anymore, and then I rip the probes out of his shirt.

"Jackson . . . Jackson! Are you okay?" I ask.

"Ct . . . ct scrtchd mmm . . ." he mumbles.

"What?" I say, rubbing at his arms like the helpers in Janice's Taser videos.

"Ca . . . ca . . . cat . . . scratch . . . scratched mmmeee . . ." he manages as control of his jaw gradually comes back.

I breathe a deep sigh of relief. "Well, yes. Jackson, meet Fancypaws. Fancypaws, this is my dumb brother, Jackson."

It takes me another twenty minutes to get Jackson sitting upright again, and ten more to reset the Taser and restuff Fancypaws. Fortunately, Jackson seems a lot calmer, or at least warier, as he recovers.

"Better now?" I ask, helping him to his feet.

"Yeah. I'm . . . I'm sorry I threw all that stuff at you."

"It's okay. Your aim is terrible. All you did was make a mess."

"What are we going to say if Mom sees it?"

I hesitate for a moment, but then lean forward and kiss him on the forehead. He makes a face like he just got tased again, but he doesn't take a swing at me or anything.

"I'll try to clean it up," I say as I carefully repack the Taser. "If Mom comes home before I can, well, I'll think of something."

I grin at him as I swing the door open. Just before I head downstairs, I glance back.

"Maybe I'll just tell her you were showing your butt."

He cocks his head in confusion, but I don't give him time to ask.

When Harriet bursts through the back door, I'm still on my hands and knees scrubbing at fruit. She's on the phone, frantic.

"Yes, I'm home! I see Charlotte, but not Jackson! I know I should've checked my messages, and I'll leave my ringer on at work from now on, but we can talk about that later. Let's deal with one crisis at a time!" Holding the phone to her chest, she shouts, "Jackson! Get down here, now!"

I sit up. "Is that Janice?"

Before Harriet can respond, Jackson stumbles his way down the hall. He's moving oddly and his hair is all over the place, but it looks like he just woke up from a power nap. I'm hoping that's what Harriet thinks.

"What, Mom?" Jackson mutters.

"Jackson!" Harriet gasps, grabbing her son by the shoulders. The phone is still in her left hand, and I can hear Janice yelling right along with Harriet. "How could you? How could you make a Facebook page? We need to—"

"I took care of it!" I exclaim.

Harriet freezes. Jackson nods.

"It's true, Mom. Charlotte deleted it."

Exhaling slowly, Harriet swoons away from Jackson, her free hand groping for a chair. When she sits, I slip over and pry the phone out of her hand.

"It's taken care of, Janice. I got rid of it."

Jackson is watching my face as I endure a round of cursing from Janice. He winces every time I do. When she's finally out of breath, I respond.

"I'm sure he realizes how stupid it was. Yes. A huge mistake." I pause, making sure Jackson's still looking. "He's a little *shocked* at how everyone's responding, but he gets it."

His eyes widen, but he doesn't say anything. Janice, on the other hand, isn't done.

"Don't defend him, Charlotte. He needs to learn, and if you're protecting him—"

"That's why you put me here, Janice! Because I get it. I get *him*, whether he likes it or not. He's angry. Angry kids lash out. Just be grateful that we caught it so quickly."

That seems to calm her down, and when I'm finally able to hang up, we take a collective deep breath. Wearily, Harriet says, "Jackson, you owe your sister one huge—"

"Thank you," Jackson whispers.

I smile, and, to my surprise, he does, too. Harriet rises from her chair and beckons us both to the kitchen, where we still have a considerable mess to clean up. We work together, scraping and scrubbing in silence. As we do, the phone rings three more times, with nobody on the other end. It's enough to have me checking the clock every few minutes to see if it's time for Brit's game to start. Finally, I say I'm going to go over early to help her set up. Harriet gives me the go-ahead, and I dash off before anything else can happen in this strange little house of ours.

Brit greets me at the door, her finger pressed to her lips. The sound of the TV blares from behind her, and I nod my understanding. Together, we creep toward the stairs, pausing with every shuffled step to see if Nancie is going to catch us. I tiptoe around yarn balls and stacks of *Good Housekeeping* magazines, knowing full well that one misstep might doom us to twenty minutes of conversation. I'm careful, I'm precise, and I'm graceful.

It doesn't matter, though.

It's just as we reach the landing that Nancie appears at the bottom of the stairs. I offer Brit an apologetic shrug as her mom starts to speak.

"Charlotte! Tell me that daughter of mine isn't forcin' you to watch her play those ridiculous games again! You'd think a girl her age would be listenin' to music, talkin' about boys, and watchin' scary movies. But no, she's plugged in 'n' tuned out. Some friend she must be!"

Brit gasps, and I jump in. "No, Mrs. Guthrie. I really like watching Brit play. She's good!"

"You're too kind to her, humorin' her like that. She's gonna think it's okay to be a recluse, never talkin' to anyone, all the kids thinkin' she's a geek or dweeb or nerd or—"

I wave my hand to disperse her swarm of synonyms. "Actually, Mrs. Guthrie, it's pretty cool. Lots of kids play games these days. And I mean *lots*."

She trails off, and I can see her eyes dart between us as she thinks.

"Lots?"

"Way lots," I assure her. "It's basically like the new quilting!"

I hear Brit sputter behind me.

"Quiltin'?" Nancie asks hopefully.

"Oh, for sure! Only Brit, you know, is basically quilting with people all over the world. It's one huge quilting bee! And let me tell you, Mrs. Guthrie . . . if it's a bee, your daughter's the queen."

Nancie casts a glance back at the yarn baskets in her living room and at the quilt hung like a Picasso over her couch. Then she looks at Brit for a long moment. Finally, she says, "Huh! Good for you, Britty! How about that? My daughter, stitchin' and grinnin' in the virtual world. Why didn't you tell me, girl? I'm proud of you!"

Nancie ambles off, not even staying to hear Brit murmur, "Thanks, Mom." When we're sure she's settled in front of the TV again, we scamper into Brit's room. I throw myself onto her beanbag with abandon and let my hair shield my face. Then I giggle. Brit joins in a second later.

"A . . . a quilting bee?"

I shrug playfully. "Knitting buddies, counterterrorists . . . what's the difference?"

"I'm pretty sure they don't give you a kill count after you complete a successful cross-stitch," Brit says, and we both laugh again. We're only interrupted by a notice that chimes on her computer: Her game starts in ten minutes. Brit settles into her chair, tinkering with some monitor settings and making sure she's in the right chat room. I look up at the constellation of glow-in-the-dark stars she's got glued to her ceiling.

"Did you fix the Facebook thing?" she asks after a few moments.

I nod. "Yes, thanks to your advice."

"Do you . . . do you want to talk about it?"

I shake my head emphatically. "Please, no. I just want to watch you win."

Brit swivels to face me, her sneakers squeaking on the plastic mat beneath her chair. She grabs a toy, a cute little Totoro, from her desk and starts fiddling with it. "Are you sure you don't want to talk? Today is the first time I've ever seen you get upset about anything. Erik was right. You were a bit of a ragebeast."

I snarl playfully at her.

"Don't worry!" she says, shielding herself with Totoro. "It was cute! I just mean that normally, you're so, you know— separate from things."

I sit up, tilting my head to the side. She continues. "It's like . . . the way you just took care of my mom—saying my games are cool. She completely believed you, no questions asked. And at school, you could sit with Deidre every day, right? But you don't. And Archer . . ."

I roll my eyes.

"Fine, fine," she says. "I won't bring up Archer. But you're different, Charlotte."

My heart skips a beat. I'll admit I went a little nuts today when Brit told me about Jackson, but was it enough to tip Brit off? I brace myself for the worst, hiding my hands just in case.

"Different . . . how?"

To my surprise, Brit hangs her head. She sets her little toy down and folds her hands in her lap.

"Things changed somehow a while back, you know?" She peeks at me through her lashes long enough to catch my puzzled expression, then drops her gaze again. "I mean, like, before you got here. Everything was fine in elementary school. Then, though . . . well, it's as if there was a huge popularity lottery in middle school. Only I missed it. I didn't even get a ticket. Like, I'm doing fine in fifth grade, and then all of a sudden, being me somehow isn't good enough."

She sniffles softly. I want to go console her, but when I try to move, the beanbag creates a cacophony of crackling, so I freeze.

"That's how you're different. You came into Loblolly, and somehow, some way, it didn't grab you. You're separate from all of it. You . . . you can actually see me. You even helped my mom see me, at least a little bit."

Heck with the beanbag chair. I stand up and hug her.

"I *so* see you, Brit."

She nods, and when I pull away, she's smiling. I smile, too, though my heart is still pounding. Yes, I was worried that she knew my family's secret, but part of me was hoping she did. I was hoping she saw *me*, too. I melt back down into the beanbag chair, watching as Brit gets ready for her game.

When it starts, I cheer and clap, adding commentary like I'm her own personal sportscaster. She demolishes the competition, and we're all hugs again as she finds out she's made the team. But after I say good-bye and slink home, I slump against the door, my mind racing. Today was the wildest yet, and not even retreating to my room or to Brit's house seemed to help. I'm still totally grateful for both, of course, but it'd sure be nice to have a place to go where I wasn't hiding something.

To: Stricker.Janice@usdoj.gov
From: Trevor.Charlotte@usdoj.gov
Subject: Almost Christmas

Dear Deputy Marshal Stricker,

Before you get mad, this IS an emergency.
Kind of.

It's almost Christmas, and our neighborhood is lit up like Times Square. The Roysters have an entire neon nativity scene in their front yard, the Guthries are sporting a strobing Santa, and the people at the end of the block have inflatable wise men that dance when it's windy. And Deputy Marshal, it's pretty windy here. . . .

I guess what I'm saying is that our house is looking dangerously drab. Can we decorate for Christmas? Like, lights and stuff? I know you already told Harriet and Jonathan no, but our lack of holiday cheer is making us stick out like a sore thumb.

Speaking of Christmas, happy holidays! Do you celebrate Christmas, or Hanukkah, or something else? Whatever you celebrate, I wish you a merry that thing, because you're sort of the only person in the world who knows all about me. That makes us familyish, and I'd hate to go through the holidays without sending greetings to my family members. Well, the ones who didn't abandon me, at any rate.

So let us know about the decorations! And tell Eddie and Dr. Coustoff I say hello!

Yours in seasonal secrecy,
N/C

P.S. We're still getting those creepy phone calls. Any luck tracing them?

To: Trevor.Charlotte@usdoj.gov
From: Stricker.Janice@usdoj.gov
Subject: RE: Almost Christmas

Charlotte,

I will inquire about the Christmas decoration issue.

We are still investigating the calls.

-JS

To: Stricker.Janice@usdoj.gov
From: Trevor.Charlotte@usdoj.gov
Subject: RE: RE: Almost Christmas

Dear Deputy Marshal Stricker,

Thanks! Happy holidays!
-N/C

To: Trevor.Charlotte@usdoj.gov
From: Stricker.Janice@usdoj.gov
Subject: RE: RE: RE: Almost Christmas

Charlotte,

Please find attached the WITSEC parameters for your decorations. Have them up in the next two days, and take them down no later than the fifth of January. Also, stop responding to these e-mails just to say thank you. We need to keep the inbox clear for emergency messages.

And yes, happy holidays.

-JS

CHAPTER TWENTY

Happy Holly Days

My fingertips ache, and I press them to my cheeks to try to warm them. That just makes my face colder, though, so instead I wiggle them around. Jackson, who is sitting in the frost-covered grass of the front lawn, sniffles and yanks the earflaps of his toboggan hat farther down.

"Hurry, Charlotte! I'm freezing out here," he whines. Then he looks up at Jonathan, who's perched on a ladder that leans precariously against our porch roof. "How much longer?"

Jonathan ignores him, instead calling out, "More slack, Char!"

"Working as fast as I can!" I reply, shoving my fingers back into the tangle of cords balled in my lap. I've got the pattern now, at least—yellow light, blue light, green light, red. "Better learn to decorate, or you'll be dead . . ." I murmur aloud.

Hmm. Maybe not the best rhyme to whistle while I work. I feed the Christmas lights up to Jonathan as he stretches to clip them to the gutter. After I navigate a couple more kinks and hitches, the festive little rat's nest unravels completely.

"All set!" I exclaim, the words puffing forth in a cloud of steam. I shove my hands beneath my armpits and slide off the front steps, joining Jackson as we watch Jonathan finish up.

"How did we do?" I ask, peering down at Jackson's phone, where he's got the attachment from Janice's e-mail open.

"No more than one hundred feet of lights. No major religious ico . . . icorn . . ."

"Iconography."

"Uh-huh," Jackson mumbles.

"We're allowed to have a wreath, right?"

Jackson shrugs. Just like I'm not allowed to dress in all black and mope my way through the holidays, our happy home has to meet the median of comfort and joy. Apparently, in response to my e-mail, they used satellites to find images of our neighborhood from the last five Christmases, and they ran some sort of algorithm that deduced the exact size, color, and obnoxiousness of everyone's holiday displays. We're expected to be right in the middle of all of it.

"Oh yeah. There it is," I say, pointing to his screen. "One wreath. Front door only. Maximum diameter: three feet."

"I'll take care of the wreath," Jonathan offers as he climbs down. "You two go get ready for school. Harriet should have breakfast on the table."

When we get in, there's a box of Rice Chex open on the counter, along with two empty bowls. Harriet is leaning up against the fridge, the landline phone pressed to her ear.

"Yes, I'll wait." She sighs. Then she mouths to me, "Caller I.D."

"Again?" I whisper back. She nods, and then says into the phone, "What do you mean the number's untraceable? Really?"

She hangs up the phone and presses her forehead to the freezer door for a moment.

"They think it's someone using a burner phone, or maybe a robocalling service that's glitching. I'll let Janice know."

I shake my head as I fill my bowl. "Another thing to add to the list."

Harriet rolls her eyes and says, "Tell me about it. What I wouldn't give for a quiet, normal Christmas."

"It can't be normal without Grandma and Grandpa, or without Bryant Park," Jackson murmurs. Then he shoves his hand straight into the cereal box, grabbing a dusty handful and cramming it past his lips.

"Tell me you're not going to pour milk directly into your mouth," I say warily.

I cringe as he inverts his head over the sink and lifts the jug. He ends up pouring most of it into his nose.

As Jackson sputters and coughs, Jonathan comes in, his own phone in hand.

"Just got the call from Quincy at work. He confirmed that our boss expects us at the holiday party Friday night. Got to go."

Harriet frowns. "That's the same night as mine."

"I already asked Janice about it. She said we really should go. Can't turn ourselves into total hermits."

"What do we do with Jackson, then? Charlotte has her own . . ." Harriet trails off, her gaze slowly swinging from Jonathan to me. He follows suit, and soon they're both staring at me, sheepish smiles playing across their faces. I put down my spoon, my eyes widening as I realize . . .

"No. Ohhh no," I say, shaking my head. "Holly's party is for seventh graders only. *Girls* only. Those are her mom's rules. Besides, what's weirder? One of you begging off your work party, or me dragging . . ." I pause, looking at Jackson. He's still blowing milk out of his nose into the sink. ". . . *him* to Holly's house?"

"Please, Char. You two have been getting along so much better the last few weeks. He can just bring his phone and play games in the corner. I'll call Holly's mom and work out the details."

I can feel a good and proper tantrum coming on; my hands are gripping my bowl, and they're shaking so badly that the spoon leaning against the edge is chiming its very own rendition of "Jingle Bells." I set the bowl down slowly. Then I take a deep breath, grit my teeth, and force a grin.

"Mother. Father," I begin, using my most diplomatic voice. "It may have come to your attention that I have endeavored in significant fashion these few months past to keep our family's secret well hidden. I have received the appropriate grades. I have gone to unforeseen lengths to ensure my positions in two extracurriculars. I successfully grounded Jackson's brief flight of Facebook fancy. In doing so, I believe I have earned a certain amount of leverage vis-à-vis how I sculpt my own social situation. I feel at this time that taking my younger brother to Holly's party would constitute a significant threat to the delicate network I have painstakingly built. As such, having him there may very well endanger us every bit as much as one of you missing your own holiday party."

"Why are you talking like that?" Jackson says, twin wads of paper towel now blooming from his nostrils.

I set my jaw, pointing at him for emphasis.

"Char," Harriet says softly. "That was very well-spoken, but I'm afraid this is where I'll need to put my foot down. We're stuck here. We cannot allow a babysitter into our home, and we cannot take Jackson to our parties. We also can't afford to miss another event. I've run out of excuses to give, and Jonathan has as well."

A lump of pure protest starts clawing its way up my windpipe. I can actually feel my own body rooting for it, too, telling me to just uncork and blow off every last bit of tension and stress. Then, though, the phone rings. Again. We all jump. Harriet looks at the phone screen and sighs.

"Unlisted, of course. Jonathan, can you . . ."

"On it, love," he says, taking the phone from her and

clicking the button. As he repeats the word "Hello?" I stalk out of the room, going upstairs to finish getting ready for school. Of course I'll take Jackson to Holly's party. Of course there won't be a screaming argument. Not from Charlotte Ashlynn Trevor. *She* somehow always makes it work.

Somehow.

I notice that I've actually swiped my own spoon only when I nearly smear toothpaste on it. I set it down on the sink and pick up my toothbrush. Maybe Holly will understand. Heck, she owes me one for the election. I just didn't think I'd have to call in the favor so soon.

I'm thinking about it all the way to school, and sure enough, Holly is beaming at me when I slip into homeroom. She beckons me over with an explosion of waves. That, or she's hyperventilating, which is possible—she's got a brown paper bag on her desk.

"Are you okay?" I ask. "Because . . ."

"Better than okay! I'm fabulokay!"

"Yeah, I'm pretty sure that's not a thing," I say, though her enthusiasm is so infectious that I can't help but smile.

"It's time, Charlotte! I've got all the names in here for the Secret Santa party. Are you ready to pick?"

My shoulders slump. "Yeah. About the party . . ."

"Oh, don't worry! I thought your idea about inviting Brit was great! I've always wanted to get to know her better, and she's, like, your best friend, so of course she can come!"

I momentarily forget about my problem. I scan the room, but Brit isn't here yet.

"Did she say yes?" I ask hopefully.

"At first, no. She gave me this look." Holly pauses, her perfect eyebrows angling in mock disbelief. "I don't know—maybe she thought I was joking? But then I told her that you told me to ask, and Charlotte! Oh my gosh! I've never seen her smile so big!"

"Awesome!" I reply. Knowing that Brit will be there makes the news I'm about to drop in Holly's lap a little easier to deliver. "But Holly, I'm afraid I have a favor to ask. A big one."

Holly winks at me. "You know I owe you big-time, girlfriend."

I sigh. "Yeah. You see, though, here's the problem. Both my parents have holiday parties on Friday night. . . ."

Holly goes from euphoric to pouty faster than I can blink.

"No, Charlotte! You can't come?!"

"Worse," I concede. "Though I wouldn't blame you if you uninvite me in about five seconds. If my parents go to their parties, and I come to yours, that leaves Jackson alone at home, and . . ."

"Bring him along!" Holly exclaims, her pout insta-banished.

"Are you . . ."

"Totally serious, Charlotte! He can hang out with us!" she says, shoving the paper bag at me. "Now pick, silly! Whoever's name you pull, you have to buy a present for. It can be cute, funny, serious, or whatever. Just not too expensive."

She holds open the bag, and I reach down. As I'm

rummaging, she tries to close it, but I manage to jerk my hand back before she can trap me.

"Hey, you're supposed to close your eyes, cheater!" Holly scolds playfully.

"I didn't look!" I retort, turning my shoulder and unleashing a devastating pout of my own.

Holly grins. "I believe you. You picked so fast you couldn't have read!"

I scurry to my seat as Ms. Millar arrives, surprised to see that Brit managed to sneak in while I was pitching my problem to Holly. I hold up the still-folded slip of paper and catch Brit's eye.

"You're coming?" I whisper.

She shrugs, then smiles. It's every bit as luminous as Holly described.

I hold on to my slip until the end of the day. When I get home, I fish it out of my pocket and smooth it on the kitchen table. I'm relieved to see MZ's name on there—she's super easy to buy for. Her favorite sport is lacrosse, she's obsessed with the Duke women's team, and there's a cool place on Ninth Street that sells that kind of stuff. I wouldn't have minded seeing Brit's or Holly's name, too, but I've already bought them gifts. In fact, the sweet plushie Companion Cube from one of Brit's favorite computer games is already wrapped and under her tree; I snuck it in last time I went over. It takes me only a day to round up what I need for MZ's gift. I have the rest of the week to convince myself that taking Jackson isn't going to be a disaster.

. . .

On Friday, all three of us cram into the back of Nancie Guthrie's Honda. As soon as we do, Nancie peppers us with questions, most of which I'm left to answer. I've grown used to it these past few months, but keeping up is made exponentially more difficult by Jackson's presence in the car. When he found out that he was going to a party with seventh-grade girls, he apparently couldn't decide which deodorant to use, so he settled on all of them. At least, that's how it smells. I'm forced to lean against Brit, who, in turn, sneaks her pinkie along the door of the car, working it like an inchworm until she reaches the window controls. Then, timing her movements with her mom's bursts of excitement, she manages to roll the window open. It gives us a few moments' reprieve, at least, before Nancie notices.

"Y'all are lucky I had this evening off. Most usually, I'm busier than a one-legged cat in a sandbox 'round holiday time. Why, just yesterday I was . . . hey, why am I freezing my pawtuchus off? Britney Aguilera Guthrie, what are you doing with that window down?"

Cowed, Brit rolls up the window, and we're still for the rest of the drive. She's probably embarrassed, and I'm left trying to puzzle through what exactly a pawtuchus might be. Whatever it is, it can't smell worse than Jackson.

Holly lives in a tall apartment building near East Campus, and Nancie walks us all the way up the stairs to the sixth floor. The entire door of Holly's apartment is covered in wrapping paper, with a massive red bow stuck just beneath

269

the peephole. When we knock, the door flings wide, and holiday tunes blast out at us, along with the aroma of baking gingerbread. The scent is so heavenly, especially in comparison with what we've endured for the past ten minutes, that I instinctively lean in. In fact, I'm so enchanted by the smell that I almost miss a true holiday miracle.

Out of the corner of my eye, I notice Brit hanging back, one hand at her throat and the other at her heart. Jackson's staring at her, too, and he dares to whisper, "Hey, are . . . are you gonna barf?"

It absolutely can't be the gingerbread, so I slip closer to see if I can figure out what's going on. Just as I do, it hits me. As a veteran of a visit from the neighborhood welcome committee, I know what's coming.

Only, it doesn't.

Nancie Guthrie does manage to wedge herself in the doorway. She stands on her tiptoes and peers past Holly, who is dressed like an elf: green dress, candy-cane tights, and fake Elrond ears. Nancie's head bobs around as she looks at all the girls who are already in Holly's living room. Then she breathes deeply, ready to make a grand entrance on behalf of her debutante daughter.

"Oh my! Look at all the friends you've got here, Pretty Bri—"

That's all she can manage, though.

"Wow. Wow! You, like, must be Mrs. Guthrie! Do you even know how big a fan I am of your black forest brownies? You made them for our bake sale last year! They were the first thing gone, and we raised twice as much as we usually do!" Holly gushes. As she talks, she wraps an arm around Nancie's shoulders and starts leading her down the walkway toward the stairs. "You're a total legend! And thanks for bringing Brit and Charlotte to our party. Don't worry—we have a nine o'clock curfew, and my parents are both home. Our number is in the school directory if you need anything. Please enjoy your evening off—you've definitely earned it!"

A quick glance at Brit reveals that she's breathing again, and her color has returned to its normal shade of pale. It's enough to make me feel positively wretched about my embarrassment over bringing Jackson. I hadn't even considered how difficult this was going to be for Brit, especially with her mom giving us a ride.

With Holly's diversion working to perfection, we scoot inside. Tanika, MZ, and a few other girls are hovering over a table covered with flour, cookie cutters, and rolled-thin gingerbread dough. Jackson quickly scuttles to the corner and slinks down between the arm of the couch and the wall, like he's a mangy cat we just brought home from the pound. Holly rejoins us a moment later. Throwing her arms around our shoulders like she did with Nancie, she leads us to the cookie table.

"We have a hundred more to make, so get to cutting!" Holly says cheerfully.

"Th-thanks," Brit whispers.

"No problem!" Holly replies. "We've all got moms."

Brit's sigh of relief is so loud I don't think anyone notices me wincing.

As if on cue, Holly's mom sweeps in from the kitchen, followed closely by her father. Both wear heavy oven mitts, and they're clutching empty baking trays.

"Hello, girls!" Holly's mom says. "*Feliz Navidad*, and welcome!"

"Thanks!" I reply. "The cookies smell wonderful."

"Yes," Mr. Fiellera says, "and it's time for another round."

Brit and I jump in, helping the others to carefully lay the cut cookies onto the trays. There are mittens, trees, angels, and this one mangled sort of spider-looking thing.

"That's a reindeer," Jessica Steadman admits. "I had trouble getting it out of the cutter."

I shrug. "It's kind of cute."

"Speaking of cute, is now when we get to talk about boys?" Tanika asks. "Like, for instance, the way Archer Brantley keeps hanging around you, Charlotte?"

I notice that over in the corner, Jackson's head has popped up over the edge of the couch like a curious, greasy meerkat. I whack-a-mole him back down with a scowl.

"Sorry, Tan," I say. "Probably not the best time to gossip with my brother here."

"Or my parents," Holly adds.

"Another subject, then," MZ suggests. "Like Brit!"

Brit, who had busied herself cutting out a gingerbread candy cane, freezes. The shape in her fingers slowly wilts down into a sad letter *J*.

MZ smiles. "Not like gossip, Brit. I just mean that we haven't talked much."

"Seriously!" Holly says. "I'm glad Charlotte brought you. It's nice to see you outside of school."

Brit blinks, then remembers to exhale. "You . . . you, too, Holly. And MZ. And everyone."

"So we were talking earlier about holiday shows. What's your favorite?" Jessica asks.

"I . . . you mean . . . like TV shows?"

Jessica nods. Holly says, "Yeah, like *A Charlie Brown Christmas*."

Brit shrugs. "I guess I have one. We watch it every year, but it's silly."

"Mine's *The Year Without a Santa Claus*, so the bar's set pretty low, unless you can beat the Heat Miser dancing around while his little fire dwarfs use shovels as pogo sticks," I say.

"I love that one!" MZ and Holly exclaim simultaneously.

Brit says, "Well, I'm a Jim Henson fan. You know, like Kermit and everyone, so . . ."

Tanika gasps. "Are you gonna say *Emmet Otter's Jug-Band Christmas*?"

Brit's eyes widen, and she nods.

"Mine too!" Tanika squeals. "It's the cutest thing ever!"

"I love that, too!" Jessica adds.

Soon Brit and I have scored invites to Tanika's house to watch her dad's VHS recording of the original airing—the good one that actually has Kermit in it. Even better, Brit opens up after that, and she truly relaxes. In truth, though I'm happy for her, I'm also more than a little jealous. How much would I like to tell everyone about Christmas with my grammy? About sucking our candy canes down to points and sword-fighting with them? Or even about holidays at the Center, where we'd eat advent calendar chocolate and light a candle in the menorah every night? I don't say anything, though, of course.

When the cookies go in the oven, Holly declares it's time for the Secret Santa presents. We wash the cookie dough off our hands and gather on the carpet of her living room, our gifts in hand. Jackson crawls up onto the couch to watch, and he even nods when I press my finger to my lips. Holly has us sit down in order of who bought for whom. MZ is to my right, and to my surprise, Brit is to my left; she must have drawn my name out of the bag. I bump shoulders with her softly, and she smiles.

"Okay," Holly declares. "Let the Secret Santa'ing commence! Pass your gift to the right and receive your present. Then, we open them one at a time. Go!"

I give MZ the lacrosse ball I bought, which was signed by six members of the 2014 Duke tournament team. It's wrapped as best as I could manage, which isn't well, but at least the signatures are hidden. Brit sets in front of me a green-and-gold gift bag with a pouf of bright red tissue paper bursting out the top.

Around the circle we go, fawning over and giggling about each gift. Holly gets a day planner for all her activities, Jessica scores her favorite nail polish, Tanika opens an ornament Jessica brought back from her Thanksgiving trip to Disney World, and Brit gets this special cloth and spray for cleaning her computer screen. When it's my turn, I shred through the tissue paper atop Brit's present, ignoring Holly's pleas to save the stuff "Because you can reuse it for Valentine's Day."

Once I've disintegrated the tissue paper, I peer down into the bag. I must turn snow-white, because even Jackson notices. From the couch, he says, "Charlotte, you look weird."

I rip my gaze from within the bag, snapping at Jackson. "I'm fine!"

I'm not, though.

"You . . . you don't like them?" Brit asks, her voice trembling.

"No!" I shout, and then force myself to take a deep breath. "No, Brit. They're beautiful. You . . . you knitted them yourself, didn't you?"

I reach into the bag to pull the gloves out. Brit has sewn an intricate pattern with pomegranate-purples and teals, a perfect interlocking of my favorite color and hers. The other girls gasp.

"Wow, Brit! Those are super-gorgeous!" Jessica exclaims.

Holly asks, "Where did you learn to knit like that?"

"From . . . from my mom."

"You've gotta try them on, Charlotte!" Tanika demands.

"You're sweating!" Jackson notes. He's not wrong; I can feel it beading beneath my hair.

"Yeah, Charlotte . . . are you okay?"

I nod. "Yeah . . . just . . . just nervous with all the attention on me, I guess," I lie. I try to throw a fake giggle in there, too, but it sounds like I'm strangling myself.

"I can make a new pair if you don't like the colors, Charlotte," Brit mutters, crestfallen. "It's just that I see you at school with no gloves, and you're always putting your hands into your pockets, or blowing on them. I thought a good pair of gloves . . ."

I shake my head. "No, Brit. You're totally right. And they are amazing. Here. I'll try them on."

Swallowing, I clench my teeth and demand that my hands stop shaking. They completely ignore me, so I gather the gloves into my lap, hiding them with my knees. Fighting off the urge to cry out, I slip my hands into the gloves. They fit perfectly, which only makes it worse—it feels like the music, the lights, everyone's stares, all of it has taken physical form and is pressing against my skin, prickling everywhere and all at once. It's so hard to breathe that I'm trying to gasp through my nose and mouth at the same time, which must look really strange. Somehow, though, I manage to squeak out a "Thank you, Brit."

It takes every last bit of energy I have to watch MZ

open her present. I nearly pass out when she hugs me, my trapped hands waving in the air as she buries me in her excited embrace. My saving grace is Holly's parents, who sweep in bearing plates of freshly baked cookies. I'm able to shed the gloves—thank goodness for frosting—and my hands calm down almost instantly, even if I don't. Fortunately, I'm able to make it through the rest of the party, though I do catch Brit looking at me every so often. I smile back every time, but I know I've got another trial coming, and it arrives soon enough.

"It's cold out there. Don't forget your jackets!" Mrs. Fiellera says at the conclusion of the party.

"Or your gloves!" Jackson adds, grinning.

I elbow him in the ribs, but the damage has been done: all the girls are looking at me, waiting for me to put them on. Wearing the biggest smile I can force, I turn around and will my hands back into their cashmere cages. They're the softest I've ever felt, but I might as well have wrapped my entire body in the scratchiest of Christmas sweaters. Still, I hug Holly good-bye, and I manage to get out the door and into Nancie's car.

The ride home is agony, at least for me. Every time I try to slip off the gloves, Jackson mentions them again. For everyone else, it's a wonderful end to a great evening. Nancie, of course, loves hearing about how the other girls carried on about her daughter, and Brit is starry-eyed. Were I not in an absolute panic, I'd be reveling in her success; if anyone deserved a great night out, it's Brit. She actually tells her mom about it and uses multiple words in each sentence.

When we're finally home, Brit walks Jackson and me to our porch. My hands are in my pockets, fingers twitching, nails digging into my palms at a fiery itch that won't go away. The frigid air does feel good on my forehead, even if my lips are probably turning blue.

Standing beneath the soft glow of our Christmas lights, Brit says, "I can't thank you enough, Charlotte, for inviting me. For being my friend. For everything. I'm . . . I'm sorry about the gloves, if you don't—"

I cut her off. "I love them, Brit. And there's no need to thank me. You did *me* the favor by coming. Watching you have a great time made my night better."

With tears in her eyes, Brit hugs me. I hope she doesn't notice that I don't use my hands to hug her back.

Once she's gone, I dart into the house and yank off the gloves, tossing them into the living room. I sink to the floor, cradling my hands to my chest. Jackson deals with the alarm, and then he strides over to pick up the gloves.

"What's your problem with these?" he asks. "Not that it wasn't fun to mess with you."

"I can't wear gloves," I reply, flexing and curling my fingers, letting them enjoy their freedom.

"But you did."

"Because they were from Brit!"

"Why is Brit so important anyway?" Jackson asks, waving the gloves around for emphasis.

"She's Charlotte's best friend."

"Huh?"

"Charlotte's best friend," I growl. "Was I wearing gloves, Jackson? It might have looked that way. Or was it Charlotte Trevor? Yeah, she can wear gloves without feeling like she's going to die. Charlotte Trevor gets thoughtful, beautiful gifts from her best friend. Charlotte Trevor *has* a best friend! What do *I* have?"

Before I can melt down any further, I spring up and dash to my room. On my way, Jonathan comes home, poking his head through the front door.

"How was the party?" he asks.

"Fine!" I manage. Then I scramble up the last few steps and slam my door shut. As I throw myself onto my bed, I can hear Jonathan grilling Jackson about why I sound so upset. He has no clue, of course, and, in truth, neither do I. Brit *is* my best friend. But something about tonight bothered me, even more than the shock of the gloves.

I was at a party with my friends and brother, and not one of them knew who I was.

A few days later, we do have a nice, quiet family Christmas, at least. Nobody gets me gloves, and I receive enough books that I can comfortably excuse myself to my room to read. Still, I can't shake the feeling that between the gloves and the guilt, the phone calls and the pretending, something is going to have to give.

CHAPTER TWENTY-ONE

What Gives?

We manage to keep our heads down through the rest of the winter, and on the surface everything seems all right . . . at least until March, when the weather starts getting warmer, the birds return, and Harriet decides to put away my laundry for me.

Holly's mom drops me off after we go to a movie on a Friday night. It's raining buckets, so I scamper up the front steps, barely remembering to jump the third one so I don't wake anyone up. It's nearly midnight, so I ease the key into the lock and turn it so slowly I can hear each individual tumbler fall into place. Then I slip inside and reset the alarm.

The entryway, hallway, and kitchen are mostly dark, though Jonathan left the little light over the fireplace on, just like he said he would. I slip off my soppy shoes and barefoot my way to the steps. Harriet and Jonathan's door is closed, but I can hear him snoring softly, even so. I crack a smile, wipe an errant droplet from the tip of my nose, and sneak upstairs.

When I get to the top, I'm puzzled—my bedroom door is closed, but there's a light on in there. I'm pretty sure I turned them all off before I left. I creep forward, keeping my feet as close to the walls as possible; the hardwood floor creaks otherwise. Stooping to peer through the old keyhole, I can see that the lamp on my dresser is on. I tell myself it's nothing, but a little projector in the back of my brain is running grainy footage of an assassin jumping on me from the shadows as soon as I open the door. Before I can muster my courage, a quiet, familiar voice emanates from within.

"Charlotte, I know you're out there. Come in."

Harriet?

"Hey, Mom," I say. "Thanks for waiting up! I'm all wet, so I'm gonna just change into my PJs after I . . ."

I trail off. Harriet is sitting on my perfectly made bed—a bed I left bedraggled. Next to her, pillowed on the comforter, is a row of neatly spaced items:

A platinum bangle bracelet.

An old wristwatch.

A pair of opal earrings.

A mother-of-pearl makeup compact.

And her rhinestone engagement ring.

"I found these," she says, her hands clasped around her phone, arms pulled tight over her lap.

I feel suddenly nauseous, a soda, popcorn, and sixty or

so Sour Patch Kids sitting heavy in my stomach. I glance toward my bathroom, then force myself to look at Harriet. As tears well in my eyes, I desperately scan her face. It's unreadable.

"Please," I beg, my voice wavering. "Please don't call Janice."

"I already did," she responds, and she sighs deeply.

I can't hold it back. My tears patter softly on the carpet, and my arms and legs start shaking. I spin and rush to the bathroom, barely making it in time before my body betrays me.

I alternate between sobs and sickness for what seems an eternity, my hands on the porcelain trembling so badly the toilet seat rattles.

"Every time," I say, coughing. "I ruin it every time. . . ."

Janice will come. She will be furious, and disappointed, and condescending. She'll make me pack up my perfect, beautiful room. I'll try to say good-bye, but Jonathan and Harriet will shake their heads and just turn away from me. I'll never see Brit again. Everything I've done will have been for nothing.

Absolutely nothing.

Another wave slams me, bending me over again. This time, though, I'm aware of a coolness at the back of my neck. It's a slip of softness that calms me, and as I slowly rise to a kneel, I realize it's Harriet's hand, holding my hair back.

"I'm . . . I'm sorry I made a mess," I whisper. She hands me a tissue, flushes the toilet, and closes the lid. Then she sits down. She takes my head in her lap and rests her palm against my cheek. The rain drives briefly against the windowpanes, then relents.

"I can leave tomor—"

"Shhh," Harriet says, putting a fingertip on my lips. "Just shhh."

We sit there in the dark, her hands upon me, my body seizing with silent sobs. Twice more I think I'm going to be sick, but I'm already empty, guilt settling deep in the hollowness.

"I found these things in your drawer," she finally says. "And I called Janice. Do you know what she told me?"

I shake my head, cheek pressed against the soft cotton of her pajama pants.

"She told me a story that I should have listened to a long time ago. It was about a girl—a confused, hurt, terribly strong little girl. A girl who I hadn't bothered to learn about, because I was so very concerned with my own life, my own hurt."

I feel her hand stroke my hair, fingers sliding softly through the rain-soaked tangles. "And I tell you, Charlotte, this girl . . . I was so sad to hear her story—but not because I pitied her. No, never that. Rather, it was because I foolishly thought I was better off not knowing who she really was, where she came from. Oh, I was wrong. What a ridiculous thought that was! To not know, to not understand where this girl was coming from . . . it was a mistake. Do you know why?"

"Why?"

"Because this girl was to be my daughter, and for a mother not to know her daughter is, in my eyes, a crime."

Harriet cups my cheeks in her hands and lifts my head. I'm too weak to do anything but let her move me. She looks down into my eyes, gray mirrored in gray, and she smiles wanly.

"Hello, Nicki Demere. My Charlotte. My beautiful girl."

I don't know what else to do, so I throw my arms around her neck and cling to her.

Still holding me, she stands up. I slip from her shoulders, and she takes me by the hand. I don't even have the strength to pull away.

"To tell you the truth, Charlotte, Janice yelled at me."

I smile softly as I sit next to her on the bed. "She'll do that from time to time." I sniffle.

"We were supposed to read your file. We should have read it. Then we would have known about your grandma, about your foster families, and your father."

I wince. "In a way, it was nice not having you know about all that. I could sort of, well, be perfect for you, I guess. Except I failed at that. Majorly."

"That's not your job, Charlotte. It isn't any child's job to be perfect for their parents. It's our job to try to be perfect for you, and that means understanding you as best we can."

I manage a laugh. "I'm thirteen. Good luck."

She smiles. "Fair enough. But there are some things we can understand. Like this," she says, and she gestures to the

284

objects lined up between us. "Your therapist's notes were in the file. We should have seen them, should have been there to help you with it."

"It's called kleptomania. I'm still working on it. I might always be."

"I know, and I get it. In fact, I've been doing some thinking in the last two hours. At first, I was very angry, Charlotte. It's important that you know that."

I nod. "I stole from you. I totally get how that makes you feel. That's one of the things I learned in therapy."

"However, after talking to Janice, I understood. Stress triggers it, right?"

"Yes."

"In that case, with all we've asked of you, I'm surprised, and grateful, that there isn't more."

I shake my head. "And there isn't, I swear. I don't have anything hidden from school, or from Jackson, or from Jonathan. Just . . ." I frown, realizing how bad this sounds. "Just from you."

Her hand comes to rest at the nape of her neck. "I thought as much."

I push all the things toward her. "Take them back, please. I didn't steal them to sell, or anything like that. I'd never . . ."

She holds up a finger. "I know. I know, Charlotte. And that's why I have a proposal for you."

I grab a pillow and hold it tightly to my chest. "Okay?"

"All these things—you may have stolen them, but you

kept them safe, just like you've kept our family safe for the past six months. In fact, they were as safe in your drawer as they would have been in my jewelry box in my room."

I tilt my head, not understanding.

"Let me put it this way, Charlotte. When I'm searching for something, I'll have two places to look: in my jewelry box and in your drawer. As far as I'm concerned, from now on they're the same. I won't ask how something got in here, or why."

"That's . . . nobody's done anything like that for me since Emmy . . ."

She says, "She was mentioned in your file, too. Emmy must have been a very special friend."

"She was."

"But Charlotte, I also need to be able to trust you. This is your end of the bargain. If I ask you whether you've taken something from me—my ring, my watch, anything—you must answer me truthfully. No secrets between us."

"What if something really does go missing?"

"I promise not to blame you. If you say you don't have it, then you don't have it. I'll trust you for as long as you allow me to do so. However, that means no hiding things anywhere else other than the drawer. And of course it would be nice if you could return the objects before I had to look there in the first place."

Smiling, I reply, "I think I can manage that."

I watch as Harriet delicately slips her possessions into her pocket. Then, just before she goes, she opens my top drawer, sneaks the platinum bracelet back in, and slides it shut.

It's a funny thing, getting caught.

Sometimes, it can be the worst thing in the world, but this time?

It makes me feel more free than I ever have before.

CHAPTER TWENTY-TWO

Testing . . . Testing . . .

Starting right after spring break, I'm wrapped up in testing fever. The whole school is. The teachers give us practice test after practice test. They take down the names of last year's winners from the library bulletin board to make space for the new honorees. We even have a pretest pep rally to fire everyone up. It's called Test Fest. I'm not saying it's the most obsessive thing I've ever seen at a school, but it's close. Mr. Jessup dresses up like a giant no. 2 pencil and chases the student council while they wear sandwich-board Scantron sheets. It's as bizarre as it sounds, but everyone in the gym cheers.

And I have to admit, seeing Deidre's disgusted face as she shuffles around in a mammoth math test gets me giggling, too. Holly, representing Reading Comprehension, seems to be enjoying it as much as everything else she ever does. After the race, which Writing Concepts and Skills wins handily, we all flood the gym floor to visit makeshift booths. At each one, we get helpful testing hints, or free pencils, or a demonstration of how to correctly bubble. I want to make fun of every part of this, but I stay quiet. Brit, Holly, MZ, and the rest of my friends are into it, so I pretend to be, too.

Secretly, I'm miffed that everything that helped me establish my routine gets shut down. Basketball ends (Zero and seventeen! Woo-hoo!), student advisory committee meetings are suspended, and even our curriculum changes. We don't go to the library in Ms. Drummond's class anymore. Nobody has flex time. We stay in our perfectly ordered seats in Mr. Alcontera's room; no trips up to the chalkboard for us. Just drilling for EOGs.

With a week to go, I've got semitanking a standardized test down to a science: On a forty-five-question test, I have to get thirty-seven correct. Every ten questions, I whiff on one. That gives me five misses, plus a buffer of two questions in case there are a couple that legitimately stump me. I try to make my wrong answers hit on questions that I'm not sure about anyway. It's like clockwork; I'm pulling in 82 percents in everything. Good enough to pass, strong enough not to hurt Loblolly's bottom line, but certainly not enough to single me out, bad or good.

When Testmas Eve arrives, Jackson and I are in bed by eight o'clock. My backpack rests against my bedroom door with eight pencils inside, all sharpened to points that put

Lewis Carroll's vorpal sword to shame. Harriet and Jonathan set their alarms for five thirty so that they can get up before us and make the breakfasts we requested. Jackson wants chocolate-chip pancakes, bacon, and OJ. I'm in for challah bread French toast, a plum, and sparkling grape juice. At the breakfast table, Jackson and I quiz each other mercilessly.

"Inferencing!" Jackson fires as he waves a bit of bacon at me.

"Reading between the lines," I declare, and I counter with, "Dividing with decimals in the divisor!"

"Move the decimal to the right, do the same in the dividend," he retorts.

Jonathan swoops in, refilling my fluted champagne glass. "Surprise writing prompt—your most embarrassing moment. What do you do, children? *What do you do?*"

In unison, we reply, "Read all the directions first, then brainstorm!"

"Harriet, I think they're ready," he murmurs, and Harriet salutes us with an oven mitt.

We get to school ten minutes early, and the entire campus is like a ghost town. Eerie breezes sway the loblollies overhead, and a single scrap of loose-leaf drifts along the breezeway connecting the art room to the cafeteria. I glance at Jackson, who knits his brow, huffs, and swings his backpack up into the two-shoulder stance. I steel myself and nod, and we both march away to our classrooms. No good lucks. No well-wishes. No signs of weakness.

I pull open Ms. Millar's door to see that the room is nearly full. Unlike on my first day, nobody looks at me, not even Archer. They're all busy arranging pencils on their desks. Some go for the perfect row. Others prefer the table setting—two to the left, two to the right. Still more go through pains to place their pencils into elaborate designs that resemble magic runes. I slip into my seat and produce my weapons, which I encircle tip-to-tip to make a floral starburst design. Holly looks up from her fractal pattern and whispers, "Ahhh, the graphite gardenia. Good choice."

I nod and cast a glance back at Brit. She salutes me, and I notice she's got her pencils aligned in three perfect squadrons, evenly spaced and ready for battle. I return her salute grimly.

At exactly 8:05, Mr. Jessup's voice crackles from the intercom. He wishes us all luck, reminds us to check our answers, and gives us the testing schedule. I mentally record it.

At exactly 8:08, we begin.

The next four hours of my life are spent locked in. I grind through three-fourths of my flower, rub away five writer's cramps, and go at least nine minutes, thirty-one seconds without blinking. Twice. I'm like clockwork, writing down all my answers on the scrap paper as soon as I bubble them, then calculating which ones I need to miss. I record the changes I make, too, and by the time I'm done, my scrap paper looks like some random cereal-box-code cypher. My test form, though, is pristine. I triple-check everything, and by the time Ms. Millar says the final "Stop.

Pencils down!" I'm certain I've nailed it. A perfect 82 percent in every section. A thing of glory.

That's not to say I'm sorry to see my materials go. All my hard work is crammed into a manila envelope, joining Archer's blank sheets, Holly's even rows of calculation, Brit's smeared scribbling, and Cuss's illustrations of tanks. We watch as Ms. Millar retrieves her keys from her purse, unlocks the top drawer of her filing cabinet, and nestles the envelope in there. Then she pushes the drawer closed with a satisfying clank. It's a sound that carries the weight of finality, and as it rings off the concrete walls and linoleum floors, we release a collective sigh. Archer high-fives Holly, and I turn around to offer Brit a congratulatory nod. We did it.

As the lunch bell sounds, we wordlessly make our way to the cafeteria. There will be dancing along the breezeways eventually, but not yet; the eighth graders have an additional thirty minutes to go, and all the kids with extended time are still fighting the good fight. It's pretty amazing, actually; I'll bet there are cloisters of monks who don't move from cell to chapel this quietly. The traffic signal doesn't even tickle yellow once.

It's not until Latin class that Mr. Jessup's voice reaches us again. "This concludes EOG testing for the spring semester. Congratulations, Loblolly!"

Forget the traffic signal; I think we might register on the Richter scale. It's impossible to feel anything but jubilant. All of us kicked our own tails to prepare for this, whether to uphold the Loblolly tradition, pave our way into a private high school, or to protect our identities and families. It truly is a time to celebrate.

For dinner, we decide to risk going out to a little diner called Elmo's. It's positively pleasant; Jackson and I mess around with crayons like we're five years old, Harriet and Jonathan smile at each other, and nobody says *awesomesauce*.

It's almost perfect—except, of course, for the five blank messages we have on the phone when we get home.

919-555-2113 ———————— No Response

919-555-2331 ———————— No Response

919-555-3321 ———————— Ruled Out

919-555-3313 ———————— No Response

919-555-3213 ———————— No Longer in Service

919-555-1131 ———————— No Response

919-555-3333 ———————— Local Business

919-555-2221 ———————— Ruled Out

919-555-2232 ———————— Ruled Out

919-555-2122 ———————— No Longer in Service

919-555-1233 ———————— No Response

919-555-1111 ———————— Local Business

919-555-1113 ———————— Ruled Out

919-555-1222   Call Back Needed

919-555-3222   Call Back Needed

919-555-3323   Call Pending

919-555-2323   Call Pending

919-555-2321   Call Pending

CHAPTER TWENTY-THREE

Scores

There are still projects to finish, movies to watch, and events to enjoy, so we don't completely check out after the EOGs are over. I'll admit, it's hard to concentrate. I even log a couple of legit B-minuses, no tweaking necessary. And I do have an excuse—most of my energy these days goes toward preparing for School Spirit Day.

The Day, as everyone calls it, is a huge celebration near the end of the year, highlighted by several key moments. There's the field games in the morning, like relay races, intergrade tug-of-war, and a massive water-balloon battle. Lunch is a humongous barbecue, which I've already been assured is not a pig-pickin'. After that, we return to our homerooms, and things get serious. Ms. Millar will pass out our EOG test scores. We're not supposed to open them until the final assembly, when our parents will be there to make sure we don't doctor up, play down, or "accidentally lose" the results. I gather it's a real agony/ecstasy moment. MZ told me that they tried once to get everyone to wait until they got home to open the scores, but the parents nearly revolted. To defuse the tension, they added a staff-student basketball game at the end of the assembly, where the boys' and girls' teams face off against the PE department and any other teachers who don't fear the thought of sweating in front of their students.

"Why can't we just dress this way every day?" Archer whines as we shuffle back to homeroom after lunch. He's wearing his yearbook staff T-shirt and blue jeans, his camera slung over his shoulder.

"Because they give you only one shirt, and you've already spilled sweet tea on it?" I suggest. He looks down and gasps, pawing at the dark, damp splotches with his fingers. Holly and Brit laugh, but all of us quickly simmer down when we see the envelopes in Ms. Millar's hands.

"Find your seats, students. We have only five minutes before we have to report to the gym, and you'll need to take your things; your parents are already there, and you'll be dismissed right after the game. No coming back to the room."

I glance around at my classmates. They're focused on those envelopes like hyenas eyeballing a wounded gazelle. Cuss is even panting like one.

"When you receive your scores, do not open the envelopes. They are for you and your parents to view at the assembly. Pay attention to—"

"Ms. Millar," Holly interjects, "we have two minutes left. I hate to interrupt, but as student council president, I need to be there on time to help with the announcement."

Ms. Millar twitches her nose. "Fine, fine. If your parents have any questions, they can arrange a conference with Mr. Jessup. Jackie Adelman!"

Jackie, first alphabetically, scurries up to Ms. Millar and grabs her envelope. She clutches it to her chest like Katniss with a care package, and she tucks it into her backpack quickly. The rest of us do the same, except for Cuss, who holds it up to the fluorescent light and peers at it.

"Atticus!" Ms. Millar squeaks.

"Awww. It's too thick to read anyways," he mumbles, and shoves it into his bag.

He's right—the envelope is full near to bursting. I do have to admit, it feels electric in my hands, like the corners are sharp enough to cut me and the whole thing might blow up if jostled the wrong way. I ease it into the front pocket of my backpack and sling the bag over my shoulder. Then I join Brit and Holly in line.

"It's worse than last year," Brit mumbles.

"I know!" exclaims Holly.

"What is?" I ask.

"The burning. Don't you feel it? In your fingertips?"

"Yeah," Brit agrees. "It's like I want to put it on my desk, whip out a machete, and hack at it until slivers of scores rain down into my hair."

"Whoa," I say. "Slow down there." I look to Holly for

support, but instead she's staring at Brit, her hands encircled around an imaginary machete hilt and arms twitching with little swinging motions.

"They do it to torture us," Brit continues. "A final test of our willpower. That's why they invite our parents in, because they know that if school was normal for the rest of the day, we'd all fake having to go to the bathroom just to lock ourselves in a stall and rip our envelopes open."

"Then we'd either sew skirts out of them and wear them as tribal dressings of honor . . ." Holly says.

"Or flush them into the deepest, darkest sewer drain in all of North Carolina," Brit finishes. They both nod at each other in unison.

"O . . . kay," I say, backing off. "I see. . . ."

The shared hysteria is even more profound on the way to the gym. I overhear one sixth grader murmuring, "Yes, Mother. I got a good night's sleep the night before. No, Mother, I did not skip a problem." He's stroking his backpack as he talks. I shudder but hold my bag a little closer, too.

In the gym, our parents are already seated on the back six rows of bleachers. We're forced to cram into the front, shoulder to shoulder. It's made more difficult because a number of moms and dads have leaped down the aisles at their kids, clawing at their backpacks and demanding to see the envelopes. When the entire gym is finally sardined full, Holly is invited up to say the school motto. I look for Jackson, who is wedged into the middle of the sixth-grade section. Harriet and Jonathan are waving enthusiastically at us from the top of the bleachers. I blush as I wave back.

"Thank you again, Loblolly families," Holly reads from the podium, pausing every few moments to bat her eyelashes at the crowd, "for your dedication to academic excellence. You are the true heart and soul of this great school. It is your motivation, trust, and, above all, patience that enables us to succeed year after year. On behalf of the PTA, the school board, student council, and all the faculty and staff of Loblolly Middle School, I, Holly Fiellera, humbly request that you exercise that signature patience now as we invite you to find your child or children, open those envelopes, and reserve your judgment for later this evening!"

Holly's words get completely overwhelmed right after the word *open*. Instantly, the entire parent section is standing, calling out their children's names. Some kids whip out their envelopes and sprint up the risers. Others make a break for the gym door.

I find Harriet and Jonathan. On my way, I pass by Cuss, who's pleading with his mother as she double-fists his results.

"But Ma, I was sure! Keel is to boat is *not* as grass is to cow! The grass! The keels! They are not as is!"

I offer Cuss a sympathetic shrug before Harriet and Jonathan sweep me up.

"So, Charlotte? How did you do?" Harriet asks nervously.

"Yes, Charlotte . . . did your expert wit and impeccable academic acumen kill us all, or are we safely mediocre yet again?" Jonathan whispers. Harriet slaps his arm.

"That's not funny."

"It is, a little," Jonathan retorts, and I hand him the envelope. With a finger calloused from a lifetime of opening business letters, he rips the results free. My hands begin to spasm as I track his eyes, which rove over the first page slowly. He scowls as he reads on, and as he nears the end, he shakes his head.

"Oh, Charlotte . . . we expected better. We know you're capable of so much more than the eighty-second percentile. Honey, do we need to get you a tutor?"

My hug buries his mischievous grin. Harriet follows suit, sandwiching me between both of my adoptive parents until Holly's voice over the loudspeaker forces us apart.

"And now, all you Fightin' Pineconies, it's time for the annual staff-student basketball game! Players, if you could make your way back down to the court, and families, find your seats. Tip-off is in just a few moments!"

As I pull away, I say, "Time to score my big two points and ride the pine! Wish me luck. . . . The bench has splinters. . . ."

Jonathan replies, "In all seriousness, Charlotte, both your mother and I understand how hard this was for you." He pauses, holding up the 82 percenter like I just nailed a perfect score. "We saw how you worked, how you've been working. This basketball game . . . it doesn't count, right?"

I glance around. "Well, it's tough to tell, but I don't think I see any WNBA scouts here."

He laughs. "Precisely. Go have a little fun. Blow off some steam. You've earned it."

Harriet nods in agreement. "Go show us what you can do, Char."

I arch my eyebrow, but then a smile creeps its way across my lips. "Okeydokey, Mom," I say. "But to tell you the truth, I don't have a clue what I can actually do. I've never tried before."

Jonathan gives me another quick hug and says, "Whatever it is, it'll make us proud, daughter. And now, excuse us . . . I finally see Jackson."

I have to leapfrog over five families to get back to the court, but I make it with plenty of time to spare. It turns out I don't even get in the game until the second quarter. When I do, we're already losing by thirty, and Mr. Jessup alone has outscored our entire roster. Everyone else on the court is so tired of his kicking their behinds on play after play that as he moves the ball up the sideline, I'm the only one left to guard him.

"C'mon, Charlotte!" he says as he crosses over six times in rapid succession. "Let's show 'em how it's done in the Queen City!"

The kids in the crowd roar at his display of skill. At least, I imagine they do. All I hear is the rhythm of his dribbling. The ball looks as big, as wide as any pocket I've ever picked. He goes into another display of behind-the-back bravado, and as he does, my limbs snake out. One hand shoots up at Mr. Jessup's nose, stopping well short but getting close enough to cause him to flinch. The other swipes downward at the bottom of the ball's dribbled descent.

Mr. Jessup is left holding his arms wide, wondering where the ball went. I'm already five steps past him. I miss the layup badly, of course, but Amanda cleans it up. On our way back on defense, I stop at half court, waiting.

My hands are ready.

"Don't know how you did that just then," Mr. Jessup declares, "but you aren't . . ."

I lunge toward his left hip, and he twists to the right to shield the ball. Naturally, that's where my hand is waiting. I knock the ball to Desiree, and we're off and running again. She scores, and Mr. Crane whips the ball in to Mr. Jessup for a third time. He starts dribbling protectively, keeping it so low to the ground that it sounds like a jackhammer. Wiping the sweat from his eyes, he begins, "Charlotte, you've got—"

Too late. Already stole the ball.

By the end of my first five minutes, I'm feeling serene, just enjoying myself. I don't really bother to keep track of what's going on score-wise; I think we're still losing big, but it doesn't matter. I get in twice more, and for the first time in a long while, I'm having fun, plain and simple, letting my mind clear and my hands do their thing.

Basketball as therapy . . . who knew?

At the end of the game, I barrel my way through the

crowd, trying not to fall down or accidentally stumble into anyone who might try to shake my hand. When I reach Harriet and Jonathan, they pull me close.

"That was amazing, Charlotte! They couldn't get the ball past you!"

"We still lost by forty points," I note, nodding toward the scoreboard.

"Yeah, but you had twenty-one steals!"

"And two points," I add. Credit where credit's due, after all.

"Twenty-one, Charlotte!" he repeats. "That's unheard-of!"

"It is?" I ask nervously. My left hand twitches.

"Absolutely! It's amazing!"

"Are you sure? Because I wasn't trying to be amazing. I wasn't really trying to be anything at all . . . just, you know . . ." I shiver.

Jonathan wraps his arms around me, holding me tightly. Together, with Harriet blazing a trail forged of polite *pardon-mes*, we manage to make our way to the gym entrance. The outside is mere steps away, and we're almost free. However, just before we slip out, I feel someone grab my shoulder. I'm pulled from Jonathan's sheltering embrace and spun around. There, inches away, is Archer Brantley's perfect, smug grin. In his left hand, he's holding his camera.

"See, Charlotte," he says, grinning, "I knew you were hiding something!"

Stepping back, he aims the muzzle of his Canon at us,

and he presses the button. The camera clicks away like machine-gun fire, taking picture after picture. All three . . . no, four of us—Jackson's slipped in right next to Harriet on our way out—wince in unison. I suppose from some sort of angle, to some terribly blind person, it might seem like we're smiling.

"There! These'll look nice on the website—the entire Trevor family, together!"

Before any of us can make a desperate grab at the camera, or come up with some excuse to get those photos deleted, a flood of families pushes us out the door. I wrench around, clambering and fighting against the surge, but it's no use. As we're swept into the parking lot, all I can see is Archer's perfectly combed hair, sinking into the masses like the disappearing fin of a well-sated shark.

CHAPTER TWENTY-FOUR

Fault Lines

"It's not the end of the world," Jackson argues as we stumble into the kitchen. "It's just a stupid basketball game."

"It *is* the end of the world, Jackson!" I yell. "Our faces are going to be on the school website. The internet-searchable, super-readable, browse-in-prisonable school website!"

"Oh," he mumbles.

I collapse into a chair. "I'm sorry. I should have stopped. I just didn't know, you know? I spent an entire season on the basketball team aggressively trying to suck at it. Besides, it's not like it was the state championship! We lost by forty in a game that's just for fun!"

"We told you it was okay, Char," Harriet says as she strokes my hair. "You can't hide everything all the time, and it's not fair for anyone to expect you to."

Jonathan comes in from the kitchen and sets down his phone. "Well, Deputy Marshal Stricker says she'll see what she can do, but she wants us to try to contain it ourselves, if we can." He pauses, his brow furrowing and lips tightened in his best Janice impersonation. "'We're not the CIA, you know!'"

"Can't we just go into the principal's office and ask her to—" Jackson offers, but Jonathan cuts him off.

"Janice said it was out of the question. It would draw too much attention. And besides, we may not have time to go through the school bureaucracy anyway. The marshals are worried that the Cercatores might be using picture-scanning software to monitor the internet. We're on the clock here."

We sit there for another awkward minute, chewing nails, drumming on tabletops, or scratching at itches that aren't there. Finally, looking at Harriet, Jonathan, and Jackson, I say, "I'm very tired."

We agree to go to bed and talk again in the morning. And I *am* tired, but I don't feel well, and I spend an hour twisting and turning, above the sheets and beneath, hugging pillows and flinging them to the floor. None of it works. So I decide to read.

As soon as I've slipped my black velvet bookmark free, I'm calmer. I curl myself against the headboard of my bed, leaning so close to the words that they go fuzzy for a moment. My hair falls around my face, framing the book and cutting the light from my bedside lamp. In that veiled space, I disappear.

I put down my copy of *The Amber Spyglass* only when I

hear movement outside my room. My clock says it's one a.m., and when I stretch out, my entire bed creaks. In response, Jackson's voice whispers through the keyhole.

"Hey, Charlotte. Are you awake?"

Opening the door, I see not only Jackson, but Jonathan as well. They're wearing matching Duke T-shirts, and it looks like both of them have been lying awake as long as I have.

"You actually seem like you're better off than you were five hours ago, Char," Jonathan notes.

"I was reading. It settles me down."

"That's good. Harriet managed to fall asleep," Jonathan says. "I figured I'd spare her my own nerves. Jackson found me on the couch. We're going to think some more, maybe over pizzelles and milk. Care to join us?"

I nod, and in a few moments, Jackson and I are seated at the kitchen counter. Jonathan slips a plate of pizzelles in front of me.

"I grabbed my best wristwatch," he says, holding his arm out. "In case, you know, you needed to . . ."

I sigh. "Mom told you about that?"

"Yep. We're kind of married. She tells me about everything."

I smile and shake my head. "Thanks for the offer, but I'm okay with cookies."

"So what's on your mind?"

I grab a pizzelle, sweeping a finger along the delicate ridges and grooves of the cookie. The scent of vanilla fills the space between us.

"I can't figure out what to do," I admit.

Jackson pulls his phone from the pocket of his PJs.

"The pictures aren't up yet, at least."

I shrug. It's only a matter of time. "This is all my fault, guys. I'm so, so sorry."

Jonathan picks out a pizzelle of his own and takes a ruminating bite. Then he waves his finger.

"Don't be ridiculous, Charlotte. You're not the one who took that picture, or the one who put us in danger in the first place. It's like I tell Elena . . ."

"Harriet?"

"Your mother . . . it's like I tell her every time she's up at night crying about destroying her family. It's not her fault they're criminals. Their behavior tore apart the Cercatores, not her. It's the same with you. None of us blames you. Not even Jackson!"

Jackson furrows his brow. "Well . . ."

Jonathan starts sliding the plate of cookies away from him.

"Fine. No. It's not Charlotte's fault."

Shaking a few clingy crumbs from my fingers, I nod. "Yeah, I know, but . . ."

"But you just really wanted to hear someone else say it."

I eventually smile; for not being my real dad, Jonathan does seem to have me down pretty well.

"So the pictures aren't up yet, right?" I mutter, rubbing at my temples like Harriet sometimes does. "What if I confront Archer? Ask him not to post the pictures? Maybe we could tell him that Jackson shouldn't be in the picture, like he's too young, or something. And maybe I can bribe Archer. I'll offer to sit with him at lunch."

Jackson grins. "I thought you said you'd bribe him, not threaten him. . . ."

"Funny. Anyway, we'll tag team it. He'll have a more difficult time saying no if we're both there asking."

Jonathan scoops up the empty plate and drops it in the sink, letting it clatter with finality. "Then it sounds like we have a plan. Put it in the corner of your minds, let it hibernate there until morning. We all need the rest."

After grimly toasting with the last of our milk and cookie shards, we head up to bed. I can't even imagine what it would've been like trying to cope with this before Harriet found my secret; knowing that my family trusts me is the only thing keeping me from completely losing it. But Harriet and Jonathan won't be at Loblolly to help me. All I've got is Jackson, the kid who spent the better part of a year punching pillows and imagining they were my face. Somehow, it doesn't seem like enough, because this problem isn't like the others. It was one thing when I was helping Holly with Deidre, or telling Brit's mom about her combat-quilting, or deleting Jackson's Facebook page. It's another thing entirely when Charlotte Trevor is the one front and center, all because I allowed a little bit of Nicki Demere to shine through.

So, Mr. Cercatore, I take it the time has come to discuss the particulars of my role in your efforts to find your sister?

-As usual, you are being retained to consult on legal matters, and particularly in my defense, should it be necessary.

You have established a plausible alibi?

-Perhaps.

Only perhaps? I do take it that you've found some evidence of your sister's whereabouts?

-Yes. A photograph, posted online this morning.

Have you located her for certain, then?

-Very nearly. There remains a complication.

How's that?

-A girl in the photo. She is identified as a member of the family, though she is no relation of Elena's.

But you are certain the woman pictured is your sister?

-Yes. Her husband and son are there as well.

This girl–is she, maybe, the same one your nephew mentioned in his Facebook post? The sister?

-I believe so. I should not have been so quick to dismiss that evidence.

Well, then, if the girl doesn't belong to Elena, who does she belong to?

-That is where you come in. You get your legal sources to answer that question, and I'll have my alibi.

I shall start making inquiries immediately, Mr. Cercatore.

CHAPTER TWENTY-FIVE

Boom

I'm peering over Brit's shoulder in homeroom. Her laptop is open, and staring back at us is one of the pictures of my family. We look like some sort of troglodyte clan, just emerging into the sun for the first time.

"We've got to get that picture down," I growl.

"No, it's okay, Charlotte. You still look pretty. . . . It's . . . it's not that weird of a smile," Brit says. I mutter a thank-you, but I can't concentrate; it's hard not to cast glances Archer's way. As soon as the bell rings, Jackson and I are cornering him outside the door.

"Hey, Charlotte!" he says as he sees me hovering in the breezeway. "Noticed you were staring at me all through homeroom. Like what you see?"

I resist the urge to throw up in my mouth a little.

"Yeah, actually, I was," I admit. "I . . . that is, we've got a favor to ask of you."

Jackson shuffles up next to me, his own dark hair falling over his eyes in a way that seems to mock Archer's perfect blond bangs.

"We? What we? Oh." He purses his lips. It makes him look like a well-groomed duck. "The Trevor clan. What can I do for you?"

"The pictures from yesterday . . . the ones up on the school website. We'd like them taken down."

"And the files deleted," Jackson adds.

"Huh? No! I like those photos!"

I breathe deeply. We anticipated this.

"And they're great photos," I lie. "But Jackson doesn't like pictures of himself online. They make him uncomfortable, and you didn't have his permission to . . ."

"Tough luck. He was at an all-school function. I have a right as part of the yearbook committee to take photos at any event that includes the entire student body. Yesterday totally qualifies."

"We're asking you to be nice, Archer."

"It's out of my hands!" he says, raising them as if to show us. "They're already up!"

With a sigh, I resign myself to plan B.

"If you take the pictures down, Archer—"

"And delete the files!" Jackson interjects again.

"Yes, and delete the files, I'll sit with you at lunch for the rest of the week. Everyone will see, and you can—"

Archer laughs, throwing his arms up in the air in a weird hallelujah. He goes on laughing until he has to catch his breath by leaning against one of the metal breezeway supports. I cast a glance at Jackson, who shrugs.

"Now?! *Now* you'll give me the time of day?" Archer gasps, his smile so wide I can see his wisdom teeth. "After every time I tried to talk to you after class? All our one-sided conversations in the library? All those times I called your house and hung up, just to see if you were home? All those . . ."

He keeps talking, I think.

All those times he called my house and hung up . . .

Jackson is tugging at my sleeve, I think.

Those hang-up calls . . .

My hand sweeps around so quickly that even I can't see it. I miss his face, but the slap pings satisfyingly off the metal support, shocking Archer into silence and probably pummeling his eardrum. It feels good enough that I do it again, hitting the metal three more times before I lunge forward.

"It was *you*," I hiss.

"Charlotte, don't . . ." Jackson warns, but I'm too far gone: The nightmares, the disrupted evenings—evenings we could have been sharing as a *family*, rather than hoping the phone wouldn't ring again.

"You can't just do that, Archer! You can't play those stupid games with me!"

"Why not? Everybody does. I like you, so I—"

313

"I don't care!" I scream, smacking the pillar again with my palm. "How? How could we not trace your call?"

"It's just an emergency phone my dad got me! It ran out of minutes last week anyway, so you don't have to worry. . . ."

I blink back tears. "We always have to worry! That's the point! You don't get to call our house like that! You don't get to mess with us!"

As my voice gets louder and louder, Ms. Millar opens her door. Jackson actually puts his hand over my mouth to shut me up. I nearly bite him.

"What is going *on* out here?" she demands. "And why aren't you three in class?"

I try to respond, but the exhaustion of the last six months hits me like a train. I swoon, and I have to grab the support. It's Jackson who saves us.

"Just doing a scene from a TV show last night. Stupid, I know. We're done. I'll get my sister to class."

"Well," Ms. Millar huffs, "this is my planning period. I need it quiet out here, and you all need to move before I call Mr. Jessup."

"Yes, ma'am."

Archer, still stunned, stands there until Ms. Millar closes the door. Jackson turns to him next.

"Go away, and don't say a word of this to anyone. If you do, I'll tell all Charlotte's friends that you made her cry. I'll tell *Holly* that you were mean to Charlotte."

Archer blanches, grabs his backpack, and stumbles off. I doubt Jackson's threats held much weight, but when punctuated by the death stare I was giving him, we probably bought ourselves a few hours, at least. I slump down against the pillar and hang my head.

"Well, that couldn't have been part of the plan," Jackson says, sitting next to me.

"I blew up," I admit.

"Oh yeah, you did. Big-time."

I exhale raggedly, wiping at my eyes with my sleeve. "We're doomed, Jackson. Janice will have to move us, and we'll have to start over. We'll have to . . ."

"Why?"

I sniffle. "Because it's not safe here anymore. I . . . I guess it never was, but it's worse now. I've been so busy trying to fit in by helping Holly and Brit and everyone else that I didn't realize that I had nobody who could help *us* if we needed it. I can't risk involving a teacher, Mom and Dad can't help, and Janice is hundreds of miles away. We really are alone here, Jackson."

"Tell Brit."

"What?"

Jackson waves his phone around. "She knew how to deal with my Facebook thing. Maybe she can fix this?"

"Oh right," I grumble. "'Hey, Brit, can you just hack the school website for me? I'd, like, totally owe you!'"

"No, Nicki. *Tell* Brit."

The sound of my own name, my real name, shocks me. When I don't respond, Jackson continues. "I saw how upset you got about the gloves—and no, I know it wasn't just your weird, creepy hand thing. You got upset because they were from *her*. Your best friend, and she had no clue."

"Yeah, so?" I manage.

"So it's obvious."

I scowl, which must look absolutely terrifying when layered atop everything else I'm feeling.

"Jeez . . . chill for, like, half a second. What I mean is, when I'm going nuts, when I can't handle it, I get to be mad. I get to freak out and have people defend me. Like Mom and Dad do. Like my older sister did."

"Harriet and Jonathan would defend me," I argue, thinking of my room, and of my drawer.

"Sure, Mom and Dad will listen, and they'll do what they can to help. But they're parents, too. There's gonna be stuff you can't talk to them about. Stuff you won't want to talk to them about. Believe me, I know."

I think of Jackson outside Harriet and Jonathan's room, so lonely and afraid that he couldn't sleep, but so mad that he couldn't turn that knob. I nod.

"And I don't want to have to be the kid you unload on," he continues. "That's what friends are for. So tell Brit, because you need her."

He gets up, shrugging his backpack over his shoulders. As he walks away, he adds, "And we need you."

CHAPTER TWENTY-SIX

Promises, Promises

"Brit," I say just as the bell rings. "Can you meet me in the bathroom during language arts? Tell Ms. Drummond I've gone to the nurse, then ask to use the restroom, like, ten minutes in? We need to talk."

"Huh? Are you not feeling well?"

I shake my head. "I'm fine . . . sort of. Late night last night, but yeah, I'm well enough. We . . . we just really need to talk is all, and it can't wait."

"Um, okay, Charlotte. I'll be there, if you're . . . you're sure you're all right."

Brit hugs her laptop to her chest. It wasn't my intent to scare her, but I don't have time to explain—especially not here.

"Just . . . I'll see you in the bathroom," I say, wrinkling

my nose. As far as good-byes go, that's about as awkward as it gets.

Those ten minutes are excruciating; every time a sixth grader rolls through, I have to pretend I'm washing my hands. By the time Brit slips in, my fingers are all pruny, and I've shredded half a loblolly's worth of paper towels.

I immediately close the door, moving the beat-up aluminum trash can behind it. It won't prevent anyone from coming in, but it'll give us some warning first.

"Charlotte, what . . ."

"Brit," I begin, my voice breaking almost immediately. My hands are shaking so badly I have to grab the sink next to her just to steady myself. When I continue, I'm looking at her face in the mirror, rather than right at her. She's blushing, breathing quickly. It's like we're staring at each other through one of her computer-game screens. "Remember how . . . how we got Jackson's Facebook page down? Can you do the same for that picture of us on the school website?"

She opens her mouth for a moment, and her glasses slip down her nose. She fumbles to push them back up.

"Oh," she says softly. "Oh, was that what . . . Wait, Charlotte . . . but why?"

"It has to come down, Brit."

She places a timid, trembling hand on my shoulder. "But it's not so bad. . . ."

"No!" I say, way too loudly. It reverberates through the bathroom, almost like the dirty pink tiles and infinitely grouted toilets had finally had enough and were rising up in protest of gossip, girlfights, and middle school melodrama. My whisper blends in with the last of those echoes. "No, Brit. It's not about that."

"You're acting like this is a matter of life and death!"

Now I turn to face her, and her hand falls limply from my shoulder.

"It is."

"But that doesn't make any sense . . . and . . . and taking the photo down, Charlotte . . . that's hacking. It's not just like getting Jackson's phone and autologging in. I'd have to get around the firewall, and even if I did, they could put it up again if I deleted it. I'd . . . I'd have to actually mess with the website itself. And if I get caught . . ."

"Can you do it, though?"

"Yeah . . . I mean, I think so, yeah, but . . ."

I step toward her, so close our foreheads nearly touch. She sees the tears welling in my eyes, and she gasps.

"Please, Brit. Please," I whisper.

"Charlotte, you're scaring me. . . ."

I try not to blink, but I fail, and a tear traces its way down my cheek. I remind myself that this is the new plan, but that doesn't make it easier.

"It's . . . it's not Charlotte."

It comes out so quietly I'm not even sure I've said it, but Brit takes a step backward, so I know I've at least done *something*. She rubs her temple, shaking her head like she's trying to clear a glitch from her system.

I take a deep, ragged breath.

"My name isn't Charlotte. I'm Nicki. Nicki Demere."

Brit simply slips her glasses off rather than mess with them anymore. "But . . ."

"I'm not from Ohio. I'm from New York City. So is the rest of my family. Only . . . only they're not my real family. All of us . . . we're in witness protection. Well, they are, and I'm . . . I'm sort of there to help hide them. Except I seem to suck at it lately."

A quick glance in the mirror shows me just how scary-desperate I look.

"This is unreal, Charlotte. . . . I don't understand. . . ."

"I can prove it," I say softly. "Take out your laptop."

Brit hesitates, like she's trying to decide whether to humor me or check me for a fever. I murmur, "Please?"

She nods and slides her laptop up onto the corner of a sink. I lean over, typing in the address for *The New York Times*. When it comes up, I do a search. I'm rewarded with a series of pictures, along with dozens of grim headlines. Below the words *Accused Killer Walks Free Again* is a photo of Arturo. I step aside, gesturing to the screen. Brit puts her glasses back on and squints at the picture.

"Remind you of anyone you know?" I ask gravely.

"He . . . he looks like your mom."

"They're brother and sister. He's a Cercatore. So is she."

"The Cercatores? Like on the news?"

I nod. Brit begins clicking on other pictures, other articles. Each one features an image of one of Elena's family members. Each one causes her to gasp.

"Oh my God, Charlotte . . . you're serious!"

"That's why . . ." I pause, struggling. I practiced this speech, like, two hundred times in my head. Not a single word of it is coming back to me now, of course, and before I can concoct something to say, I'm interrupted in the worst way.

A spine-shivering screech claws at our eardrums as the trash can skids across the rough concrete floor. Our heads turn simultaneously, and we see Bethanny Karstens there, staring at us from beneath her blond bob. After she sizes us up, she slips inside.

Sniffling in a desperate attempt to shift gears, I step in front of her. "Do you mind? We were kind of talking."

She smirks. "I can see that. You two, like, need to get a room."

I glance back at Brit, who is just stricken. She hasn't stopped gaping at me.

"Hellooo, Bethanny," I retort, waving my hand across the bay of sinks. "We kind of did get a room. This is our room."

"The bathroom . . . is your room?" she mumbles skeptically.

"Yup. This one's claimed. Find another one . . . or I'll tell Deidre you misplaced her ballots."

The merest mention of the election has Bethanny

scurrying out so quickly she nearly trips. After the door closes behind her, it cracks open again a second later. Her hand snakes around, grabbing the trash can and dragging it back into position. Then the door thuds into place. As a precaution, I yank a nearly finished roll of toilet paper off the holder, bend it in two, and shove it beneath the door like a jamb. It should keep anyone else from coming in, but I leave the trash can there just in case. Brit watches me, dumbfounded.

"So, yeah," I manage, "I'm serious. And I'm so, so sorry to drag you into this."

"All those nights you came over . . . eating lunch every day . . . the mall, study breaks, all of it . . . that wasn't really you?"

I can actually see the hurt beginning to coalesce in her, and I take her by the shoulders, like a field doctor trying to stem the bleeding. "It was me, just . . . just with the mother of all secrets. I wanted to tell you, you more than anyone, but I couldn't."

"So why now, Charlotte?"

"Because I can't do this without you. And I'm not just talking about getting a picture off the school website. I'm talking about all of it—the hiding, the lying, the distance. You said you like me because I'm not a part of what's here. I'm sorry, Brit, but I can't be separate from everything. I need something that's real. And my time with you? Our friendship? It's been the closest thing to real I've had. That's why it's hurt more than anything to keep myself from you. . . ."

She reaches up, lifting her hand in the closeness between us. It stops the spill of my words, letting the silence scar over the space.

After many moments, she finally says, "So tell me."

I can't reveal everything—I know that. It's too much, and I can't risk scaring her off or bringing her any closer to the danger we face. So the Sicurezzas, the trial, Janice, Glynco: I can't tell her about any of it.

But I can tell her about me. And so I do. I start from the very beginning—the Center, my hands, my grammy, all of it. Brit listens, and as I empty out the truth, a heaviness lifts. All my bad things, all my disasters are adventures again, stories to share instead of secrets to keep. It's better than hiding, better than stealing, better even than the feeling of Harriet's arms around me.

For the first time in a long time, I am known.

When I'm finished, she hugs me. The combined thumping of our heartbeats feels strong enough to shake the walls. It's a long time before I find my voice again.

"Yeah, so if that photo doesn't come down, they could relocate us—make us disappear. Or the Cercatores could find us."

Brit scowls. "I don't want you to disappear. I just re-found you. No. You can't disappear."

"Or die. Don't forget the dying part."

"Yes, both, Charlotte. Promise me you'll never do both. Or either."

I sigh. "I can't promise that, Brit. If there's one thing I've learned in my life, it's that things don't always work out, and then, well, you know . . ."

She straightens, her arms folding before her as she steps away from me. "You've gotta promise, or I'm not doing this."

In that moment, I can see Emmy back at the Center, wondering where I've gone. I see Erin and AJ, waving goodbye in Glynco.

I see myself, finding out that my dad could've come for me but never did.

"I promise," I reply.

We walk out of the bathroom a few moments later, arm in arm, and we stay like that all the way back to Ms. Drummond's classroom. When we both enter at the same time, she looks up just once. I think the combined intensity on our faces is enough to keep her from mentioning all the mentionables. A dozen times through the rest of her lesson I catch Brit's eyes, and we nod. It feels good to have her on my side, finally and for real. I just wish I could take the time to enjoy it. There's still that nagging little issue of the picture on the website, after all, along with a much, much bigger problem.

I have to tell Harriet and Jonathan about Brit.

I watch as Jackson reaches for the saltshaker. He taps a few grains into his palm and flicks them around with his

324

thumb. Then he upends the shaker over our kitchen table, slapping the bottom of it until he's got a fair-sized drift in front of him. With the tip of his finger, he smooths the mound flat and draws a tic-tac-toe board.

"*X*s or *O*s, Charlotte?"

I scowl, showing him my left hand. It's shaking so badly that I'd obliterate the board if I even tried to play. He shrugs and turns to Brit, who scoots away a few inches.

"Um, when your parents say 'stay right here' . . ."

Jackson presses his finger into the center square, drawing a perfect *X*. "They mean *stay right here*. And you're gonna want to. This one time when they were angry, I tried to sneak over to the bedroom door to listen. They caught me."

"A bad scene?" I ask.

"I believe the words my mom used were, 'You're so grounded that the next party you attend will be your own wake.'"

I swallow. "And were they . . ."

"About half as mad as they looked when you told them Brit knows our secret."

"But . . . but they didn't yell," Brit offers, biting her lower lip.

"Yeah, you see, my parents . . ." Jackson pauses, glancing at me for a moment. "*Our* parents are the kind that have that extra gear of angry. They go right past yelling and into—"

"Seething?" I guess, shuddering. Jackson nods, and we fall silent. I strain to hear anything from down the hallway.

I'll admit, it would be so much better if Harriet and Jonathan *were* yelling. It's what Jackson, Brit, and I had planned on when we talked after school: I'd tell our parents that trying to get Archer to take the photo down didn't work, and we got desperate. They'd yell a bunch, we'd weather it, and then they'd see that it was the best play in an impossible situation. After all, better to risk getting help from someone I trust than leaving the picture up there.

When we finally hear Harriet's and Jonathan's footsteps, all three of us wince. Jackson quickly brushes the salt into his lap, folding his arms over the mess. I notice Harriet's eyes first. She's been crying, and not a little. The explanation I was going to offer gets swept away right along with Jackson's salt, and we're left staring at the floor for a solid minute until Jonathan speaks.

"Brit," he declares, and she jumps.

"Yes, sir?"

"You took the picture down?"

"Yes, sir."

"How?"

"Well," she says sheepishly, "it was actually, um, pretty easy. I did it in study hall at the end of the day. I just found out when the firewall was due to have its update, waited for the two-minute vulnerability window, hacked in, and changed the website's HTML code. Now every JPEG they upload will automatically get covered by a new CSS, so that it looks blank. I also went ahead and deleted the photos from their servers, but if Archer or anyone else tries to upload them again, they'll just be hidden behind walls of nothing. It's kind of cool, because they'll think the upload failed, but they won't get an error message to help them figure it out. I guess . . ."

She trails off, blushing furiously as Jonathan stares at her stoically. I jump in to try to save her.

"See? Brit knows what she's doing—"

"Which is more than we can say for you," Harriet interjects. I slump down in my seat.

"It's more than we can say for any of us," Jonathan says, and he puts his hand on my shoulder. I stop breathing for a moment.

"We talked, your mother and I," he continues. "We don't blame you for what you did, Charlotte. You made a choice, and it was with our best interest in mind. Know that we appreciate that. We are deeply concerned, however, and we're disappointed that it seemed to be the only option for you, but we understand—getting the picture down was the priority. Even now, it may be that the damage has already been done. It may be that you've saved us. It may be that we've traded one danger for another. Time will tell, I suppose."

Harriet wags her finger. "What is clear, though, is that we can't take risks anymore. We were wrong to relax, and to encourage you to do the same at your basketball game. From now on, we play our roles every single moment of every single day, no exceptions."

"But we're not grounded?" Jackson asks hopefully.

I shake my head. "She's saying we're permanently grounded. All of us."

Jonathan squeezes my shoulder softly, letting me know I've hit the mark. Jackson scowls.

"This was a good plan! And it was my idea, by the way. Charlotte didn't know what to do, so I told her to tell Brit. It's like you said, Mom! It isn't fair for anyone to expect us to hide everything all the time."

Harriet glances at the ceiling; I can almost hear her counting to ten in her mind. Then she exhales softly. "You're right, Jackson. It's not fair. But it's our lives now. This can't be a slippery slope. There is no 'Oh, telling Brit solved one problem, so telling someone else is okay, too!' Regardless of how much good your plan did, it was a mistake. You both need to swear to us right now that this will never happen again."

"I swear," I say quickly.

"I swear," Jackson grumbles.

"And you, Brit," Harriet adds. "I fear Charlotte has brought you into a dangerous situation, and we must beg your confidence."

"I understand, Mrs. Trevor," Brit says. "I'm not going to pry, or anything like that. And I won't even tell my mom or dad. Charlotte is my best friend. She's . . . she's kind of my only friend. Or was. Is. I mean, because of her I have more friends, but she's . . . she's just really important to me."

I can see Brit growing more flustered, her hands wringing like she's trying to mold the crumbly clay of her words

328

into something recognizable. Under the table, I find her foot with mine, and I give it a little tap for support.

"I guess it's like this, Mrs. Trevor. . . . If Charlotte got hurt, or you all disappeared suddenly, and I ever found out that there was something I could have done to stop it? I couldn't live with that. So I'm glad Charlotte told me. I'd hate it if she didn't, even though I guess I wouldn't know that I didn't know . . . you know?" She grimaces and gives up, sinking into silence as she picks at a little crack in the wood of the table.

Harriet sighs and looks at Jonathan, who shrugs. Then she walks around, taking Brit's hands in hers. Brit flinches, but she doesn't pull away like I would.

"We're grateful for your help," Harriet says gently, "but it needs to end here. Charlotte is not to tell you anything more about who we are and what we're dealing with, and you are not to attempt to help us in any way beyond what you've done already. Do you understand?"

"Yes, ma'am," Brit whispers. "Can . . . can Charlotte and I still be friends?"

"Of course. Based on what I just heard, I doubt we could stop you, and that's a good thing. But in any case, it's quite late. Best you head home."

Brit nods, glancing out the window at the gloom between her house and ours. She grabs her backpack and slips from her seat. At the door, she pauses, looking at me. I muster a smile to thank her, and she smiles back. Then she's gone.

Harriet takes her place at the table, staring at Jackson

and me in turns. I brush the hair from my eyes and ask, "Are we going to tell Jani—"

"No. That would only invite more drama. It's time to close ranks and put this behind us."

Jonathan mutters, "So . . . crisis averted, at least for now. I need cake."

It's an awkward ten minutes worth of German chocolate to be sure, but by the end my heart isn't beating so hard. I even manage a snicker at the gentle sound of salt sifting through Jackson's shirt and onto his shoes when he stands. As he sputters through an explanation, and as Harriet stifles a giggle with the back of her hand, I allow myself to think that we may have just survived. Yes, it was scary, but we got the picture down, and I know I can trust Brit with our secret. For now, we're still the Trevors, and we're okay.

I only hope it's not too little, too late.

Incoming Text Msg
From: EnriCercat
To: Rtur0

Touch Yes to Accept

YES

--(start message)--

Li abbiamo trovati.

Address confirmed:

491 Bestel St.

Durham.

--(end of message)--

Do You Wish to Reply?

YES

Outgoing Text Msg
From: Rtur0
To: EnriCercat

--(start message)--

Eccellente.

--(end of message)--

CHAPTER TWENTY-SEVEN

Too Little, Too Late

At Loblolly the next day, I'm forced to deal with the fallout from my nuclear explosion. In fact, the rest of the week is basically high-stakes hide-and-seek. I'm constantly ducking Archer and his friends, not to mention the girls from the basketball team, who have every right to wonder why I didn't bother to go all defensive diva until the game didn't count.

By Friday, I'm exhausted—we all are. I could have gone over to Brit's for the fourth night this week, but I beg off, and instead curl up on the couch under a pink fleecy blanket. Jackson is asleep across from me, and Jonathan is slumped down in his chair, the lamp above him illuminating the copy of *Fahrenheit 451* perched on his chest. I've got my eyes closed, but I'm listening to him read aloud, and every time he drifts off I chuck one of the little embroidered pillows at him.

"Stop that," he murmurs, and glances at his watch.

"They're called throw pillows for a reason. You were falling asleep again."

"It's past midnight. Of course I'm falling asleep."

"Not until—" I interrupt myself with a tonsil-baring yawn. "Not until we finish. We're almost done."

Jonathan stretches, takes off his reading glasses, and sets them on the coffee table.

"I am done. Your mother went to bed two hours ago. Let's finish tomorrow."

"It *is* tomorrow," I say snarkily, pointing to the clock on the DVR box.

"All the more reason to go to bed."

I relent, slithering out from under the comfy fleece and slinging an arm around Jonathan.

"Should we get Jackson?" I ask.

"Nah. Leave him. He gets grumpy when we wake him up."

"It's not just when we wake him up. There's when we say good morning, when we're eating dinner, when we walk by his room, when we . . ."

"You forgot alternate Tuesdays, just because."

He chuckles and starts toward his bedroom. He only makes it a few steps, though, before the phone rings.

"Who could be calling this late?" Jonathan grumbles.

"I bet I know," I fume. "Let me get it."

I hurry over to the phone and rip it off its dock. Sure enough, the number is unlisted. I press the button and bring the phone to my ear.

"Listen, Archer. I'm sorry for freaking out at you, but this stops now. We're not ever going to—"

"Essi sono all'interno."

I pull the phone away in confusion. *"Essi sono all'interno?"* I echo.

Jonathan's eyes widen. Trembling, he translates.

"They are inside."

"Shhh!" I snap, and I cock my head toward the front door.

The third step creaks.

Jonathan scrambles to the switch and cuts off the lights. My fingers hover over the phone, ready to key in Janice's emergency number. When I hear the jostling of the front doorknob, followed by the sound of a quiet curse, I dial.

"I'll use the alarm to call nine-one-one, too," Jonathan whispers, and he creeps toward the hallway. I follow closely behind, the phone up to my ear, and eyes riveted on the windows. The blinds are closed like always, but we can see shadows thrown by the streetlamps. Jonathan and I both freeze as a patch of darkness grows. It slowly climbs the ladder of the blinds until it takes the shape of a man.

Then two.

Then three.

Jonathan bolts toward the front door, and I'm right behind him. He tries to push the blue police button on the alarm pad, but his finger never reaches it. Our mad dash must have made the noise the men were waiting for, because the door explodes inward, knocking Jonathan back against the wall.

Standing in the frame, flanked by two darkly dressed figures, is my bogeyman. My cancer and my killer bees. Somehow, some way, Arturo Cercatore found us.

Just the sight of him hits me like a punch to the chest, a full-body shiver jolting me, paralyzing me. I watch as he steps through the splinters of the shattered door casing, watch as he looms over Jonathan, as he raises a gun.

It's Janice's voice that sets the second hand to spinning again. In my ear, I can hear her: "Charlotte? Charlotte? I just got a message that your alarm system was breached. Are you okay? Charlotte?"

I scream in response. No words—just a scream. And I launch myself at Arturo. I honestly don't know if he's pulling the trigger as I move, or if my movement, my sudden shout causes him to fire. It doesn't matter, because I'm too late. I can't push him down. I can't knock the gun away. My feet aren't fast enough to let me do anything to save Jonathan.

But my hands are.

I snap my right hand out just as I reach him, the phone gripped tightly between my fingers. There's a blinding flash of light, and I turn my head. Someone curses—

I think it's Arturo—and I collapse atop Jonathan, who wraps his arms around me as we both fall to the floor. My ears are ringing. There's a hot slipperiness beneath my fingers, and I can't seem to close them; I can't even move them.

The pain comes as a single, massive throb. I gasp like I'm drowning, and I see Jonathan beneath me. His shoulder is covered in blood. I hear a voice in my head: He's been shot. Find the wound. Put pressure on it. I try to slide my fingers over his shoulder again and again, but there's too much blood, too much pain.

Too much fear.

"Daddy!" I screech, pure panic blurring my vision. "Jonathan! Daddy! I can't find it! I can't find it! I can't . . ."

Jonathan's arms raise, and I feel myself held, crushed to him. At the same time, my head is wrenched backward, and I'm forced to look up into Arturo's face. He's got a hand tangled in my hair, and he's ripping me away. I try to turn, to fight him off, but I'm weak all of a sudden; Jonathan has gripped my right wrist, and I can't seem to pull back. And through it all, I watch this man's face—his horrible, calm, still-eyed face.

Jackson is screaming; Harriet bursts from the bedroom with a baseball bat in her hands, and she brings it down over the closest man's head. He staggers, and she hits him again, and again, until he folds like a crumpled blanket. With a rage I'd never seen, the woman who held me so gently, who forgave my worst mistake, turns against her brother. She lifts the bat again, leaps forward . . .

And freezes.

Arturo, who has let go of me, levels his gun directly at Jackson. Regarding Harriet coolly, he twitches just the tip of his weapon. She flinches, dropping back a step.

"*Saluti, Elena,*" he purrs. "Nice hair."

"Please, Arturo . . . please," she manages, and she puts the bat down. She lifts her hands wide.

"In a few moments, the alarm company will call to ask about the front door?" he asks her. She nods rapidly.

"You will tell them everything is okay. Just a false alarm. If you don't, I'll shoot them. In fact, I'll start with the girl. Maybe it will go through her and into your husband?"

"Okay, Arturo. A false alarm. Whatever you . . ."

Harriet doesn't get a chance to finish. The third man, carrying a crowbar and wearing a hoodie, shouts over her.

"Damnit, Arturo! Who *are* these people? You said this was a simple B&E on an empty house!"

I gasp.

I know that voice.

In the deepest, rawest places in me, those places behind and beneath my heart, I know that voice.

CHAPTER TWENTY-EIGHT

The Bottom of Things

I force myself to look up. He has a full beard now, and his nose is different—flatter. Maybe someone broke it in prison? I don't care. I still recognize my father.

"What . . . how?" I mumble.

"Christian," Arturo says smugly, "say hello to your daughter."

My father reaches up to pull back his hood. His mouth is moving, lips forming words that just don't come. His feet shuffle like he can't decide whether to run, collapse, or take a swing at Arturo with his crowbar.

"That . . . that isn't possible," he says finally.

"Look at her. This is no trick," Arturo commands, and he gestures at me with his gun. I wince.

The only light in the entryway is the bare glow of the streetlights, and my father steps to the side to allow it to wash over me. Then he stares. Hard. I stare right back. His eyes cast about, like he's a sculptor mentally chipping away seven years' worth of change to get at the little girl he knew. I can actually see the moment when it clicks for him.

I didn't have a memory of what my father looked like when he was terrified.

Now I do.

"What the *hell* is she doing here?" he spits, his voice cracking. He points at me with the crowbar like he's warding off some pale, blood-soaked ghost.

"You are right, Christian, and I will admit to a bit of deception here. This is no robbery. What it *is*, though, need not concern you. You have a new task. Take your daughter, get in the second car, and leave."

"What?"

"At our rendezvous point, you will find the remainder of your payment for this job. I have taken the liberty of increasing it tenfold, enough to allow you to hide, comfortably, for the rest of your life—both you and your daughter. And you get to leave here now, before you become either an accessory to murder . . . or a victim of it."

My father presses his palm to his forehead, his teeth bared and gritting. He curses several times under his breath before responding.

"And . . . and what do you get out of this?"

"A scapegoat," Harriet says softly. Arturo smiles, nodding appreciatively at his sister as she continues. "Someone to take the fall. Oh, this is cruel, even for you. . . ."

I expect Arturo to bow, but he doesn't.

"What does she . . . what do you mean, a scapegoat?"

"You're his reasonable doubt," Harriet tells him.

Arturo turns his gun on my father. "My sister, the lawyer. She is correct, Christian. We both profit from this deal. You get your daughter. You get the money. You get a running start. Maybe the cops don't catch you. And if they do, you tell them about us. Perfectly plausible that Arturo Cercatore came here to make a message out of his turncoat sibling, just as it is perfectly plausible that an ex-convict might find that his only daughter has been taken by a family that is not her own. That man might very well seek her out. He might find that family, and when he goes to reclaim his flesh and blood, things could turn violent. Two stories, each one believable. What is a jury to do? Especially when the police find ample evidence of that ex-convict's presence here. . . ."

As his words trail off, Arturo points at the crowbar in my father's hand.

"Drop it. Right there on the ground."

I watch as my father grips the metal so hard his knuckles turn white. He knows his fingerprints are all over it. Still, he lets it clatter to the floor.

"Good. Now you have two hands free," Arturo says. "You can get your daughter."

"What if I don't? What if I just leave? The girl doesn't know me, and I don't know the first thing about . . ."

Arturo levels his gaze. "Christian, my family spent considerable resources to set this in motion. We bribed people. We threatened them. And trust me when I tell you that this is not the first time; we've grown quite good at this. So, given our efforts here, to what lengths do you think we might go to find a man who disappointed us in the manner you're suggesting? One who might conceivably testify in court to what he's seen here?"

It's hard to tell if my father nods or if he's just trembling so badly his head shakes. He wipes his sweaty palms on his flannel shirt and steps toward me.

"No," I manage, and I try to stand, try to push off Harriet and Jonathan so I can fight.

"Charlotte," Jonathan whispers, "you can't. Your hand . . . you saved me, but your hand . . . you've lost too much blood already. You have to be still."

I tear my gaze away from my father long enough to look at my right hand. Jonathan has wrapped his shirt around it, and he's squeezing tightly. A thick ball of pain rolls up my arm, blurring my vision. I can taste the acid on my tongue, like I'm going to throw up, but I resist.

"I'm not going with him."

My father heaves a sigh. He kneels by me, daring to touch my face. I jerk away.

"Honey, I . . ."

A shrill ring from the bedroom interrupts him. The alarm company, calling Harriet's phone. . . .

"Nephew," Arturo croons. "Do be so kind as to go get the phone for your mommy?"

Jackson, shaking worse than I ever have, stumbles his way over the unconscious form of Harriet's bat victim. He emerges with the phone moments later and hands it to Harriet. She grabs him and pulls him into a tight, protective embrace.

"Answer it, Harriet," Arturo says, and he aims the gun at Jackson. As she obeys, woodenly telling the operator that everything is fine, my father leans close to me.

"Can you move?"

I can—just enough to kick out at him. I wish I had the strength to make it hurt. To make him feel my anger. To do something. All I get, though, is a laugh from Arturo.

"Still so much trouble from this one! Do you know, little girl, how many problems you've caused us? Our accountants, our Realtors looking for three people buying homes. One child enrolling in a school. We simply didn't account for you. And my nephew's Facebook page—a boy with a sister? I almost dismissed it entirely. Christian," he says, placing a hand on my father's shoulder, "I can shoot her again if she's too feisty for you to corral."

"Don't touch me, Arturo," he warns.

"Fine. You're right. We are not friends. Take your wounded little bird and fly, or I will kill all of them right here, right now. As for you—" He swivels his gun back on Harriet. "Do what you can for my man there."

I twist to escape my father's grasp, slapping at him with my good hand while Jonathan tries to calm me. As I squirm, though, I catch sight of Jackson. I've never seen him so afraid, so hurt. So I close my eyes, and I breathe deep. Then I grab my father's shoulder. He wraps an arm around my waist and hoists me up.

"You . . . you're going?" Jackson cries. "You're just going to leave us?"

"I have to," I murmur. My words slur together, and I slump against my father.

"No you don't! You're part of this family!"

Harriet strokes his hair. "It's okay, Jackson. She can go."

"And leave us to die? After everything?" He pushes Harriet away and stands up.

Through blurred, bloodshot eyes, I level a vicious stare at him. Arturo does considerably more. I watch as he calmly approaches, lashes out with the back of his hand, and catches Jackson on the cheek. The force of it knocks him into Harriet's lap, where he lands, weeping.

"We do not have time for these theatrics, boy. Even if the alarm company is satisfied, the marshals won't be. You're only distracting your mother, who is now reviving my associate."

He points to the slowly stirring man, and Harriet lets go of Jackson. She kneels, swabbing the thug's cut and bleeding forehead with the sleeve of her pajamas.

"Come now, Nicki," my father says, and he leads me away. Every step feels shackled, every heartbeat pulses fresh pain through my arm. I cling to my father, though, feel his strength, and with his help, manage to reach the door.

Then I stop.

"What is it, honey?"

"Please, Dad," I whisper, turning around as best I can.

"Nicki, we have to move!"

Gripping my father's shirt, I point up the stairs. Then I find Jackson's eyes. Miserable and furious, he meets my gaze.

"We can go," I promise. "But not without Fancypaws."

CHAPTER TWENTY-NINE

Arrivederci

"What the hell is Fancypaws?" Arturo says, though his attention, and gun, never leave Harriet. She has the man sitting up now, and he's angrily pushing her away.

"Her stuffed toy. When she was little, she took that cat everywhere. Honey, we don't have time. . . ."

"She's just . . . just on my bedside table. I can get her if you carry me."

My father looks at Arturo, who shrugs cavalierly. "You have until he's ready to go. If you're still here when my man is standing, I shoot you both."

The injured man grins and immediately tries to get up. However, he swoons, crumpling back down to the floor and groaning. With an exasperated growl, my father picks me up and strides to the stairs. Every thudding step jostles me, and the narrow passage forces my feet and head to scrape along the wall. He tries his best to maneuver, but I still take the brunt of it.

"To the right," I murmur when we get to the top.

As we slip into my room, I grab poor Fancypaws by the ear. I press her to my chest with my wrapped hand, being extremely careful not to squeeze too tightly.

"Got her," I say, and my father spins about. Before leaving, though, he gives the space a once-over.

"I would have liked to have given you a room like this, Nicki."

"But you didn't. And I waited."

I can feel the breath leaving his body as he sighs. "You're going to ask me why I never came, aren't you?"

I look at him. Even in the dark, I can see that his beard hides several scars along his jawline and cheeks, and I can't remember if they were there before. I search for signs of something to hate, a feature or tic to make him the demon I'd convinced myself he was. All I see, though, is a confused, tired, and trapped man, and I find that there isn't anything there *to* hate.

Or to love.

"No, Dad," I say softly. "There's nothing you could say that makes it okay."

He closes his eyes. "I suppose not. I just wanted to keep you away from my world. I can't really tell you why. To protect you? To make my life easier? So I could forget about the mistakes I made? It doesn't matter now, I guess."

"No, it doesn't," I reply, and I rest my head on his shoulder. He adjusts his grip, and I use the opportunity to say good-bye to my hexagon, to my crystals, to my hiding drawer, and to my beautiful maple. In the hallway, I have to squint; I know it's more than just the darkness that's making it hard for me to see. When we reach the steps, I have to count them from memory.

Five.

I twist my childhood forever-friend around in my arms.

Ten.

I use my left hand to tug her paw away from the tear beneath. I mutter a silent apology as more of her worn fur rips, enlarging the hole.

Fifteen.

We arrive downstairs, just as Arturo's man stands up fully, his hand against the door frame to steady himself. With the widest, cruelest smile I've ever seen, Arturo shrugs and lifts his gun.

An instant later, he has two electrified probes dancing in his cheek.

His smile snaps closed into a grimace, and his entire body locks up. He pulls the trigger of his gun involuntarily, but the bullet just slams into the staircase behind us, stinging us with splinters. Then he falls to the ground, dragging Fancypaws from my grip as the cords tug her free.

Jackson leaps forward, picking up the bat and smashing it over the last man's head. Jonathan dives for Arturo's gun and pries it from his still-rigid hand.

"What in the . . ." my father yelps, but he silences himself as Jonathan jumps to his feet.

"Put her down, Christian."

"I'm her father," he says, and he holds me close. My lips brush his ear, and I can whisper.

"You need to go, Dad. Police will come. The marshals know."

"Not without you. You heard Arturo. Doesn't matter that he's down now. Won't even matter if you kill him. Those people won't stop coming for this family. I leave you, they won't stop coming for me, either. I'm saving both of us here, Nicki."

I force myself to kiss his cheek, and his eyes widen in surprise.

"You can't take me," I whisper. "I'm hurt. I need a hospital."

He shakes his head, but there's a violence playing out across his face, and it's agonizing.

With a whimper, I unwrap my hand. The blood flows freely from the hole, near the very center of my palm. I almost retch just seeing it. Harriet jumps up, wrapping the shirt back around.

I watch a tear roll down my father's cheek, and he blinks more away. Then he looks at Harriet.

"Got no choice. We're going."

"Dad," I plead, but he hushes me, and a wave of dizziness forces my eyes closed.

"The nearest hospital is Duke," Harriet says, "Down

the road, take a right, and follow the signs. Please. Please take her."

I can't tell if my father heard Harriet or not, but I do feel the sudden jagging as he carries me out onto the front porch. I hear the creak of the third step and his aggressive, awkward fumbling to open the car door and hold me at the same time. He puts me in the passenger seat, buckles me in, and slides in next to me. I open my eyes enough to see the key already in the ignition.

"Nicki," my father says, "I'm going to try to get you to a gas station. We'll find bandages there, fix up your hand, and then . . ."

"The hospital, Dad. Please."

"Can't go to the hospital. I take you there, I get caught by the police. I'll go back to jail."

"Then take me inside. Let Jonathan or Harriet call an ambulance."

"Back inside? Nicki, we have to get as far away from that family as possible. It's not safe."

He starts the car and peels away from the curb. As he drives, his hands twist around the rubber of the steering wheel, eyes darting toward every side road. In the half-light of the streetlamps, he looks hollow. Haunted.

"I *am* safe, Dad," I say softly. "I have a family who wants me. I have a friend who knows me."

"Damnit, Nicki." He sighs, glancing down at my hand, at the way my hair clings to my cheek. "Look at you. There is no *safe!*"

"Maybe not a normal safe. Maybe not. But Dad." I shiver, resting my head against the window, my hand cradled in the cove of my lap. "This is *my* safe. You say you want to keep me away from your world? Then help me make my own."

He does not respond. I whimper through another wave of pain, and the urge to close my eyes, to fall asleep, is suddenly overwhelming. Before I do, though, I allow myself one more glance at my father.

It lasts just long enough to see him stop beneath the hospital lights.

CHAPTER THIRTY

Nicki Doesn't Live Here Anymore

I don't get to see them take my father away, and I'm not allowed access to newspapers or the internet in Glynco. It's part of my debrief. At least, that's what Janice tells me.

"When can I see Harriet and Jonathan?" I ask from my infirmary bed.

Janice steps gingerly over the pile of bandages on the floor.

"You need to keep these on," she says sternly.

"They make me feel sick, like gloves," I argue. "My hands shake with them on, and the doctors said I need to keep them still as much as possible. Besides, the gauze pads cover up the hole enough. Wanna see?"

She grimaces, but she sits down at the edge of my bed all the same. Looking through her folder, she takes out a photograph and holds it up.

"Is this the man who was with Arturo? Look closely."

I roll my eyes. "Janice, it was only three days ago. That's him. Did you figure out how they found us? Found my dad?"

Janice growls, closing the folder and slapping her hands down on it. "They broke us down bit by bit. A clue here, a lead there. Jackson's Facebook page didn't help, and the picture on the school website sealed it. They even threatened Deputy Marshal Harkness, though you'll be pleased to know he didn't give them anything."

I smile. "He wouldn't. And I know you wouldn't, either."

Janice pauses, pursing her lips.

"Thank you, Nicki. As for your father, once they had the picture of you with the Trevors, we believe they distributed it to their entire network. Perhaps one of your former foster relatives or a teacher somewhere recognized you. Once they had your name, it wouldn't be hard for an organization with their resources to find a parolee."

"I wrote him a letter," I say. "Had to use my left hand."

Janice sits bolt upright, nearly dumping her folder on the floor.

"Don't worry. I'm not going to send it; I don't even know where he is. Probably for the best."

The deputy marshal relaxes maybe, like, a half inch, but she continues giving me the hairy eyeball.

"It's best to avoid attachments, Nicki, particularly now. Things are going to be . . . unsettled, maybe for quite a while."

I glance over at Fancypaws, who has had a patch job

and no longer packs heat. "Unsettled is okay. I'm used to unsettled. I can even help Jackson with it now; I'm pretty sure he'll let me."

Janice fingers her starchy collar, her neck and cheeks suddenly red. She's blinking a lot, too. I sit up.

"What, Janice? Is Jackson okay? Is there a reason I haven't seen . . ."

"You'll see them tomorrow morning, and yes, Jackson is fine," she replies curtly, standing up and gathering her things.

"Tomorrow morning? Why not now?"

"It's ten o'clock. And besides, I said things would be unsettled. It's best not to press the issue."

To punctuate her words, she taps the bedpost with her folder.

"Good night, Janice," I say as I pull Fancypaws over, resting her in the crook of my shoulder.

"Get some rest," she says, smoothing a hand along my sheets. When she reaches the door, she cuts off the lights and turns to go. Before she does, though, she glances back. In a whisper, she adds, "You've earned it."

The next morning, the marshals try to load me into a wheelchair, but I wriggle away; my legs are working just fine. As soon as I hear from Janice which room the Trevors are in, I skip ahead, ignoring her protests. When I burst into the room, they're already seated at a table. They seem exhausted and spent, but all three stand up. Janice bustles in behind me.

"Now that we're here," the deputy marshal says matter-of-factly, flipping through a sheaf of papers, "we can—"

"Quiet," Harriet murmurs.

"Excuse me?" Janice snaps.

"I said quiet, for a moment, please," Harriet responds, and she glides toward me.

"Hi," I whisper.

"Hi, my girl," she says, reaching up to brush a fingertip along my cheek.

"Are . . . are you guys okay?"

She nods, and then she indicates my hand. "And you're . . ."

"Okay, too. It's still hard to move, and it itches terribly. The doctors said I'll need to do six months of therapy, and then we'll see. On the bright side, it means I get to play video games and stuff to build up the nerves and muscles. So there's that."

Harriet smiles and reaches out for my good hand. When I flinch, she pulls back. "Oh yes. That's right. I forgot. I just wanted to—"

I cut her off with the most ferocious hug I think I've ever given. By the time we're done, Janice has already finished her coffee. She tells all of us to sit down, and then starts reading from a prepared statement.

"On behalf of the United States marshals and the WITSEC program, I'd like to officially apologize for the failure of Project Family to ensure your safety," Janice begins. "While it has met with success in other regions, we feel it is too destabilizing to continue in your case. Although Arturo Cercatore is no longer a direct threat, your family's reach remains considerable, Elena."

"You're moving us again, aren't you?" Jackson grumbles.

Janice scowls at him, but answers. "In short, yes. We will proceed with a standard relocation, which has proven effective numerous times in the past. Granted, your experiences with the Cercatores show that criminals' methods of tracking down witnesses in our program have advanced considerably, but after discussion, we have decided that our tried-and-true strategy will serve best here."

"Where are we going this time?" Jonathan asks.

"I'm not at liberty to say in present company," she remarks, glancing at me. "Only those directly involved may know, as part of the safety protocol."

My jaw drops. "Wait, you mean . . ."

"Nicki, you'll be placed into a reputable foster system in another district. We'll provide you with a new social security number, new papers, and a new identity."

I pull up my legs, curling them around my shaking hands. My injured palm burns.

"Don't be petulant, Nicki. We'll get you placed shortly, and we'll assure that you've moved on."

Jonathan stands up. "Like hell you will."

Janice opens her mouth, but Harriet slaps the table. "No, Janice. No. This isn't even a discussion." She points at me. "See that girl in the chair there? The one who has endured more than any child should ever have to? The one who saved me, saved my husband, saved my son? That's my daughter. She's *mine*, and I'd rather share a cell with my psychopath brother for the rest of my short life than be the mom who sends her away."

Janice leans forward, raising her hands. Jonathan looms over her, though, and even her pinched brow wavers in the face of his expression.

"Leave this room, Deputy Marshal, and don't come back until you've found a way to make this work. I don't care who you call, what you say, how many signatures you have to forge. My wife helped you and yours cripple one of the biggest crime syndicates in the world, and we've asked for nothing. Nothing. Now, we're asking for this, and you're going to give it to us."

Slowly, Janice pushes back from the table. She straightens her uniform jacket and neatly arranges the papers in her stack. Tucking it underneath her arm, she holds out her chin defiantly, looking down her nose at Harriet and Jonathan. Then she pivots, and with a stabbing step marches toward the door. Before she slams it shut, she twists her head to the side.

"Mr. and Mrs. Sicurezza," she mutters, the corner of her mouth perhaps, just perhaps, curling slightly. "I was hoping you'd say that."

We wait together for twenty minutes. None of us says much. When the door silently swings open, we all tense. Janice is there, a fresh cup of coffee in her hand and a stern look on her face. She breathes deeply, then sits in her chair.

We watch as she takes each piece of paper out of her folder, one at a time. We squirm as she arranges them in a perfect overlapping row. She sips her coffee once, puts the cup down, and clears her throat.

Finally, she says, "How do you all feel about Arizona?"

STEAM ACCOUNT INFORMATION FOR USER:
BR1TN3YSP34RGUN

You have received one (1) new friend request.

See below to accept or ignore this user.

BR1TN3YSP34RGUN >> Invites

You have 1 friend invite | Ignore All

ACCEPT	IGNORE	BLOCK

MISSRAGEBEAST91

(You have 0 friends in common)

• • •

• • •

• • •

• • •

-FRIEND REQUEST ACCEPTED-

Acknowledgments

I'd be a pretty poor excuse for a writing teacher if I didn't acknowledge the many people who helped make this book possible. Liz Szabla and the magnificent team at Feiwel and Friends—thank you for giving Nicki a home, and for helping with repairs when the manuscript needed it. Thanks, too, to my agent, Rebecca Stead. You are a Renaissance woman of the first order, and I feel blessed to have your experience and encouragement to guide me.

Nicki's adventures were also tweaked, fine-tuned, and immeasurably improved by the input of my second readers, to whom I am deeply grateful: Adam Solomon, Jennifer Shaw, Carol Maoz, Caroline Huber, Caitlin Simon, Greg Huber, Ruthann Gill, and Donald and Donna Burt.

Finally, all my love to Elizabeth and Lauriann, who have encouraged me in every phase of this journey . . . possibly because when I'm writing, I'm not playing the banjo. Your support could simply be an act of self-preservation, but I treasure it all the same.